Pass Me the Lip Gloss

Pass Me the Lip Gloss

Surviving the Challenge with Fashion

ROSINA RAMÓN

PASS ME THE LIP GLOSS
SURVIVING THE CHALLENGE WITH FASHION

Author Credits: Rosa María Ramón Purón
Cover Credit: Prince Láuder & Renata Alarcón
Photographer Oswaldo Gonzalez

iUniverse books may be ordered through booksellers or by contacting:

iUniverse
1663 Liberty Drive
Bloomington, IN 47403
www.iuniverse.com
844-349-9409

ISBN: 978-1-5320-9912-0 (sc)
ISBN: 978-1-5320-9914-4 (hc)
ISBN: 978-1-5320-9913-7 (e)

Library of Congress Control Number: 2020908421

Print information available on the last page.

iUniverse rev. date: 11/26/2020

I dedicate this book to first of all to so many women
in my life that taught me resilience, specially
Rosa Maria, my gorgeous mother
Who was an expert at making the ordinary extraordinary

Dearly
To Pepe, my father
Who was a master in the art of sense of humor, teaching me that
it was ok to talk to strangers and make lasting friends for life
I Love and miss them so much…

To
Alexis and Alejandro
My beautiful daughter and handsome son
The two most important people in my life.

And of course to all those brave women who have beaten
the "challenge" and to the ones that lost the battle,
Especially for my cousin
Maria Esther
My Love

Contents

Preface

I write from the depth of my heart, where feelings are stuck somewhere in my being lingering in a hidden dark secluded corner untouched, out of reach to only me and myself.

I write for the sheer pleasure of recording my memories, which seem to lose light as the years go by, a time, a space, and a different life.

I write with the yearning of a heart overflowing with love that merely longs to share it.

I write to empty my brain of senseless thoughts, and to rearrange the good ones.

For the use of words that turn into pictures of a reality that once was or an event we want to recreate, the way we arrange the sentences or paragraphs in the end, it is a translation of a glimpse of the past.

Sometimes as I close my eyes and remember a particular face, I can even recall the smell and feel the cold or the heat of the moment, maybe that face touched my heart as the temperature felt on my body.

Two people in one. One who reason's another that expresses what is going on in that brain. I have so many thoughts at the same moment and feelings inside me that it would be unreasonable not to let them all out, in the hope that my journey can be of value to others.

In association with time in which particular events became a way of life as I glimpse back to the crucial moments in my life, it is funny but still now I can even remember what dress I was wearing.

Time

As I am facing the long oblong full body mirror, seeing not my actual early fifties reflection but a plump eleven-year-old playing with her Barbie and Tracy dolls from out of a black vinyl suitcase that is opened to reveal a very well organized closet.

Tracy, the long-haired brunette blue-eyed and one of my favorite dolls is wearing yellow rubber boots on her long thin legs sealing the look with a bright fuccia plastic hooded parka over a multicolored miniskirt and a bright orange turtleneck.

Finally, realizing how the yellow boots paved the road to my love affair with fashion constructing my way of life, saving me even in my worst personal crisis.

When confronted with the most unexpected challenge, I came face to face with my unknown vulnerability. Starts then my search of understanding how I became this particular person I am today. In such a pursuit I will begin traveling back and forth thru time to work with the pain claiming not only my body but choking my whole being, in my relentless search for the strength needed for survival.

Amid all the unraveling of my most exposed and shattered naked self, I find a characteristic that kept repairing in the background of my memories my obsession with beauty and fashion.

Being an only child, I grew up in a sort of protective glass bubble sheltered from harm's way. I never even learnt how to ride a bike, for my mother feared I would fall, hit my head split it in half or break a bone, and become paralyzed for life. She had a way of describing danger around me as a Greek tragedy.

Over my mom's objections, on my seventh birthday, my grandmother's present of a red tricycle was heaven-sent, providing the first glance at freedom.

I jumped to my mom's horror pedaling rapidly the engine-red bike. Wearing a new blue and red checked cotton dress with a white Peter Pan collar and with the season's shiny black patent leather Mary Jane's, pristine white lace socks, and the bow on the dress's waist flying untied in my haste. In mom's mind, I was exposing myself to the danger not only of falling,

1

but also of ruining such a cute looking outfit and messing up my perfectly groomed sleek "Dippity-Do" ponytail.

Riding happily around the block for what seemed hours, with my mother anxiously walking steps behind me, and grandmother laughing at her overprotectiveness.

Being cuddled and taken care in such a way, I was never really prepared on how to deal with one of my life's hardest experience. Even my mother could not have predicted with her fantasy crystal ball the terrifying outcome, she had had to overcome, and thirty years later will also attack me her only child.

As in my mother's case, illness arrives with no warning an intruder inflicting a sensation of dread.

Then all of a sudden this person I have grown up to be stares back from the mirror unable to comprehend what is going on inside this body, I cannot recognize how my reflection is the same person who is processing inside her head irrational thoughts that tamper with life and death.

The situation is as if a tsunami struck my brain immobilizing the process of understanding, bursting waves of shivers all thru the last cells of my being. The loss of clarity is in vain as I try to focus on the next step ahead. Even after several deep long breaths I cannot find an answer.

Experiencing it now in my own self, feeling it in my skin, understanding now, after almost eight years, the shock my mother had to cope when fighting against this horrible disease. Facing days without answers, nights without sleep, months of treatments, and years of discomfort when a permanent colostomy disrupted her feminine body.

How does one really handle pain? Which type is more upsetting the physical, which sickens and distorts the flesh or the psychological one, that hunts the brain? Which one plays more with loss or inflicts more devastation and helplessness?

As I was to experience, I fought pain with medicine but mostly with crazy ideas inside my head.

Years before I was sure when I saw my mother's coffin lay to rest and the dirt shoveled onto her lavender casket would be one of the hardest things I would have to brave out. I was very wrong.

Normalcy stops, with this silent invasion inside my body, incoherent to "Me" a control freak who spends her days monitoring perfection of fit, the right color combination and deciding over boots or pumps, pearls or diamonds, or gold instead of silver.

What to do when needles substitute stilettos, vintage dresses replace washed drab aqua green robes? I merely took refuge in the only topic I blindly know, fashion.

Strangely, experiencing in my entire journey thru all the different phases I mostly followed my mother's road to survival. Clearly she just never let go of her most precious belief, beauty with fashion in the mix had always been her mantra, and now my own to adopt and cherish.

Fashion, turning out to be a suitable occupation that permitted me to use the tools of being pretty, and stylish as a way of disguising what had crept without an invitation inside me.

Starting every day, my private daily fashion show, and an adventure on what I will wear and how. While the forced transformation of my body evolved, so did the way I would play with my clothes and my overall appearance.

Now, how do I dress for being sick? Well, I had to analyze first my state of mind every morning, which at the time was one of the loneliest of places I had ever visited.

My world stopped. I had been forgotten, left without air, drowning in a deep pool unable to stay afloat. Going against the high wave of desperation I seized on to the first thing, which gave me a chance, to grasp at some needed oxygen; beauty and fashion.

Reasoning, dressing up makes me happy, this evil makes me scared, very scared. Sensing being trapped and alone in an empty room with high walls, no doors or windows, and no chance for escape. Only me, with big dreadful thoughts, minimized into a tiny and defenseless creature.

Glancing at my terrified reflection staring back from the mirror, a thought pops like lighting. A simple idea. What if I play with this fear and dress it up a bit, what more do I have to lose?

A pretty dress will surely give me confidence. I will mix it with attitude and add some subtle makeup to cover my drab sick complexion. Providing me with the necessary courage, to cope with the beast lurking around called panic.

From now on my fears will be covered in gold and sequence. Any intruder ready to attack, will have to untangle itself from lace and crochet, spitting feathers from my long red boa. Besides taking a tremendous fall from my high-heel black stiletto boots.

Fashion

All of my life, I been working around respecting and honoring an image's evolution, beautifying people around me. Fashion has been my sole profession for over 30 years, representing models, coordinating fashion shows, styling photo shoots, and generally consulting on trends and image.

My daughter Alexis and my son Alex grew up between clothing racks, crazy hats and large impressive necklaces and earrings that were designed exclusively to adorn the model and enhance the outfit. Being a dress a simple piece of cloth that hung on a hanger coming to life on the models body.

The dress has to fit, first the model, and in the end you have to make it work for the client it is a precise unison of sensibility and creativity. A combination of original and glamorous ideas to provide a total look, without ever losing the respect of the body.

Clothes for a specific type of figure, makeup to boost the features, it is a construction of a unique "persona" who conquers as she walks with the swaying movement of the skirt or the right cut of the dress as it touches the skin.

An image becomes a process of learning about who we are and who we want to become. From our elders, we are influenced by our upbringing, and by our surroundings, yet it is only up to ourselves to fall in love with our image, crucial now for surviving with dignity.

Fashion is the most important tool one can use as the foundation for a beautiful and attractive self. We must understand I am not talking only about trends of the moment, as Coco Chanel used to point out:

"Fashion passes, and style remains."

Fashion becomes the elemental tool for nourishing the person we want to be, but most of all having fun in the process.

The answer to my predicament was simply in the management of the art of transformation, and at that I had become an expert.

The Challenge

Having this philosophy which enables me to find refuge in fashion came in handy when I hear the worst news no women ever wants to hear:

"You have breast cancer."

Referred from this point on as the "Challenge"

Why?

The "Challenge" seems to be the perfect word, as soon as I forgo the denial stage, I face one of the toughest trials in my life. Knowing I ought to fight with whatever it takes, starting an open war against all the odds coming my way. The other word gives me the creeps. Fear is not welcome at the moment, at all.

Silly as this may be all thru the time of struggling with the disease I learnt to concentrate on beauty and clothes while even throwing up after chemo. Feeling a lot worse on seeing my sick face staring me back on the mirror without any lip-gloss.

Establishing my theory on lip-gloss, concluding that besides softening my lips, it firmly brightens my complexion, giving an effortless lift to my face. So no matter how tired I might be just the act of dabbing it on, is as if transforming into an entirely different person.

Lip-gloss for me is a type of push-up bra to a deflated squashed up ego.

Adopting the tools of beauty has assured me of enhancing myself physically and mentally. My determination on looking attractive has been a permanent way of life, and no matter what the emotional turmoil I might be experiencing it was out of the question to change the habit.

Dressing

The fun in dressing is a must in my life, practicing it now more than ever to keep me grounded for the person I am, and for the life, I now have to lead. Every day of the week I play with new options on how to dress, making my own specific rules as I go along to meet the "Challenge" face to face.

For me fashion has always been "My" fashion since it lives my own life I certainly have not had to compete with anyone but myself. Using it always to my advantage, and also to regain some optimism during this daunting experience.

My closet is a mixture of what feels right for me and also feels comfortable, if I make blunders it doesn't matter since I dress only for myself. Anyway it is harder in life to have a personal style, than just thrive on what is in fashion.

As much as I love the fashion on the cover of magazines which I diligently devour every month, I am an expert at developing my own rules with some added flair. The whole purpose is to keep my mind busy and distracted from the harsh, reality the "Challenge" implies, and play along as when a child.

Beauty

My mother's closet was fantasyland. I grew up playing with long evening dresses from the 50's. Her drawers filled with necklaces of crystal colored stones of enormous proportions, looking like candy to my child's eyes.

My grandmother's crocodile bags from the 40's with a little lizard looking oddly alive lying comfortably over the flap, accompanied me on my imaginary adventures.

Stoles with head, feet, and tails of some exotic furry animal from my great aunt's attic will complete the look of what at eleven I thought was very chic, fashionable, or just dreamy.

Only children live life very differently from other kids, my mind will wander to places no one had ever heard. Somehow discovering them thru the constant company of books or Sunday at the movies.

Never will I forget one time the air conditioner broke down in my bedroom, camping out on the foot of my parent's bed. For three nights before falling asleep I traveled on a make-believe Safari, laying on my sleeping bag envisioning a sky filled with bright stars, the sounds of lions, and chimps all around me.

Dressing for this fictional journeys wearing long wide pant-skirts in earth tones, some soft white gauzy shirt-like blouse worn with a multi-pocket jacket, combat boots, and of course a large-brimmed straw hat.

All thru those nights, my thin, dark-skinned friend huge-eyed Yahir kept me company in my make-believe adventures. Impeccably attired with a turban on his head, long off-white linen tunic, and matching harem pants and pointy slippers.

At eleven years of age, I was still the chubby, large-nose little girl of this tall, beautiful lady. The granddaughter, of this grand, imposing dame of delicate features, and the grand-niece of an extravagant sophisticated widowed great-aunt who well past her 80's never stopped polishing her nails bright lacquered red.

Mother's porcelain beauty, patrician nose, and imposing height were the constant delight to anyone meeting her. Possessing the ability to turn an ordinary dress into an extraordinary ensemble. Be it the way she placed a pin, a necklace, or a scarf. Her choice of jewelry was preferably big but nothing someone else would wear. She loved as I do unique pieces, having very narrow feet, she would have her shoes custom made with bags to match, considered a big splurge in the early 60's.

Comparisons abound about physical beauty in any family, creating at an early age shadows of insecurity of the person I perceived I was, and uncertain of the person I wanted to be.

Passing long hours in front of the mirror effortlessly trying with scotch tape to make my nose daintier. The dilemma over my looks at that age was at its peak. With great effort I stopped eating chocolates, to lose the plumpness, which made my cylinder body shape exactly like those push-up ice cream orange pops I craved in the sixth grade.

In my middle teens I had my first love affair with shoes, opting the norm of walking in very high heels, sometimes experiencing uncomfortable pain. A sacrifice at that particular stage I felt compelled to make, forgoing discomfort for the sake of fashion.

My self-doubts in those days were more related to trying to be as tall as my cousins from my mother's side, height being the pride of her family. The necessity of belonging or being accepted as an equal was also due to my only child status. Even if I saw them more often than not quarreling between themselves over insignificant issues, I dearly yearned to be their sister of sorts.

Finally, I do not remember if by accident or destiny, as I was reaching fourteen my body started to readjust itself, settling my insecurities in the process. My relationship with shoes changed after falling from tall platforms and breaking a stiletto heel or two, caring less every day not having grown to be 5.10.

I even stopped fretting about my nose and started to really, loving it. I had role models to look up to, meeting them thru fashion magazines, which I devoured. I never will forget Angelica Houston saying:

"There were days I hated my nose, but as you grow up you realize it is not that bad not being born a Barbie".

Becoming for me this phrase hope, and an opening to the world of uniqueness as a possibility to beauty, changing the perception I had of myself. Somehow born of harsh comparisons, with perfect little-chiseled noses.

Discovering Barbara Streisand's beauty made me recognize I will keep my distinctive nose forever, understanding this in the early 80's when my

College friends started doing nose jobs ending all with the same nose surgeons at the time had to offer. Finally accepting I did not want to be a part of a cookie cutter nose world.

A great advantage has now been to accept my individual type of beauty, one of the pillars of my image and modeling courses.

My plumpness also turned out to be unimportant. Growing up my body reshaped itself, boobs and hips to the eyes of boys enhanced my sex appeal, even though I would have preferred not such a curvaceous figure. I became pickier in my shoe addiction admitting flats without shame, though loving heels has always been a balancing act and part of the game.

In the acceptance of my so-called flaws, one day the mirror and I started a love affair with each other, one almost ending with the "Challenge."

The "Challenge" faced me with a prerogative on the matter of ideal beauty where a positive opinion of myself as a woman was essential. Soon I will be forced to stare in the mirror and confront my crushed feminine self, deciding to keep playing as a little girl with fashion in order to survive, as I will constantly repeat physically and mentally.

The Beginning

Mexico City, October 2008

I have a great new haircut short and flimsy and blonder than it has been in ages, it looks fresh after years of red. I am wearing, a khaki colored circular Marbella trench with a huge bow at the waist over a slim Theory strapless dress in the same color, looking much like an ensemble. Complementing the look with tall over the knee black suede boots I am feeling spectacular, and an attractive guy across the room seems to agree, introducing himself and joining the group that whole weekend.

Attending a Stuart Weitzman auction of celebrity-designed shoes benefiting Breast Cancer Research. Moet Chandon flutes are swirling around me. I am too preoccupied with meeting up with friends I haven't seen in quite a while. Lucia, one of my best friends, has just moved into the city with her husband, we have a lot catching up to do.

Hardly paying attention to the video of the foundation missing some heart-aching stories, a reality in someone else's skin, not in a million years in mine.

As mother used to say: "Wishful thinking."

Monterrey Mexico, Monday

October the 6th

M onterrey is a city surrounded by mountains where nothing is typically of what you would expect a Mexican town to be or you might picture in your mind. I often tell New Yorkers during the cold February fashion week days:

"No, we do not have a beach, just truly enigmatic mountains."

A modern Americanized industrial town, driving on one of the most used express-ways you will spot on the side roads a Chili's, a Sirloin Stockade, a Starbucks, a Macdonald's an office Depot, and even an American post office. As you are coming in from the airport, you are faced with a Sam's Club a Wall Mart, a super huge HEB supermarket, more American and now some European hotel chains.

After a great weekend of dining and partying in Mexico City and Monday filled with successful meetings with some clients I fly back to Monterrey.

Arriving home around 9:00 P.M. tired and hungry from the trip, as I am pulling off my sweater, and unbuckle my bra, in order to take a bath. I accidentally feel what seems to me a pretty big lump on my right breast.

Startled, I scream for Juanita, my live-in maid who is more a sort of second mother, (after 26 years in our house she has lasted more than my ex-husband, any lover, or boyfriend to date) as she touches the lump I can see her tan skin almost turn white.

"It is immense," she says.

Precisely at that moment things take a fast turn for the unexpected.

As soon as Juanita is up the next day at 8:00 A.M. she has already scheduled a mammogram appointment. I have learnt not to go empty handed to any doctor, who will surely order tests before confirming anything.

Shock

Getting the results two days later, the words on the paper mean nothing until I type Neoplasia on the computer. The Internet shouts back TUMOR, and it looks it is not the friendly KIND.

Breathing stops, as a grey cloud assaults my brain without any logical understanding. Slowly deeply inhaling, I try to think. My friend the oncologist, Jaime Garcia comes instantly to mind.

After reaching him, I stammer the overview of the report over the phone. In a hurried horsy voice I hear him say:

"Come in at noon tomorrow," a Saturday. First warning sign, he does not give appointments on Saturdays.

Jaime is not a very tall person but he is in excellent shape with dark hair, fine features, and expressive brown eyes a typical Latin heartthrob. He could be in General Hospital anytime.

This particular day he seems to lose his normal composure shuffling nervously with the results of my mammogram sheets, scrutinizing them on the light screen, when he almost mumbles not finding the right words:

"Yes, I am sorry, it is the Challenge."

On this perfect given Saturday, I am faced with the unthinkable hearing the words coming out of my doctors mouth, turning around to see if maybe by some chance somebody else is in the room, almost foolishly I feel like asking:

"Are you talking to me?"

My inner self almost shouts at him:

"You must be wrong. You see I have plans, lots of plans, and lots of things to do, besides my son wants to go to Australia for next semester."

In reality, my talkative self-falls speechless, as when in a dream, straining to shout for help, and the words are stuck unable to make a sound.

I somehow hear him:

"Let me explain it is a little bigger than 4 cm in dimension."

My brain hears:

"It looks mean and ugly."

The final blow comes like an explosion inside all of me when he almost falters with the worst words no woman will ever be prepared to hear:

"Rosina, you have to understand a mastectomy is in order."

At this point logic leaves me, even when I hear his next sentence of hope:

"You are really lucky we caught it on the first stage."

On listening to this, it does nothing to change a feeling in the pit of my stomach, it is similar to being turned upside down, and someone is holding me by my feet and at any minute will lose his grip, living me to crash head on to the ground.

There seems not much else he can say, so putting his arm around my shoulders, accompanies me out of his office. Walking me in silence to my car, I guess part for regaining himself, or at the same time to offer some comfort. He must be very used to this type of disbelief, which at the moment must be plastered all over my face.

My brain at this point is trying to process the words to understand it's meaning, hard to believe something is wrong with me, a second opinion is in order, and basically nothing hurts. I feel fine there has to be some mistake.

"I just don't get it? I have plans you see."

An incoherent mess is taking place inside my head, as I am driving a couple of blocks to the house. Just thinking how, am I going to drop the bomb on my then 21-year-old son Alejandro, and my 24-year-old daughter, Alexis? Another problem is my 83 year-old father Pepe, and of course Juanita. Worst of all telling my friend Lucia whose own brother has been fighting the "Challenge" for several months, and it looks like he is not getting any better.

The rest of the day is blurred. I do not remember to this day how I told everyone at the house, a blank space on my memory bank.

Alejandro's dream of going for a semester to Australia shatters like crystal pieces to the ground, he feels he is the man of the house and declares there is no way he would leave me at a time like this.

Alexis, my daughter, has a harder time understanding and settles for the comfort of avoiding the truth, until one of my dearest cousin, Abe makes her slowly come to terms with the harsh reality. I guess no one is prepared to hear this, ever.

Dreams

From now on, nightmares or messed up thoughts become the norm. I am incapable of knowing if I am dreaming or thinking awake, it will become hard to tell them apart. In the end, I will wake up sweating from all the craziness going on inside my mind.

My dreams at this point remind me of a poem I wrote for Mr. Green's creative writing class in my High School sophomore year in 1973:

A king on a horse
A clown with red nose
One running one jumping,
To get to a door?
The coins of the rich
That made a great ditch.
A little boy crying
A little girl flying
The queen with her laugh,
Nobody could stop.
Images of people long gone
Pass over a looking glass.
Thru fields of green grass,
I am at a loss.
Chased by horrible black birds
A panic attack.
In layers of blue chiffon,
I end up in shreds, on the seas shore.
Falling down an endless wishing well
Why sometimes a dream
Really makes no sense?
And yet..

The relation to this long-forgotten poem and my dreams was such a reflection to what I was experiencing at the moment, in all of the stances I am trying to find my way out of something, there is always some anguish or fear.

Translating it to "the moment" I would say the little boy crying was my son on finding out about my "Challenge," the little girl flying was my daughter's inability of facing up to what was happening.

Images of people long gone, relates to my great need of being able to have my mother around at this terrible moment, I crave desperately for her embrace.

My recurring dreams of running thru woods chased by my worst fear ever, since a kid, being birds, (no I did not watch the movie). Relating those dreams to the "Challenge," this terrible thing invading my body, I tremble with fright.

The thought of ending up in shreds not only on my clothes somehow relates to the upcoming mutilation awaiting my body. How strange the interconnection of it all, life, with all its fears, mingled in our dreams, you cannot separate them.

Hospitals & Cold Rooms

Deprived of sleep, I arrive at the chilly hospital waiting room Sunday at 8:00 A.M., with my Guardian Angel, Juanita.

Wearing faded jeans a loose knitted sweater with a long scarf and cowboy boots I brace myself for another mammogram of my boob. Waiting my turn, the mind races into high gear of positive thinking, "I am going to be all right it is a big mistake I will prove it." Sadly I was wrong.

The first exam takes fifteen minutes lying on a bed while some jelly crystal goop is spread evenly on my breasts and an artifact traces every fiber on a screen. I am sitting in front of the photographic device for the mammogram my sick boob is squashed between two plates as if it were some soft rubber ball.

The technician has no visible reaction on her plump face, as much I try to get a conversation going on with her in order to distract myself. She appears rather unimpressed with my incoherent babbling. An impartial bystander apparently devoid of feelings, minding her own business, not paying me any attention, as if I was not even there, silent, just doing her job.

Envisioning her as a witch maneuvering a broomstick out of the window with my positivism dangling on her hands, scattering it all over dirty waters, a tear rolls down my cheek.

Finding many insensible creatures as her along the way, but I will also meet caring ones who will try with humor make me feel better, at this point, I need very much to be comforted. Feelings of understanding are something I will be seeking a lot from people in gray hospitals. I start craving reassurance that worse will become better.

All hospitals in town are mostly white, but at the beginning of those creepy days, they looked the dullest of gray. The fluorescent lights seemed to transform the rooms to a grayish blue tint, and the air conditioner will be blasting cold. For God's sake in the middle of October I could not understand why they could not turn them off.

Doubts start popping inside my brain as I take a hard look around me:

"What if I start to look like him, walk like her?" Panic hits hard, dread choking me without words, breathing is paused, and sweat appears on my forehead and hands. Shaken on facing the sickness of others, battling the vulnerability of my mere human existence.

Confronted with the probability of death for the first time, a harsh jolt to my confused self. Thinking of death was not an option for me.

Then the recollection of a sentence written by Ayn Rand in the book from 1943 the Fountainhead, spoken by Dominique, one of the main characters:

"We actually die a little every day."

Nevertheless, I shall put on a fight!

Work

Monday after this time bomb fell into my life, things start like an ordinary week with lots of activity.

After a quick shower, my uniform today consists of skinny jeans in dark blue with a lighter blue work shirt and lots of turquoise, necklaces and bracelets. Cowboy boots in leather imitating jean material and my distressed sand colored suede and jean jacket, a big brown leather fringed bag, and a finishing touch of subtle makeup and pink gloss for glow.

As I am piling on the necklaces and bracelets sort of adorning a Christmas tree I am on an automatic mode. The alien image in the mirror is suspended completely from the terrible news it has received avoiding feelings and suppressing thoughts of what seems to be my new reality.

The day starts with selecting the clothes for a photography session, I will be styling for the new boutique Hotel Habitat, where my daughter now works. After I will also be selecting some more outfits for the two courses in fashion for two groups of executives and society ladies.

Programing my mind with work, I will not be bothered with anything else but clothes at the moment. I sincerely rejoice in the scape my job brings, and love doing this now more than ever.

Getting on with my day numbness becomes me, on reviewing the shoot's details:

A cocktail dress for her, and for him semi-formal suit from Zegna, for the restaurants romantic mood. For the lobby a sport jacket with jeans for the guy, an ivory Max Mara pantsuit for the girl and some Vuitton luggage.

A last assessment of all that is needed:

Bathing suits for the pools scene, other takes require shoes, bags, and accessories, sign loaning releases, arrive at the hotel, fit models, check with makeup artist and hair stylist the image mood board of each take.

When finally everyone is ready at the hotel's pool, for the first shoot we are rushing since the natural light is playing tricks on us, and the lady photographer flown in from L.A. seems to think we are kind of responsible for the cloudy weather, artists and fashion people we are impossible as always.

Already mid-afternoon and only two takes have been completed. We are running very late after an hour has passed, I get them ready for the third take for the next location.

As I am organizing the rest of the shoot, unexpectedly I have an anxiety attack, triggered by my oncologist confirmation of an appointment tomorrow with a surgeon. I start to hyperventilate, shaking and sweating all over. Hearing a loud voice almost shout:

"I cannot do this by myself, face an unknown doctor on my own. How will I even be able to think straight?"

Understanding

M y beautiful daughter Alexis at the time is a 24-year-old with long dark brown slightly wavy hair, lightly tanned skin left from her days living in Playa del Carmen, expressive olive-brown eyes and a small delicate nose I would have died for, but most of all she is gregarious with a charismatic nature. After dropping out from art school to live few years on the beach, she mastered the art of people, building a successful career in public relations.

As I am facing the "Challenge" she has become responsible for this hotel's Public Relations, she is too preoccupied with the photography session going well. Being one of her first big assignments. My problems at the moment are not something she can handle, shutting it from her brain like a bad joke is being played on her.

With some difficulty, along the way I will have to understand I cannot expect the same reaction or comfort from all my love ones, every individual faces tragedy in an entirely different manner. Many days I will become selfish in thinking only of what was going on in my brain and body, forgetting that my loved ones are coping with a worse scenario, called helplessness.

Seeking sympathy from others, or compassion feels unhealthy for my overall well-being, leaving me defenselessness and more alone.

At this precise moment I think what anyone in my situation needs, is to find some inner force inside in order not to completely lose it. Still it is inevitable at this early stage not to lose it, as I did today. Fear is a nasty enemy to fight. My composure crumbled similar to a sand castle when brushed by a sea wave.

My friend Lola is a cautious and super organized attractive brunette who looks like Bianca Jagger when she stepped out off Studio 54 on the famous white horse back in the 70's. She is as composed and calm as anyone one can be in a critical situation. Insightful, and inquisitive more like a private investigator than a mother hen she is cool, and aloof when asking questions no doctor will be able to escape her meticulous formulated inquiries.

She was exactly what I needed at the moment, and the official backbone of my support group. This support group essentially made up of friends and family, worked for almost four years around the evolution of my "Challenge." Everyone needs one in order to survive.

This support system helped me get ahead thru the hardships and ups and downs of the sick me. With their help I got up after each stumble, and because of them I worked on facing them with a nice looking dress and lip gloss on. Looking nice for me was essential, but having the acknowledgment of others was vital. For many my idea of trying to be pretty when ill might sound crazy.

Just tell me when holding the hand of someone in a hospital bed and telling them how nice they look or how much you love them, a smile flashes like a ray of light thru their faces and for a brief moment they rejoice in that. Meaning that second, offered hope.

Lying, cheating or even steeling in the sake of feeling beautiful, is worth it for me, so I hope also for others.

Doctors

O n our arrival to the small cramped doctor's office, by the look of Lola's face, I could tell we are not making a connection with him. The doctor's evasive answers could not prove our perceptive self's more right sensing an uncomfortable uncertainty to every word he uttered.

From here on the ritual would be the same as with all the other doctors: undress from the waist up put on dull cotton robe with opening on the front, sit down arms up, lay down arms up, dress again.

Always a complicated task, with my pilling necklaces, bracelets, scarf's, sweaters, jackets, and on cold days even gloves, I am a very complex dresser.

I am adamant the act of dressing will keep me grounded even if I get strange looks from normal individuals the idea was to make it fun for me.

Examining my breast like a tedious ritual and looking at my eco and mammography charts he blurts it out, for the second time in less than a week confirming:

"It is the Challenge, of course."

As I am dressing, I overhear his mumbling words and the steps to be taken, absentminded and listening to Lola's relentless interrogation. I just hate his answers, I just hate his crowded little office, totally disliking his old shiny suit and crumpled white shirt, I just want to run out from there.

As I nervously sit down facing him I feel my eyes well up with tears, which for some unknown reason are not rolling down my cheeks. How I did not start screaming like a raving lunatic is beyond me.

I am doing it again like when mother died, little old hysterical me appears to be under control against my better judgment. Again taking a look behind me even though the office door seems to be just inches from my back I want to be sure there is no one else there.

I want to think his explanation unacceptable, he of all people will not invade in any way my body, I will make sure of that. To this day, his features have vanished from my memory he looked to be in his early 40's or late 30's.

What bothered me was he never answered a question without being evasive or doubtful and never maintained direct eye contact with any of us.

Learning over time when someone is having a serious conversation and is not looking straight into my eyes, a trust bond cannot be formed between us, it is intolerable.

Maybe it also had to do with his bluntness, cold demeanor, and yes, very important for me, the shabbiness in which he was dressed. Blocking him forever from my mind. Even forgetting his name, unsettling me to the point of driving us to get a six pack of beer just after leaving his office.

My Rock Star

After much thought, a little research, by way of Lola's recommendation, I make an appointment with another doctor, only two weeks shy after discovering the lump.

At 10:05 A.M. the next day my cell has been blasting on and off for almost ten minutes. I am driving and cannot pick up the phone. I am just one block from the doctor's office and know it is, Lola by her standards I am running late. The appointment is until 10:30 A. M. It starts to unnerve me. Doesn't she know doctors always make you wait. Sure enough, a little over half an hour later we are ushered finally into his office.

Dr. Canavati greets Lola with genuine fondness (he operated on her mother years ago). A warm looking man in his early 60's, without being extremely tall, his imposing presence makes him look big. With long gray hair, combed back in a sleek way, giving me the impression he is hooked on the radical 60's.

I will later find out he liked to write romantic pop type music, forming a band with some friends. I feel these are the best credentials for any highly recommended surgeon, cool and looking like a retired rock star.

Maybe it was his bohemian background that made me like him immediately. Acting fatherly and very comfortable with himself, when I ask if the other diploma on the wall of a preppy younger handsome man, is his son he almost shouts: "My nephew Mauricio," heard of him? "Yes" I answer," He almost shouts:

"Two for the price of one."

Replying with a natural sense of humor, and sounding proud. So I have fallen for him on the spot. Again the same drill starts for the third time in less than ten days.

So I take off my starched white shirt, which I have worn over my brown skinny suede pants with a lot of long beaded necklaces and wide bracelets. All of it seems inappropriate and not at all functional. Beads getting entangled with one another, and bracelets clinking loudly against each other, complicated me! Mechanically donning on a bluish-drab robe opened on the front, there goes my fashion statement.

The routine starts, arms up, lay down on the bed the doctor examines both of my breasts carefully. Tells me to go back and put my clothes on. I take a long look at my attractive reflection in the bathroom mirror.

As I am buttoning up my shirt and putting back on all the strands of beads around my neck. Fluffing up my short blond hair, I still do not look or feel sick. Nothing hurts only my spirit is heavily damaged and squashed.

Sitting back at the doctor's desk, he is rearranging the results of my mammogram in front of the light box. Turning towards me he looks me right into my eyes with the warmest sympathetic expression on his face as I start to hear the words coming out of his mouth:

"I am very sorry; it has all the characteristics of a malignant tumor."

Again the word "Challenge," strikes harder than before being the third person to confirm the diagnose, as I am processing all of this, he starts drawing the procedure, outlining where the specific incisions will be performed. I am cringing at the gloomy scenario.

The blunt translation is my boob has to go, but there have to be other alternatives I ponder trying to take it all in. Explaining to Dr. Canavati I do not want to come out flat looking like a cutting board, he pays little attention, to my nervous rambling as I hear him say:

"We will do what is the best for you, I promise."

My chest feels heavy, this is not what I want to hear, and I am having trouble breathing. Sensing a nagging need again to run out of the office, and start screaming, with all the force my lungs can muster.

Surprising myself, with my calmness, sitting very lady-like, back straight hands folded on my lap, feet together to one side, (Emily Post comes to mind). Deeply locked inside me dread hovers like a beast, tears cleverly controlled.

I am acting exactly the contrary of what my brain is thinking, maybe I am going crazier than usual. Understanding later, the impact of shock.

Meantime, Dr. Canavati sets up an appointment with his nephew, for a thorough scan test the next day. As we are about to leave his office, he reassures me comfortingly everything will be all right and gives me a needed fatherly hug.

Trapped inside me the wave of tears ready to explode, are put on hold, unrecognizing my toughness I embrace Lola goodbye.

She reassures me I am in great hands, and that she will be just a call away.

Driving home in a partial state of blurriness, finally there seemed I had found a ray of hope. Recognizing the importance of feeling conformable with now my doctor. I felt safe and sure I had found someone I could trust I was in the process of building my team of physicians who would work together for what would be the best for me.

Home

J uanita is a character all of her own, sometimes she reminds me of Scarlet O'Hara's nanny's manner in Gone with the Wind. She is not as huge but big and cushy with caramel colored skin, black hair and very dark warm eyes.

Growing up close to a river in small mining town lost in the heart of the state of Coahuila, Mexico, called Aura, (just like the Carlos Fuentes novel). Learning resilience at an early age since facing the many trials of a mining town, is enough to help you survive anything in life.

Working both with my aunt, and my mother before coming to work with me after the birth of Alex my second child. Twenty-five years later, Juanita is more family than a worker, sometimes unsettling me to the point of exasperation, extremely talkative, noisy and of course terrible bossy.

Still she never fails to be there in time of need, she shifts from our house to her family of children and grandchildren. Doting totally on my son, staying with us for so many years, is all about him.

Our home is more hers than ours, running every single aspect, down to making the perfect "Cuba" rum, lime & Coke, excellent vodka tonics, and of course "micheladas," (a beer and hot sauce concoction). She has also mastered the art of Mexican gourmet cuisine, including several international dishes, taught to me by my mother and grandmother.

Juanita's remaining with us over the years has made it easier for me to work in the craziness of fashion shows, and photo shoots. I have always been confident my kids were well-taken care for, and she made sure I would not forget them at a birthday party, or leave them of at school after soccer practice. She has kept the house afloat even following my divorce.

After the doctor's appointment, and the third time of being told I have the "Challenge" I arrive at the house asking her to please fix me a ham, cheese, and mushrooms omelet.

I guess hunger strikes like an alternative to calm a worried mind since tears are not coming out. I am still a size four dress, and not in bad shape for my early 50's so I deserve comfort food.

Slumping my body down in front of the TV, immersing myself at 11:30 A.M. with the problems and affairs of the Young and the Restless, a soap opera my mother used to enjoy watching, making me feel closer to her. Oh how badly I want her now!

A melancholic sigh escapes me, as Juanita walks with a big wooden tray into my cozy family room were masks made by Mexican artisans deck the walls. My alternative mother to the rescue.

All energy has left my body, but if I stay on the sofa for one minute longer, I will start feeling sorry for myself. From this moment on I pledge to do everything I am asked by the doctors and somehow go on with my usual activities, the "Challenge" will not intrude on my daylily life.

Such a compromise with myself was a tough one since I just wanted to fall asleep through the whole ordeal. Honestly, some days I did but mostly I forced my life to go on as usual.

Family

U nderstanding you have to draw some courage where there seems none left, I confronted my son after the third doctor's appointment with the hard facts. Australia was left behind on a corner of his dream board. Facing the fact it was left to only the two of us to brace the storm by ourselves.

My father has not much to offer with his years and my daughter has to fight her own battles before she can help anyone.

Raising my kids on my own has been an enormous task. Sitting with my blondish, tall, thin, handsome son Alex, light brown eyes shining with hidden tears, behind thick-framed glasses, a heavy weight falls on my chest as we hugged.

Alex is in College majoring in architecture, being a man he is more realistic knowing we have had good times, and many hard ones. My business sometimes great others not so, but things will always have a way of coming out right at the worst possible time.

Talk of the recession started to loom high in the air. I am not only facing the "Challenge" but also a rocky financial road ahead. So sitting on the couch doing nothing is not even an option, luckily I have been paying a very expensive health insurance for years, one less thing to worry about knowing I will be getting the best possible medical attention needed.

So between the coordination of fashion shoots and fashion shows, teaching modeling, and fashion courses, I squeeze in blood tests, scans, and many x-ray exams. Some days I am so exhausted from lack of sleep. Getting out of bed by 9:00 in the morning is an ordeal, making me feel guilty since I have always been an early riser.

Somehow my body badly needs sleep, I just crave it, and it is also a way of escaping reality. Sleep turns out to be a field trip, you just let go and try to have good dreams.

As Jaime, my oncologist says:

"You need sleep to recuperate from the stress of what you are experiencing. The mind takes in the disease sometimes harder than the body."

Waking up to reality is a tricky affair, there are days I don't feel like putting on makeup or cute clothes. On those days when I feel I can't take another test, pink lip-gloss and a pair of tall boots with skinny jeans, a black turtleneck, and leather jacket does the trick.

Even though I will probably never get picked up like Pretty Woman!

Grasping at my inner struggle against this imaginary 100-pound weight over my back pulling me down. An illness without the discomfort of sickness, nothing hurts but my heart feels like it is coming undone into teeny little pieces.

This to a point becomes a tricky affair, when pain is not manifested, comfort sets in, and this may take us to the brim of danger, so attention to the problem can't be overlooked, time is a crucial friend or a terrible adversary.

With a lot of care, I start concentrating more on what to wear every day specially to tests or doctor's appointments I decide if all my life I have been talking image and fashion so this is not a moment to let my guard down.

Working on looking attractive, is a booster to my self-esteem, besides people around me treat me with a lot more respect. Not a good time for sweat-pants, not even if they are Juicy Couture.

The Team

Already twelve days have gone by after I had first visited Jaime, my oncologist friend. Reaching him had been on my mid to explain what I was up to, when the call comes from my office. Jaime is there wondering if I am still in shock and knowing by this time I had not liked the doctor he had recommended in the first place.

Arriving at the office, Jaime listens to my reasons for looking for another surgeon and then he starts to describe his idea on how we could make my operation a conservative one. Taking me a while to understand how it would work even though the explanation was simple as he goes on, Hope:

"You see you are in stage one, so with chemo before the surgery the "Challenges" dimensions will minimize in size, preserving your skin. Being then a less invasive procedure. Coming out of the operating room with a temporary implant, which will not look as you have lost your breast. From here on, next step, the reconstruction process".

What I am listening to specifically is what I have been asking all along, knowing from my readings there had to be a better way out.

My very experienced Dr. Canavati is first all a surgeon and from his point of view it is better to get rid of everything looking murky and evil. I had been very clear on telling each of the doctors on my team my needs, stating again and again I did not want to come out looking like a wood cutting board. Being utterly essential that everyone understood this.

So we contacted my surgeon explaining Jaime's suggestion over the phone, agreeing all, that a catheter will be installed at the same time of the biopsy surgery.

Arriving to my appointment with Dr. Mauricio Canavati my surgeon's nephew and partner, I can see he is as handsome as the picture in his uncle's office. A preppy kind of guy in his mid-thirties with semi curly light brown hair, white skin, and kind brown eyes. He is subtle where the uncle is rough he is quiet where the other is loud. He listens carefully to all my doubts. Clarifying again precisely the procedure his uncle tried to explain when I was too numb to understand.

With each doctor, I start to realize I am creating a bond, so this is the way I start building my team. After he checks, mammograms sonograms, echo-s, x-rays and blood tests. Just like his uncle, he starts drawing pictures of my boob and the incisions to be performed if we want to save the skin, before reconstruction.

I am in a trance struggling once again with acceptance, sitting in front of this cruel reality, which appears alien to me. Listening, to the explanation, it appears like he is talking about someone else. I don't feel sick, nothing hurts, my whole being is submerged in this vast irrational abyss.

Shivers go thru my spine, as all will depend on the pathology reports after the biopsy which is to be scheduled a week from now. My brain is trying to get a clear grasp of his detailed account. When suddenly I acknowledge the connection of the drawings as belonging to my boob.

The raw awareness of reconstruction, triggers a wake-up call from my dark thoughts. This is hope in a silver platter. Many will probably not see it like this, but for me getting rid of the "Challenge" is a first but without reconstruction the meaning of all the struggle will be useless, I will not be able to cope without a little ray of light.

So I ask Mauricio "Who do you recommend for my reconstruction?"

Just saying the word out loud seems to come out hoarse as if it was trapped inside my throat.

For the first time he becomes nervous giving me only two names: "Walberg or Narvaez but, you will have to make an appointment and interview both to decide"

He answers not trying to influence my choice. "No, Mauricio I want you to tell me with whom you and your uncle feel more comfortable working with?"

I see he is feeling pressured, so I make a crazy sort of comparison, drawing a witty smile on his face: "It is easy there are some makeup artists I hate to work with, and some I just love, it is the same."

The result is how I came to meet with Dr. Francisco Walberg the fourth part of the team, the plastic surgeon who gave Lola and me a whole hour course in the evolution of breast reconstruction.

Walberg is also in his thirties gregarious good-looking guy with an enormous sense of humor and always impeccably dressed. Considering always the positive side of things and the best at narrating a procedure without skipping on any detail. Specializing in New York, and is accredited by the Breast Surgeons of American Association as are my two other surgeons, I have felt quite at ease with him to this day.

So I find my perfect dream team of doctors, one in his 60's, one in his 40's and two in their 30's, experience mingled with a new outlook in the end, the best combination for my survival of body and soul.

Barbarella

B efore the biopsy, a lineup of tests, are necessary, the worst one a sonogram. Letty, a dear friend from my new support system, accompanies me to the hospital. Acting like a pro as soon as she sees me turn white as the needles get inserted into my arm and the blue fluorescent goop starts going all thru my body.

After waiting outside the exam room for more than an hour, her presence of friendship only inspires my courage and triggers my gratefulness.

I am strapped face down boobs embarrassingly plunging down like melting candles, enclosed in a sort of Barbarella capsule inside a very cold room. Recalling the 60's futuristic and scandalous science-fiction movie, which made Jane Fonda into a sex symbol and a female force to reckon with.

Considered at the time indecent since Barbarella's naked body, boobs included were only partially covered by her long luscious reddish mane. I remember sneaking into the movie theater without parental approval, during my early teens, and became in total awe of Miss Fonda, to this day.

Totally uncomfortable, being in the same position like forty minutes, with the constant sound of this tick, tack, as if listening to some heavy metal music. Piercing tunes hover loud, clobbering my brain after every picture was shot, with the technician's voice pounding inside my ears:

"Rosa don't move"

How I hate them calling me Rosa, I never know they are talking to me (my real name which I never use). Moving my little finger is not actually moving. Well for him it was, and stillness has never been one of my fondest traits.

Reasoning

I have come to realize how important it is to like my doctors to feel they are trustworthy, and answer my every question. They patiently take the time to explain the procedures, so I ask, what is going to be done to my body, many times over. Reasoning it is the "only body" I will get, I have to guard it and cherish it with all my being.

As complicated as the medical technicalities appear, they start to unfold under my own eyes in a clearer light. I will feel the pain of needles, the sickness in the pit of my stomach. Later the scars will start changing how my body looks, and there will be times I will hate it all, even if it justifies maintaining me alive.

Evidently life has to go on as if nothing is happening. Only my close group of friends at the moment know what I am going thru. I first had to take it in myself, before putting it out there, I am still too stunned to discern how to handle this. Some days I honestly try to block the whole "Challenge" from my mind as if it is a foggy dream and that very soon I will wake up to my old life.

Things start getting more complicated as my 83-year-old father arrives in town, explaining to him what is going on is quite a difficult task. After going thru my mom's long illness he was left in a sensible spot. Besides I am his only child.

As hard as it was telling my kids, telling my father was more heartbreaking. I would achingly observe him withdrawing to a painful place of silence and solitude.

To some extent, it helps he has a hearing difficulty, which needed to say his ear device is most of the time inside one of his coat pockets. An excellent excuse when he does not want to be bothered by whatever problem is going around him.

Evasion is permitted at his age, even if at first I feel a sharp stab of resentment. In my selfishness I take for granted how dad settles himself into those prolonged quiet phases throughout my ordeal.

Being the funny witty and dynamic man he always was, he began carrying his pain on his plump short frame moving in slower paces. Painful to see his light brown eyes constantly watery.

Taking time in understanding what may look like his lack of interest or compassion for what I am experiencing. I finally realize it is too much for him to handle. He is with tied hands unable to do anything for me, to stunned just dealing with his own pain.

Recalling now when my mother was diagnosed with the "Challenge," twenty years younger than today, it took him a while to comprehend what was happening to the love of his life.

At times being insensitive of her needs, in fact too overwhelming for him as it is now. Men are obviously less resilient when faced with a love ones illness, putting on a protective armor to hide their fears and worries.

My daughter Alexis at the time was only three years old, so a support system was built to help us out including, my mother's two sisters and my father's sister Eddy. The five of us will take turns accompanying my mom to her chemotherapy and radiation sessions, flying in an orderly fashion to San Antonio, Texas.

We knew my dad could not have survived all the pressure of her illness by himself if he had lacked the assistance team we all became for both of them.

Courage

Postponing work, is not an option and I am really glad to be kept busy, forcing me to focus on something outside of myself it would be too dangerous to have any moment for self-pity. Fear on the other hand is inevitable, it is always teasing and poking big holes on the little courage that is there to be rescued.

Time has worked to my favor since I have taken fast control of the situation, not a day has gone by since finding out about the "Challenge" have I wasted in feeling sorry for myself.

Standing faithful to a pact made in the beginning, not ever bothering to ask:

"Why me?"

Work is my therapy. Starting a course with a group of executives from the local brewery, enjoying the process of explaining how they can learn to dress with key pieces, work with the right hair color and perking their overall look.

Advising also a group of society ladies who with a great amount of sense of humor are very open to my suggestions. More like when in my teens, gathering with friends before a big night out and we would start comparing what we were going to wear that night on our special date.

Having the opportunity of explaining how a cut fits a body type and a particular color can enhance a certain skin tone, my audience ended with more options on managing their fashion dilemmas.

As women we inexplicably bond in times of need even when you are not the best of friends, so without their asking my clients turned out to be a big support. Together, transforming into an army of fortitude helping me in the fight against my worries and self-doubts, filling my whole being with a well required dose of strength.

Essential, this support group of women sprouting from everywhere, old friends, new friends, clients, and strangers kept appearing as the stages of the "Challenge" evolved.

Image

U nderstanding there are two of ME. The sick ME tires, and aches the fighter ME tries to take one day at a time with as much normalcy as I possibly can.

Remembering from the beginning when told of the "Challenge" I promised myself "it" would not stop me from my everyday life and work. Swearing never, ever to looking sloppy. Besides my work does not give me the chance to appear lousy, it is really out of the question.

Working a lot with teens in our modeling and image courses, it is important they see me as a role model. Dressing with fresh ideas, cool looks not slutty or like their mother's may dress.

I rejoice watching their surprised faces which feels so great, when they see how I mix and match things they never thought up they could wear. A real gratification to have a job which I highly enjoy, and forcing me to be creative every single day. I focus my mind daily more on what I will wear next day, than what my body is going thru.

My dream is to transmit to all of this girls, the appreciation of their unique beauty. Also for them to accept, that the only competition is not with anyone outside of their inner-selves, it is only with the image facing them in front of the mirror.

Our unique image is what is given to us to work with, and only us as individuals can make it grow and flourish.

I share this with Mrs. Dianna Vreeland, my fashion guru and the legendary fashion columnist and editor, from the 30's to the 60's at Bazar, later at Vogue and then at the Metropolitan Museum of Art in New York till almost the time she died in 1989.

Mrs. Vreeland was not a beauty in the traditional sense of the word, she just simply made herself look attractive She avidly managed flair, not only the way she dressed butt the display of her attitude, which to a certain degree forgoes beauty. She knew well that beauty without attitude has no real power, and I believe, it is her fundamental legacy to all.

At the time of her funeral the designer Oscar De La Renta had this anecdote to prove what I am talking about:

"Inviting her for a holiday in my native Puerto Rico, close to the house there was this duty-free drug store, so every day she would walk down there, at first just to buy something or other."

"On the second day Dianna returns thrilled having discovered the town's natives were in awe of her, for more than a week at a given hour, a big group would gather around just waiting to see how she had dressed that day."

"Over dinner, one evening she tells me with her famous exaggerated accents and adjectives:

"Oscar my dear, I am afraid I will have to go back home before everyone, I simply have to confess I have run out of "dazzling" ideas on what other "glamour's" outfit to wear." "You do understand I cannot disappoint my audience?"

Like her, I became so engrossed on the skill of dressing first before the surgeries and obsessed after each one, for my changed body needed the art of camouflage.

So when it was decided by my team of doctors to install a catheter for the administration of the chemotherapy (nasty word) and also the biopsy (cuss word) of the tumor would be in order, I had to start to brave myself for the outcome, clothes wise of course, for my hospital stay.

I shopped like when you are going to a special event, and cannot decide what to wear. I went overboard with my selection, of velvet leopard pants with a wraparound robe, a green silk open front tunic with black silk pants, red silk men's button up style pajamas.

An array of kaftans, some in animal prints, others in Indian-inspired graphics and a special metallic powder pink pleated number. This one was more for wearing to the Grammys than to my bedroom, but when finally raising my arms was possible I felt like a big pink butterfly.

Hospital robes in drab colors, are not a so great effect on any complexion combined with the bright iridescent hospital lights. A dose of some extravagance is essential in order to survive all the drama.

God

Without warning I realized I had to go look for God. Strangely before the biopsy, I ended inside this beautiful church in the middle of a fruit market in an old downtown neighborhood of the city, of Monterrey, the church of the Virgin Mother of the Perpetual Socorro, my grandmother's namesake.

Guided by my Grandmother's hand to this particular place of high ceilings, and beautiful stained glass windows. Lost back into my childhood's memories, this same image was almost in every room at Grandmas Coco's house, her great devotion drove her to persuade my uncles to build a unique marble altar in our home town's main church with an image of this Virgin Mother brought from Italy.

A shame it mysteriously disappeared with no recollection from no one at the church or even my cousins living in town. Recalling all this as I am kneeling down praying in this peaceful place in the middle of a racket outside from the fruit vendors

Out of no specific place a priest comes up to me as if he knows I am dealing with some heavy load, kneeling besides me, and asks about my troubles carefully listening to my story as he crocheted a thread rosary, which lasted on my left wrist all thru the ordeal. Left as a reminder of his bad judgment.

At first, he was so comforting, until he said something, which astonished me, and later I would prove him wrong when I hear him in disbelief:

"What need of you to worry about losing your breast since being divorced and with no apparent partner why worry who is going to see your body?"

It was like being stabbed straight into the heart. Unknown to this priest, to me the relevance of maintaining my attractive self-intact. In no way was I, giving up on my sexuality. His advice was unjustified and a very outrageous, proclamation.

First having to look "great" for only myself, not for anyone else. I am the most important "being" who is going to be facing the mirror every single day for the rest of my life. Then if a man comes along well, it is an extra bonus. As a matter of fact I had three relationships in the process of recuperation, but let's leave that for another chapter.

I was now more certain than ever that no one, not even a priest could minimize the importance of my feminine self. Experiencing critical anguish as a "woman" when facing being told my body was going to be mutilated especially in one of my most feminine parts.

On leaving the church I was outraged at his insensitivity, still the burning anger gave me the strength I was looking for, let's say I found the core-training program for my fight.

October 20th

B eing admitted to the hospital at 6:45 A. M. with just my son Alex, and Juanita my guardian angel. My daughter is quite unable to understand the ordeal just yet, so she could not refuse to attend a Madonna concert in Vegas.

After much crying about her lack of concern, as mentioned before, I realized that I could not expect all the members of the family to react the same way. One may always be there to hold my hand, while the other will be unable to cope with the ordeal at hand.

Pondering on this matter, when finding out my mother was dying only after less than a month of leaving my house with my father, to Piedras Negras, I just froze. First, I felt Alzheimer had already taken her away from me a long time before. I could not bear seeing her drift off from this world without even recognizing me.

In dealing with the pain of loss, selfishness is sometimes one of the things one day may cause us the worst regret of all, and in order not to suffer we can become self-centered brats.

We sometimes make excuses or find places to escape and hide from the reality at hand. My daughter was just acting as I had done on my mother's last New Year's Eve. I never wanted to remember her being frail, or looking ill. Desperately wanting to recall her beautiful, with her smiling face, and her amazing stunning presence. I was a coward too engrossed with my own pain, to have the courage to see her slow deterioration, so I drove to San Miguel de Allende, and would never see her alive again.

The same was happening now with my 83-year-old father he will excuse himself by saying his earpiece was not working, and could not hear what was going on. The truth being he apparently was too damn scared of losing his only child, so the place of silence was his best way out.

On the other hand my 21-year-old son as nervous as he might be adopted a grown up attitude. Today he appears older than his real age, concentrating carefully on all of the documents to be signed, as I am checking into the hospital.

A big support for all is Lourdes, my famous model friend who astonishes the few people working the hospital rounds at this early hour. Storming into the lobby looking fabulous even without a hint of makeup, her beauty shines. Thick eyebrows frame her eagle hazel-olive eyes, and ash light straight blond hair past her shoulders cascades freely as she walks.

As she hugs me she tries to hide her nervousness with her funny giggles, (which always give her away). Approaching the doctors, giving them all kinds of orders, asking question after question about my operation in her rushed and authoritarian, characteristic manner.

As I say my goodbyes before being wheeled into surgery, Lourdes decides to take her first mammogram. At the time in her early 40's my ordeal is a scary wake-up call. Confronting, what she has never considered and should have, some time ago.

So this brings us face to face with prevention an activity most of us women take for granted, scheduling mammograms should be a priority on our to-do list every six months starting in our late 20's.

Being my first surgery, my team of doctors reassures me, everything will be all right. I am a cluster of nerves, before sensing the anesthesia take hold of my mind and body. Slowly I start to slip into the unconscious world, where it starts to transform into a mass of whiteness, without dreams.

Wakening an hour later, with a time-lapse I have no account for, entering to a different and cold world I hear myself say:

"I am freezing."

Faces all around peak from above as I am something strange to behold, I hear laughter and chitchat. All the nurses clad in sparkling white head to toe dresses, one of the many giggly ones covers me with another too thin white sheet, before rolling me out from recovery.

Hanging outside my rooms door I find a bear stuff animal wearing a pink frilly dress and a straw bonnet with the letterhead:

"It's a girl."

Surely the reason for all the whispering and commotion the nurses had going on in the recovery room. The idea must be Lourdes, who also managed to have two more stuff animals decorating the inside of the room, with even a white furry singing dog.

"You are just too good to be true can't take my eyes of off you."

The dogs mouth sort of quivers, like a real person, seeing this makes me appreciate and love her even more, my dear crazy friend.

Having friends of every age and gender brings certain stability to my chaos. My reliable one Luis Felipe, a short and light of built witty man always impeccably well dressed, just like an English gentleman. Looking ten years younger, than his actual seventy years, he is busy traveling the world and being on the board of several organizations.

Our friendship has grown over the years, always around to give me his affection and support. His presence is always a joy to my heart, especially today since it must be hard for him to be here, after losing his wife more than ten years ago to the "Challenge."

Having friends and family support is an unexpected show of love.

Tears

As everyone goes off to lunch, I face my solitude and without warning it hits me. Only a month has passed since my confrontation with the "Challenge" at this point actual sobs leave my body. I cry trembling unable to control myself, I am shedding tears by the second, I hide my face on the pillow, but I cannot stop.

What I have been avoiding for days is facing me with bold black letters my battle, has started against the "Challenge."

As he leaves the room I see my son's pale face movements stiff, like controlling himself not to break down before me.

So I sob for him, for my friend Lourdes who hides her qualms behind funny remarks, for my father's fears, which show on his watering eyes, for Alexis absence.

I cry at the sight of my ex-husband who is stricken with worry and Juanita who has never looked so somber in all the years at my side

I weep also, for the many women who have had to face this "Challenge," for Luis Felipe's wife and for all the others who passed away, living their families and loved ones behind. Tears flow freely, drenching my drab hospital robe.

With a trembling force I continue my crying storm which seems to have no end. Overcome by an indescribable sadness and a profound heaviness inside my chest I cry also for the survivors. Like me they will have to face a new image in front of the mirror.

Sobbing still, believe it or not, I reach for the lip-gloss as a way of comforting myself, the first reason my super chapped dried lips, and the second is obvious, vanity. I sincerely consider "vanity" the only thing able at this moment to keep me sane.

I doze off for a while exhausted from my emotional outburst. Only to be awakened from my deep sleep, to be taken for a TACT exam. Being cold has become a way of life. My feet seem to be always freezing, even when covered by unsexy thick socks.

Again as I am wheeled to the exam room the cold travels thru my bones, even the little warm granny blanket Lucia my dear friend gave me two Christmas ago, does not help much. I smile remembering joking to her about it when unwrapping her present:

"Does this mean I am old lady now?"

I remember her laughing hard at my remark, her blond curls bouncing from her head like admitting in our joking manner the answer to my question.

On my arrival to the exam room, it is as icy as the technician's attitude, my small talk gets hardly a peep from him. Total detachment and lack of warmth have become characteristic of most of the people involved with medical equipment. They even seem to have a hard time smiling.

I begin to think it has to do with the lack of color in their surroundings, gray and dull white seem to be the norm of decoration in all hospitals. My theory, is it drains their energy and infuses automatic gloom. Color to me gives life, we cannot survive in the melancholy of a black and white world, and it is too depressing.

Inside again in the Barbarella's like space capsule as the tick-tock sound starts pounding all thru my body I distract myself counting one, two, three and so on.

Lola, who acts as my sounding board, greets me, on the arrival back to my room, Luis Felipe is back with flowers in hand. Lourdes arrives making one of her grand and noisy entrances accompanied by her mother Rose, and her sister Viv. The room starts to feel small on the arrival of my friend Marcus, and my photographer friend Luz Maria. I am overwhelmed by all's reassurance of their total support and love.

Phil another of my group of crazy friends arrives clad in one of his Hugo Boss suits, and Ferragamo shoes obviously worn Italian style, with no socks. He starts making jokes way past midnight, starting with the "it's a girl" stuffed animal at the door. Biding his time, not wanting to live me alone, until the last drop of sedatives go thru my veins.

On feeling I am fading away I barely hear him tiptoe out of the room, still a foggy glimpse of him makes me almost laugh out loud. I see him with his Louis Vuitton portfolio in arm, carrying it the way only Queen Elizabeth always manages to hold her bags, and very ceremoniously he shuts the door behind him.

In the middle of the night, a sharp pain awakens me on my left side where the catheter now rests, a now strange being inside my body. A not a very nice look for strapless dresses, resembling a bulky pimple the size of a cherry tomato, only covered with skin. On my right side, the incision made for the biopsy stings a little less.

Feeling helpless I start on another crying rampage. Fear is the worst feeling you can have, and sleep is the only solution so like a little girl I cry myself to sleep.

My Body

A few weeks before the surgery I had asked my friend Luz Maria Vales one of the official photographers of deceased famous Mexican painter Julio Galán to take some nude photos of myself.

I felt I needed a reminder of my body before the operation, this turned out to be a great experience on self-appreciation. I should never have taken for granted the body given to me by God. So being naked in front of the camera was at the beginning intimidating but in the end very stimulating

Nakedness faced me with a new found freedom, the form of my body seemed a sight to behold cellulite and all. For the first time in years I felt less critical about my wide hips and my C size boobs which I had considered as a burden. My breasts now looked lovely, flawless, and the central elements of my feminine figure. My body was only mine to cherish.

Appreciating my body with all its shortcomings and qualities as the only one I will have. Funny it took the devastation of the "Challenge" to open my eyes to its imperfect beauty. The pictures became my first step in preparing my mind for the process of transformation.

A straight message to the priest, who wanted me to suppose the marring of my body, was unimportant.

Going back to when I heard:

"Your boob has to go?"

An explosion had gone inside my brain, sparks of uncertainty hovered. A death threat had been tossed with a closed fist ready to knock me down. Then I was thrown a rope for salvation, called mutilation, and realized the blow will be slow.

Being my femininity under direct attack, grabbing at this rope is one of the toughest things I would have to hold onto, to ease the quiet pain of loss.

As the catheter was installed inside my body I began to realize the nature of my crying attacks, first it was the stress of the operation, the ordeal it implied and second my body had started to be disrupted.

Facing Life

A gain my color theory is put to a test. I would think instead of drab looking greens and faded blues there should be hospital gowns in bright, happy colors. Like emerald green, fuchsia, orange, deep-sea blue, and sunny yellow. Color offers so much positive energy, it should be taken into consideration in the future by all hospitals.

The doctor arrives after 8:30 A. M. surprised to see me ready for checking out. An hour ago I had convinced the nurses to help me take off the dreadful colorless robe.

After washing and drying my hair, I dressed in a new yoga like pant-suit, with a matching zippered jacket in cobalt blue, embroidered on one side in sequences with a big silver heart. A much better look than a dull tunic, the final touch, lip-gloss.

Dr. Canavati has his long white hair neatly arranged away from his face, controlled with some mousse the rest is curled up at the back of his neck, looking more like a celebrity, than a doctor. He is noisy, bossy, with the nurses, with a very optimistic vibe, he seems bigger than life with his brilliant, sense of humor, in a horse thick voice jokes about the stuff animals, balloons and flowers all over the room:

"Looks like there was a great party in here." And laughs loudly.

He starts commenting how my friend Lourdes interrogated him about the steps of the procedure. Like everyone meeting her, he became enchanted by her beautiful, enigmatic presence. Under chuckles he says:

"Coming out of surgery, she even gave him a high five and a hug, making my colleagues all green with jealousy."

Signing my hospital release after clearly instructing the steps to follow, and pointing out that we will wait for a couple of days for the biopsy results. Just an official procedure since we all know what the outcome already is, still holding my hand, whispers:

"Well, miracles are known to happen."

On hearing this, checking all of this to be real, my hand goes to my left side under my collarbone. I touch the catheter bump, then to my right side were the biopsy was obtained. Tears are about to start escaping from my eyes as the door opens, there is my beautiful son Alex arriving to take me home. I quickly regain myself.

Alex almost loses his usual calm when realizing he has to make several trips back and forth from the room to the car. So of he goes battling up and down with all the balloons, flowers, stuffed animals, and chocolate boxes.

As we are driving from the hospital, the car looks more like a party with wheels. Stopping at a red light the people on the other lanes look at us with mocking expression making us roar with laughter, losing the mornings tensions.

We detour to the office to check on the image course for an executive group of ladies, Miro's my longtime makeup artist is teaching the ten-minute technique, for close to an hour, I start explaining new ways to use the new color trends of the season for each skin type.

Out from the corner of my eye, I glimpse at Alex expression on his face, as if shouting to me "I cannot believe you are doing this, just now?"

I take my cue and wrap up my participation, say my goodbyes and as we are walking to the car I hear his agitated sermon:

"You are exhausting yourself you just had an operation what are you thinking?"

I stop him as I put my hands on his shoulder and looking straight into his watery eyes, I say:

"Alex bear with me I will not have this "Challenge" prevent me from doing what I love."

He was of course right as I start to feel little pinches of pain as the sedatives start losing effect, so when we arrived home, fatigued I go straight to bed.

After the ease of the hospital's automatic bed trying to accommodate in a standard one is quite a process. Discomfort arises from having two cuts one on my right side and the other on my left side. Finding the only option is to be propped on a lot of pillows laying down completely straight Dracula style.

Facing the vastness of my bedrooms roof seems to be the only alternative left. A heavy silence reigns in the house. I been left to rest, only with my dark thoughts taking hold of the peace I crave.

As my hand touches the bump, reality strikes again this is happening to me I am a prisoner of a dragon inside my body, and my prince charming has put this device as a hope of chasing the beast away.

After little-brooding sleep creeps in until I lose the day. Waking in the middle of the night from a sharp pain, and the feeling of a strange artifact inside my body. Surrounded by six pillows almost unable to move like an Egyptian mummy I fall back to sleep.

I have to admit I am more tired from the stress, of the operation than anything else, sleep seems a good way out.

Dreams this first weekend are long and weird with a lot of strange faces, and a lot of familiar ones in which mother pops in giving me a needed support, missing her aches so much. Understanding, you are never too old to miss your mommy.

Waking up to a very calm Sunday I spend it reading a book and dozing off eventually. Reading lets me worry about someone else's problems instead of mine. I grab the energy I can from sleep. Tomorrow I will fix a closet for a client, yes the doctor said I could work, I cannot sit by and do nothing it is unthinkable.

Day to Day

O ur daily life is predictable no matter what profession we are in, sticking to a particular schedule trying to follow it in an orderly manner, we become creatures of habits, and maniacs of time.

When life becomes unsettled by an improbable outcome like mine has, incorporating this trial into my normal life is not an easy task. Crucial are the daily confrontations with this ambivalent person inside my head, having to guide her to a certain normalcy path.

Optimism stands as fundamental for survival since failure for me is not an option. Tedious as my life might be now, more than ever I have to spice it up with whatever makeup I can find.

Just two days after my operation with a sunny disposition my friend Deborah from my support group drives me to a client's gorgeous house up on a hill for a closet makeover.

My client Clara is in her early fifties in great shape and handsome face, her clothes are excellent quality, of high-end brands, but somehow she hates her legs wearing pants always, with granny like shoes, making her look a lot older.

As I am listening to her reasons for disliking her to thin legs; I remember how the not so long ago "Me" thought:

"If only I had smaller boobs?"

Engraved in our senses is the relationship with our body image, related to our family backgrounds, our culture, and media influences. Sometimes taking for granted our beauty aspiring for a false perfection, an "idea" of the reflection of what we desire of "Us" to be.

Irrelevant to our body structure, our height or metabolism, or to our health, we dream of thinness, of a flat stomach of narrow thighs, of bigger or smaller boobs, but never in our wildest visions do we dream of the "Challenge" and never to the prospect of mutilation.

After pointing out my newfound wisdom to Clara, I see her assessing her body in a totally more appreciative way. Accepting her imaginary flaws in a different light. I say imaginary because usually our perception of ourselves is a false image we have created in relation to a comparison alien to our reality.

We have the tendency of wanting to look like someone we are really not. Losing ourselves when striving for a false perfection.

For years I had repeated this in my courses, but not until now had I really experienced the true meaning of loving and respecting my body to the fullest. I was excited I had accomplished of throwing down Clara's barrier and passing the torch of self-appreciation to her.

So after we do some cleaning and rearranging, I left Clara homework of buying booties with more stylish heels to perk all the pantsuits in her closet.

I also convinced her to get a pair of tall under the knee boots so she can revamp some practically unworn great suits and dresses, so her legs will stop being an issue at least in winter.

To my surprise before I am about to leave she takes out a very familiar shoebox she had almost hidden away in her closet, and say's:

"Thank you, as you suggested I will definitely wear my Manolo pumps with my little black dress this weekend."

Arriving home emotionally triumphant, but exhausted, limbs aching from everywhere. I cannot place where the pain is coming from, a disturbing drilling noise inside my head finally drives me to seek darkness, under the covers of my bed.

Spending a quiet afternoon to recharge energy, learning to take one thing at a time, my speedy-self has to slow down, only for now.

First Chemotherapy

S o how do I dress for chemo? It was my first silly thought in the morning. Choosing comfortable warm clothes, jeans a brown turtleneck, brown middle heeled suede boots and a brown knitted cape from Michael Kors, and on my arm a present from Lucia my security blanket, since I know it will get cold.

As I am walking inside the chemo facility, with Juanita on my toes, flaunting my cape with every movement, as if ready for a photograph at the end of a long runway. Self-confidence on the outside, vulnerability is at its peak on the inside.

I am having trouble not to fall to pieces at any given minute. Then everything seems to start to go wrong from the moment I give them my name, a mix-up on part of my insurance something to do with the date of starting the treatment, hysteria seems to be creeping inside me.

An hour goes by until the authorization comes thru, delays trigger my nerves making me get into awful mood swings. Recognizing there will be a lot of red tape, along the way in medical services, patience has to be part of my game, something I surely lack.

Having heard so many stories about the procedure, I hardly know what I am in for and the anxiety builds as I wait. Maybe if I had been Marie Antoinette I would have been glad to come back tomorrow, to have one more day before being beheaded. I just wanted everything to be over fast, and it better be today.

Juanita and I were left on our own devices, Alex had an important test at school, besides I did not want him to get involved in the ordeal of it all.

The pressure of seeing the appearance of some of the members of my "Challenge" club will have been too much for him to bear, so I kept him at bay. Alexis was busy at work, and knowing her state of mind would probably have fainted when the insertion of the needles started.

The nurses here were a different breed from what I had been experiencing beforehand, friendly, considerate and very careful while doing the procedure, explaining in detail how they will connect the needles to the catheter.

For almost four hours I lay down while this poison kills the bad cells of the "Challenge."

I am left in my private curtained room and on facing the ceilings fixtures, I start recognizing the building, originally from the 50's. This used to be the home of a very prominent family where important social gatherings took place. A period when lady's dressed with hats and gloves and pointy heels with martini glasses on their hands, conversing in the large foyer.

On closing my eyes to distract myself. Traveling back in time, picturing myself swirling around, in a pistachio raw silk wide circular skirted dress, with a tight bodice detailing my slim waist, a figure enhancing cleavage, with the famous almost round cut neckline and small cap sleeves, a very Christian Dior's New Look.

Only to be awakened from my imaginary fairyland, with a funny, acid heavy plastic smell one to be registered in my brain forever. Being this smell one of the hardest things to take about the whole affair before every chemo's ordeal, I just start to loath it.

As the clock ticks and boredom looms, Juanita falls asleep, watching an old Mexican movie on the TV. I reach for my book and read the last pages of Angels and Demons' without feeling a thing, until the last drop of the medication travels thru my body.

On the clock at six in the evening Silva, my assistant arrives looking somber, usually perky and always happy in manner, she seems stressed by the surroundings. She hands me several checks to sign, a regular Friday activity, and then offers to drive us home.

Two hours after I start to feel sick, throwing up as if my insides are coming undone. Anything I had ever experienced can't compare to this perspiring, cold sweat on my forehead I feel like spinning down into a tunnel.

The poison has activated my sense of smell to an incredible and sensitive degree, even in my bedroom with a closed door. The smell of cooking filter's from the kitchen triggering attack after attack of nausea.

Wanting to cry for help, is useless since no one will hear me I feel being pulled down to ground level, a vast emptiness with no end to fall to, I start making myself believe it is a sort of cleansing of my body.

Just think how flat my stomach will feel and how strong my abs will look?

Incoherent thoughts speed in and out as if driving a racecar and in front of me I am losing control, as I push the pedal in deeper trying to avoid a dangerous curve.

Kneeling almost embracing the toilet seat I vomit till I suppose there is nothing left in my insides, I lie on the bathroom floor to feel the cold tile take the heat from my body. The antique small chandelier seems to swing inches from my forehead ready to strike.

Suddenly above me in a blur I see Alex stricken face, staring down at me as his tall frame lowers down, pulling me up embracing my ragdoll-like body, I appreciate just being alive.

After a long bubbly soapy bath, my limbs relax my brain starts focusing more clearly, and my stomach takes a break from nausea. Getting into a dark purple silk nightgown, I jump hiding under thick, cushiony covers in an instant I am off into one of my travels to the world of dreams.

Early dawn some unknown force taps me awake throwing me off from the bed and off again to the bathroom, another seizure of queasiness hits and the drill becomes familiar until again after a shower I pass out naked on my bed.

Waking up Saturday as though I had a big night out, and after having too many tequilas, the hangover makes my head throb, hearing a constant oozing sound as if a bee is swimming inside.

Sleep seems to be the only way out, falling in and out of it thru the day, not wanting to get near the kitchen afraid the smell would trigger more vomiting. Food at this moment is my worst enemy even if I feel a bit of stomach emptiness.

Sunday, renewed, a beautiful sunny day greets me outside with a hint of crisp coldness making me feel very alive, and walking the three blocks to the beauty parlor to do my nails appears to be my greatest option. Even though my growling stomach has a revolution still going inside

Taking long deep joyful breaths wrapped in a cable- knit brown sweater with a long velour rust skirt and my favorite olive colored beaten up cowboy boots, warmed by the coziness of it all. I concentrate on my walk, grateful for this gift of another day is far more vital. Seems like when a heavy thunderstorm hits, sensing the wet air but around it has turned peaceful and quiet. Nevertheless I am so happy in the moment with the sun caressing my hair the brisk air framing my face. Rejoicing in the freedom of just being able for this, warmth and coolness, a hint of hope.

Fortunate to appreciate the mountains around me, grasping in their magnificent beauty, I am here now and I am not going anywhere anytime soon. Even if I have to puke every day I am going to fight this dam "Challenge."

The Show

Only two days after my first chemo, with all the will power I can muster I arrive at a store for the selection of the outfits for a fashion show, to be held at the end of the week.

As I pull the rack around to hang more clothes on the other side, I get hit by a nauseating feeling, as my stomach rumbles loudly I feel a cold sweat on my forehead, my reflection in one of the mirrors is ghostly.

How embarrassing, I am going to hit the floor.

I hear a voice asking me "Are you ok"?

Someone rushes toward me pulling me onto a chair, hands me a small can of coke. Slowly after taking a sip, I start regaining strength, my composure and mostly the will to keep up the fight.

With a growling stomach most of the week I continue to pull out the clothes, do the fittings, select the music, do rehearsals with sixteen models, and have a great show with sixty-four outfit changes.

Afterward, of course I drop exhausted for one whole day in bed, but it is so worth it like they say the show must go on and not without me.

November 30th

With a new asymmetrical haircut in a short black dress with batwing sleeves by Custo Barcelona worn with strappy pewter ankle open toe booties and black tights, off I go to my friend's Marcus's birthday bash.

I worked hard on trying to look good for tonight, my first big coming out party after chemo, besides the news is out, all my close circle of friends already know about the "Challenge." So I put a lot of energy into first convincing myself to do my nails, get the cut, put on makeup and get all dressed up.

On arrival to the party's venue the view is mesmerizing from the rooftop terrace, the city stretches before my eyes as a carpet of lights that seem to be preparing us for Christmas. My vintage mink jacket goes out from hiding since the wind chill up here is getting into my bones, still rejoicing from a great tingling sensation as I am filling my lungs with long cool breaths.

There is a certain thing I have come to discover in the past weeks, the great act to "feel" cold, heat, rain, sun, touch, smell, hugs and kisses. Having now a more powerful meaning, reaching under my skin and targeting straight to the heart.

Compliments from everyone at the gathering made me comfortable in my skin, and even if a lot of the audience was gay, they are the experts on the art of flattery, lifting my spirit to extraordinary heights. It was as if I was the belle of the ball, watch out Cinderella.

Whatever you do, do not shy from a compliment grab it and don't dare let it go. The boosting of our ego is oxygen to our self-esteem, feeling lovely about ourselves makes us more beautiful people.

My Beauty Idea

The idea of Beauty helps me through the rough days when frightened I will muster the strength from within every fiber of my body, not to fall apart, and when even washing my hair seemed to be a major task, I will force my head under the shower, never forgetting to dab some lip-gloss on. When feeling I lacked the strength to do something on my own, I didn't shy away from getting someone's help.

The magic of perfume on the back of my ears is a wakeup call, to my senses. The habit of applying some sweet smelling cream all over my body, especially on that part the "Challenge" struck it's blow. A caressing act, in preparation for the outcome.

From October to March, I would come out of the shower as part of a ritual, look at my naked body in the mirror and will say things to God like:

"Thanks for letting me have this body for so long, now I await a new body hoping it makes me a new person, more appreciative of what "You" granted me in the first place."

"You Lord have chosen me over so many, and I am one of the luckiest that have been given time to get prepared to meet the "Challenge" head on."

This sort of became my daily prayers in my preparation for body and mind.

For me the first chemotherapy would be by far the worst of all the sessions, still to this day I will have negative memories of what I ate before or after each ordeal.

Being a healthy eater I had never been picky with food. The night before my first round of treatments. Over dinner with friends at this Latin-Oriental fusion restaurant, the food left an aftertaste, a negative experience till this day. So my relation to food turns out to be tricky for a while, also smell required a respectful alertness since it would somehow trigger nausea.

My Support System

As I mentioned before I relied on my support system, operating successfully thru out my chemo's, in every single one I was in the company of one or another friend or relative.

Even Lucia tough it out after her brothers funeral, Nancy arranged her husband take care of their one-year-old twins for a whole afternoon not to mention Macarena, who took charge twice in a row.

Marcus, who broke the rules of only one visitor driving the nurses crazy with his charm and charisma to sit with us for more than an hour and gossip to his heart's content of what was happening in the local media of where he is a TV personality.

Being my body treated for the "Challenge", I found out in each step I couldn't do this without a support system. The help of friends who kept appearing from everywhere, Alicia called from Germany, Angelica from Laredo, Texas and Natalie from New York.

Lucia and Lourdes will call almost daily from Mexico City, my cousins took turns visiting, the phone rang the emails came, as did the stuff animals, balloons, flowers, and most significantly the love.

Strangely this sickness, reminded me about the importance of human relationships. Aware of the great power of friendships, and sometimes how just a casual acquaintance in trial times can lend a helping hand and stay friends forever.

Hope

O thers will bring hope, or some kind or comfort here is where Paula comes along.

Figuring that losing my hair would drive me nuts, after seeing it slide to the floor as my comb went thru the blond dyed strands after each shower. Facing baldness was not as bad as experiencing a burning sensation on my skull, and on scratching more chunks of hair will fall onto my hands.

Paula is as beautiful on the outside as she is on the inside, tall and slim with thick black hair beautiful green eyes and translucent white skin, she used to work with me as a model, now she is molding the character of three boys ages 12 to 6.

She calls unexpectedly in the middle of one morning all rushed, like any mother with tree kids. Talking rapidly of the wonders a German priest is accomplishing by healing people with prayer

Jaime my oncologist, had warned me the many things people will suggest for me to get better, but when Paula talks she is very convincing, so down to the point you have to pay attention and listen. In her authoritative tone, she makes me drop whatever I am doing and in less than half an hour we are speeding in her super Mom SUV to a neighborhood in the city you might never choose to visit.

Like in a cop and robbers movie tree black cars pulled together at the same time, in an empty lot close to a government hospital, where the priest is expected for a special visit.

As we all get down, I glimpse at a blond, tall, sturdy man walking towards me. Father, Tom's bright blue eyes penetrate my entire being, without his asking covers my head with his hands. His hoarse voice with a thick German accent uttering prayer after prayer. A warm light sensation covers my body, and the burning itchy feeling starts to disappear. For five minutes I surrender myself in his holiness, as if there was no one else around us. A proven fact, faith is a strong medicine.

December

C hristmas since childhood has been quite an affair, as a kid, my parents always found a way to do something spectacular with an element of surprise. At age five, Santa must have had a lot of trouble maneuvering the swings in the middle of our hallway close to the Christmas tree.

The next Christmas, I found under the tree just a beautifully wrapped little box in red and gold with only a key inside. I remember the details vividly as if it was yesterday. Seeing my parent's happy faces encouraging me to venture outside on a crisp December morning.

My then natural golden hair bouncing under my chin in soft waves, clad in a princess thick red velour robe with matching nightgown and fluffy slippers. Polaroid shots were taken by my father, of my excited face as my eyes opened wide, in disbelief on discovering outside the pink wood dollhouse standing in the backyard. On opening the door, furnished with a dining table for four, stove and cabinets for the china set with a rose pattern a similar replica to my mum's own Bavaria dishes, a dream come thru for any six-year-old little girl.

Strange how we find out things after so many years. I am now sure it was my father who orchestrated all of those happenings and can hear my mother saying:

"Pepe, how on earth are we putting the swings on the hallway? Think of the mess they are going to make."

"Do you realize the dollhouse is big enough for four people?"

I can hear him roar with laughter, and his answer will be as evasive as always:

"Rosa, everything can be arranged. It is Christmas."

Most Christmas's, he will be in charge of secretly hiding presents on the top shelves of our dens closet, covering them with distracting items. Like every other kid, I dreamed Santa Claus was as real as our image of him. Unfortunately, around age ten, my cousins and I discovered his hiding spot, destroying the magic.

Recently after watching an old home video, my three-year-old frame is plump and happy dancing around the Christmas tree. I am wearing a green velvet dress with a white lace collar, black velvet Mary Jane shoes, white tights, and an off-white sweater embroidered with tiny pearls and sequences.

A nostalgic feeling, as my mother's image, seems so alive looking gorgeous. Dressed in a black to the knee pencil skirt, red sweater set, her two string pearl necklace, and black leather pumps. With a joyful gleaming face, she waves to the camera operator, my father. Teary-eyed, I now remember my lovely childhood.

The family coming together for the holidays was a special affair. Always closer to my mother's family, the setting for Christmas day was the big two-story house where she grew up with her two brothers and two sisters. Family and friends made up of almost forty people at one time or another, including cousins, aunts, a great aunt, and great uncle. My grandmother Coco a long-time widow, will be holding court like a queen bee.

There was also the alternative family made up of neighbors, gray-haired Eva, one of my grandmother's bests friends from just across the street, and my mother's and aunt's official chaperone to dances. I have integrated into my courses the advice she gave them before entering into any social affair:

"Tuck that tummy, and raise high, those boobs. You might meet an interesting stranger tonight."

Eva, in my mind, will always have her platinum Nice & Easy gray hair and thick-framed glasses. What made her stand out was her loud-mouthed attitude and her witty remarks about life in general. Eva's sons and daughters, and a lawyer's family next door to her made up what would be our extended family unit. An unbreakable bond formed through the years, sharing births, christenings, first communions, graduations, weddings, and deaths, they lived alongside, no need for an invitation.

Christmas was a particular time in which celebration of life brought everyone together. Forgetting grievances or failures, it was merely a time of coming together and appreciating each other, and to this day, we honor the memory of tradition.

Alternative Bonds

B eing an only child, I have learnt to rely on different types of relationships filing in the blanks with friends and cousins as substitutes for brothers or sisters.

As Christmas draws near nostalgia arises, as so many key players from my childhood have passed away. On keeping the tradition alive, only my family and three other families living in town get together to honor the holidays.

My cousin, Abe's beautiful Spanish style house, has become the fitting backdrop of our reunions, exchanging presents, with lots of laughter, great food, and of course, funny stories from our childhood days.

My cousins are like my substitute brothers and sisters, of the 18 on my mother's side. I would say I am very close to 14. Still, the trio living here in town is an exception, we all have been there in the best and now the worst times. My news about the "Challenge" had left them stunned to the point of living them almost speechless.

Abe and Paco have a particular type of sense of humor, which includes making fun of everyone since we were kids. They still joke with such ease, you crack up. Celine, their sister, goes along with the pranks, squeezed between two boys who make fun of everything around them, given her a long leeway on patience.

The way I dress has been a particular topic for their silly comments. Knowing well, I may walk into the room, with the latest fashion or a vintage dress belonging to someone in the family. Only last year, I walked in wearing a wool coat from the early 50's, owned by my great aunt Pilar. A very ladylike coat with big flashy buttons, a mink collar, and cuffs. One of the nieces is out of her way, complimenting on the coat:

"Wow, it is so amazing you look like you are coming out of an old Hollywood movie!"

Cousin Esther, her mother, and Abe's wife, says:

"Gosh, Rosina, your aunt Pilar was like 84 when she died, over 60 years ago the coat must be now ancient!" The room fills with laughter.

A sort of excuse for my vintage mania, I always say I am "the keeper of the torch," since I own quite a few belongings from my deceased relatives.

I am a collector of things past, from clothes to furniture. My persona as my house is a mixture of antiques, with a few new things mixed like in a blender, making me and my surroundings unique.

My fashion is all about excitement and amusement, sometimes striking some raised eyebrows on how I may dress. The adventure and joy of playing with clothes and breaking "fashion rules" to this day, is my form of communicating who I am or want to become.

Facing the "Challenge," the mirror in this ordeal is going to be a close friend or my worst enemy. I will trust for advice or will not accept its criticism on the way I look.

Facing the mirror this morning was a tricky affair since today is the cousin's Christmas luncheon. Deciding what to wear is even harder since I have just a few strands of wispy hair left. Thin like bangs coming out from under my turban only covering part of my forehead.

Reluctant to shave it off, since I had been confident it would not fall off. My mother had fought a stricter type of "Challenge" and had not lost even a strand. I was so sure as her I would be one of the chosen few. Then when it started vanishing after each brushing, I had to take rapid action.

Brooding about this remains a helpless situation. I get dressed in a long grey wool turtleneck shift, a turban to cover my head, suede purple boots. Then grab a chunky circular grey sweater and jump in the car, driving a couple of blocks to a wig store.

Marcel, the owner, is just opening the shop upon my arrival. A professional hairstylist in his early thirties, plump and short, makes a surprised face when I specify my needs.

"Hi, you see, I am losing my hair over chemo and want to try a couple of wigs, but I need loud music from the 80s to get in the mood."

He gives me a stare like he is talking with someone just out from a mental institution, but agrees to my crazy request, turning the music loud.

As he sees me trying wig after wig and disco dancing in front of the mirror, changing lip-gloss color at the same time, he cannot help but ask.

"How do you do this? How is it you are so positive and cheerful with this terrible "Challenge?"

Bluntly he is questioning my being sane.

"Are you sure you are feeling alright?"

My answer went on something like this:

"Look at this red-tinted Cher-like with bangs almost past my boobs, is an exciting happy piece, and goes great with all my vintage long skirts."

He looks incredulous but listens intently.

"This cute short asymmetrical blond bob a la Vidal Sassoon, remember him?" Like a bright pupil, he gives me an affirmative nod, as I continue.

"Well, it just needs a Mary Quant type mini skirt to go with, it is going to be fun with short dresses."

"This straight shoulder length in light brown a la Ali McGraw in Love Story is a reminder of Love."

"You see Marcel, there are two things I can do, one is be depressed every day, and the other is play like when I was a little girl with fashion. I pick the last alternative as my best option."

Moving his heart, my purchase of three wigs gets a considerable discount. Looking like Cher, I cheerfully stroll out from the store, with my new friend waving good-bye.

When Alex my son sees me walk into the house, he does a double-take, and of course, he cannot sustain his laughter.

Proving my point that playing around with fashion may be a little wacky. Now my loved ones understand gloom has to be left in a comer if I want to survive this "Challenge."

I then hear Juanita with one of her quirky observations.

"Alex, your mom, is not just sick, she is also crazy."

Undecided on what to wear for the luncheon, I change several times like any other female dwelling on a fashion decision.

After much thought, I opt for a semi-circular silver taffeta Marbella coat with black velvet appliques. Tying it with its matching velvet belt at the waist, and wearing it as a dress over a black turtleneck sweater.

Considering a little scandalous to wear a wig at such an early stage, I choose my mom's black velvet turban from the 60's, finding a vintage velvet bag from the 50's to complement the look, and seal it with over the knee suede black boots. Finally, content with my reflection in the mirror, I am set to go with my father, Alex, and Alexis, to my cousin's luncheon.

Over the years, a commotion always starts when I am walking into the living room of Abe's house for our Christmas reunion. Always the inevitable funny comments arise on what I am wearing, and of course, a lot of laughs.

My cousins, are careful about making any silly comments today. The disbelief over my "Challenge" is still a sensitive matter, which no one knows how to handle. I start to break the ice by narrating my morning experience at the wig store. There was laughter all around, after telling them of my dancing in front of Marcel, the store's owner.

Alex, my son, tells his part of the story:

"Here I am waking up after arriving at four o'clock in the morning, from a party. When I see this stranger with long red hair in the hallway at first, I do not recognize her. I think who this showgirl, and how did she get inside the house. Was I that wasted that I brought her over?"

Amused, we continue all through the evening until just before dinner, we honor Esther's tradition of seeing who will take the Baby Jesus home this year. To our luck, dad is the winner. So now I have an accomplice on my side to help me fight my battles.

As the evening draws to a close, I appreciate the vast army of loved ones on my side. I understand now the love medicine you do not get it in a prescription. It is a drug you get from people's s warmth.

Thru it all, it will have to be Love what will hold me together.

The Christmas Tree

C hristmas has for us unique family traditions like decorating and
preparing good food, the setting of tables a ceremony all of its own.
Tree shopping since the kids were little was an adventure to find the right
real Christmas tree.

Like in all families quarrels will arise over the height, or the width of
the branches, you name it. In one of our many outings, Alexis clad in a
pink hooded imitation fur jacket firmly stated:

"That tree looks sad and ugly, I don't like it."

She was five at the time, and she was right, the tree had been there
almost a week, so it was beginning to look old.

Alex being only three years old just agreed with his generic word for
naming everything: "PAPA" sounding more like the Spanish word potato
than father.

After the cousin's dinner, my enthusiasm had sort of worn off, so as
perky as I tended to be the "Challenge" sometimes overshadowed my usual
excitement, and being mom's favorite time of the year I felt like in a vast
empty gloomy abyss, missing her.

Some days what was going on inside my body took hold of the state
within the layers inside my head. For the sake of my family, I had to force
me back to the Christmassy spirit. Two weeks before Christmas, shoving
away any state of gloominess off we went in search for our dream tree.

Confronting the cold, I wrapped myself in the big blanket rust-colored
coat over a long vintage Vittadini camel-hued buttoned-down sweater
dress. Wool hat on my head, thick knitted gloves on my hands, a long
scarf to match, and comfy brown fringed suede boots, I felt elated, just by
being there.

The melancholic mood was fading as soon as the smell of the pine
trees spread thru my nostrils. I even started to laugh on seeing my father
sneaking with my son Alex directly to a food stand for hot chocolate and
churros (a doughnut-like pastry filled with caramel). Traditions for him
will always be food-oriented, and in his book, the primary purpose of any
outing.

Rosina Ramón

Happiness overcame me as the coolness of the evening touched my face, this simple act of feeling has become a thriving awakening. My senses are keen to all around me, music, smell, and the touch of my love ones. As I see them all Alexis, Alex, my Dad, and Juanita. I thank God for allowing me to cherish such enjoyment of the moment, and again just to feel.

Everyone has an opinion about the tree but after a long deliberation and my bargaining abilities, we all agreed on a beautiful, noble one. A little over three feet tall, branches happily spread out, with a thick trunk, a sight to put anyone in awe.

Transporting takes almost four people to tie the tree to the rooftop of my son's car. On arrival at the house, we had to tip two handymen to get it inside our living room.

Sometimes peace comes in the simplest of objects, this tree is one of the most beautiful trees we have ever bought taking my breath away, and to a certain degree filling all the family with much hope.

December 5, Chemo Day

Awakening to a sunny, blue sky, but an icy day, I get ready for a meeting. Dressing in jeans a black turtleneck distressed brown leather jacket, a belt with copper serpent tips emphasizes my waist. Jeans tucked inside my 80's vintage Karl Lagerfeld tall black suede boots with thick killer heels, and a large brown sac style soft leather bag. To complete the look I construct on my head an Arab like turban in rust hues made from a large wool pashmina, upgrading it totally to an exotic, not your everyday wear, but crazy-chic.

Walking from the parking lot to my appointment in the downtown area of Monterrey, I feel the stares and hear the whispers. I have never minded what people have thought of how I dress, and indeed by now, I could care less, besides I am enjoying to the max their astonished faces. Clothes and accessories are my way of expression, my very personal need to be me. I am ecstatic to stand out in a crowd as an individual, under my own terms with my flaws perfectly aligned as qualities.

Friday's are always hectic with the signing of checks, and going to the bank, now to add to my activities I scheduled my second chemo for the afternoon. Figuring I will have the whole weekend to recuperate, even though I might be still messed up on Monday, I can organize my days all a little better.

So roughing it out the whole weekend with nausea and exhaustion, I looked at the week ahead as expecting a holiday. Who ever thought just thinking of work could force me to try to program myself to actually act on feeling better.

Recognizing again it all has to do with this thing called attitude, an actual awakening force plays positively or negatively on the senses, and the decision of with which ball to play with, is only mine.

Mirrors

N ext day as I stand with my now usual confrontation with Mr. mirror,
I can hardly accept the thin ghostly reflection of my image as mine.
I punch negativity a blow of self-confidence. Juggling with makeup, and
realizing the look has to be little more made up than usual. Wearing a
turban or a wig forces a more dramatic look it is not the same as with my
own hair, being outlandish requires a bit more work.

Playing with makeup now is a must, the eyes need to be accentuated
with darker liner, smudged with smoky eye shadows, lots of mascara and
a matte pinkish lip. My skin needs to be perked with color at the moment
since it has turned light translucent yellow with hints of white. Gaspar the
ghost comes to mind!

A priority is having fun with fashion, jeans with boots of rare skins and
outlandish colors, work nicely with beaten-up leather jackets. Turtlenecks
work better than open collar shirts since they act as a pedestal for the face,
long scarfs and pashminas are an essential adornment on my head.

My go-to option of long skirts with comfy like sweaters and cowboy
boots, to balance the ethnic touch. I pile on accessories of big bracelets,
and necklaces, in turquoise, and amber, as my trademark and anchor.

Somehow every other day I am taken out of my comfort zone, and as
confident as I try to be there are days it feels like my whole world has been
turned upside down.

A feeling of being kicked on my butt falling headfirst on a dirt road,
trying to find my way up, while still something is trying to pull me back
on the ground, a constant struggle with myself, and it is just up to me to
get up or lie on the mud.

Tough to take in I have to accept I am going thru the "Challenge"
feeling this in my skin and processing it in my mind. Waking up frequently
in the middle of the night soaked in sweat, not to a mess-up dream, but to
a real-life happening.

Tree Decorating

L ove from others has kept me grounded, I did not know I was so cared for, silly it has taken this severe blow to find out, feeing loved even by people I took for granted.

Sunday afternoon a trio shows up Phil, Lola, and Marcus, came not only to see how I am after the second round of chemo but also to help put the lights and decorations on my spectacular tree.

So needing warmth and a proper perspective of the action, I sit in one of the living room sofas in front of the fireplace. I take in a dose of love dressed in a dark brown velvet skirt, ivory turtleneck sweater, a pashmina on my head made into one of my outrageous turbans, and vintage taupe colored fringed Navaho Indian suede boots.

Scattered all around are boxes filled with decorations I have collected over the years, petit everything's: bells, shoes, horses, angels, dolls, houses, nutcrackers, bows and Christmas balls.

As I open one of the boxes I reach for one of the eight plastic pastel colored carrousel structures, a fan inside starts swirling around, as I blow into it automatically picks up speed. My four-year-old image flashes momentarily, as my little girl self-gasps in awe when for the first time my mother gave me this same box, and patiently helped me put every carousel after blowing into each one, before settling them on the tree branches. Memories are what Christmas is all about.

My friend's chatter and Juanita's noisy entrance to the room brings me back to real life, carrying a tray with hot chocolate, and brown sugar coffee cake, she almost loses her balance as Phil jumps up to grab his mug and cake. With plate in hand and between each bite Phil bossily coaches Marcus, who is on top of the ladder on where to correctly install the lights, Lola laughs at their squabbling.

Everyone is trying to act as normal as possible. Aware all, my hair has fallen almost entirely, and perceiving clearly the toll this has taken on, my vanity.

My stomach is still kind of upside down, remnants of Friday's chemo, feeling touched by my friend's sensitivity of being just there no questions asked, merely making jokes, and lending a helping hand makes me forgo the discomfort.

Christmas Eve

I am trying to get into the Christmas spirit, but somehow a gloomy feeling makes me concentrate on something else altogether.

Tackling my jewelry closet, which suddenly looks a total mess, I am not talking diamonds, or real pearls but a collection of vintage paraphernalia inside my antique wood and glass cabinet. Tall flower bases filled to the rim with colorful huge bracelets, and baskets filed with gold and silver cuffs, my trademark. Necklaces, earrings are another essential category, doing this helps me get rid of the grey cloud over my head, which at this moments is being hunted by nostalgia.

Taking also my time as not to interfere with Juanita's cooking and interrupt the control of her kitchen, which at this precise moment is out of bounds to anyone, her own private domain.

So when finished I turn the stereo to an old CD of Rudolph the Red Nose Reindeer and start to get cheery setting the table, for eight. Mixing vintage colored crystal goblets with clear crystal ones, depression glasses in pink with two floral china patterns, my gold angels in front of every plate for holding name cards, and the golden flatware adds a festive, merry touch.

Instead of a formal centerpiece, Red roses are intertwined with short colored crystal candleholders in reds and greens strewn across the table making quite a nice warm set up over my mom's antique lace white tablecloth with white matching napkins, held by gold rings that are part of the flatware.

After finishing I sit in one of the armchairs from the late 1800's taking a deep breath and appreciating my finished work. Enjoying the moment, I drift into my usual trips to the past:

Since I was twelve, my beautiful widow and childless great-aunt Pilar taught me how to set a table, what each shape and size of each crystal glass, plate, or utensil, were for. A ritual before every Christmas dinner to be her personal assistant.

She had been the one in her family who married well, to José, a wealthy Spanish gentleman who spoiled her with lavishness, from clothes and housewares ordered from French catalogs, an unheard thing for someone living in a dusty border town with Eagle Pass Texas, Piedras Negras.

Never having children of her own she was not very used to young visitors. I became an imposition from her younger sister, my grandmother Coco who was twelve years younger and considered her older sister as a strange and lonely being.

Still, to my eyes, she lived an independent and luxurious life, in her two-floor Spanish style house. A mysterious sort of enchanted small Alhambra with colored floors, and walls of ceramic painted tiles.

The house furnished all with antique furniture from the 20's to the 40's, with magazines and books spread casually all over the place, a sort of replica as my own house looks now with some of her things.

Tia Pilar, as everyone called her, was, slender and always elegant looking. In her late sixties at the time, her face showed visible remnants of having been a great beauty. White unlined skin, delicate features and almond-shaped eyes with a clear brown touch, which met me with a kind of warm, sentimental look that never gave away what she might be thinking or feeling. She fiercely guarded her privacy and her own special world was her safe-heaven.

Her precisely choreographed graceful movements set her apart from the rest of the ladies in town, being cast as arrogant, but to me, she had a captivating and original presence. Now I know she was a natural lady of style.

With me she was strict yet very formal, a real perfectionist in all her endeavors and straight to the point in her teachings. Gaining her trust by age fifteen, she left me to my own devices allowing my creativity to take its free course, while she fussed with her maids in the kitchen.

Remembering this, I sighed over my finished work I had become her great apprentice, enjoying doing marvelous tables, to this day.

It was almost the middle of the afternoon when I walk to check on things into Juanita's kitchen. Turkey, meat stuffing, green bean casserole, spaghetti with spinach, and cream sauce all done. Finally, I am allowed to start working on the pumpkin pie and the antipasto, savoring the moment and the warm smell of home cooking I feel happy now, then again, more memories.

From tranquility and order, I walk the half a block from my great-aunt's house to chaos. Grandma was large of built, bold and loud where her sister was quiet and composed, her home always filled with all type of visitors. A noisy environment during the Holidays, what to me was my second home now was invaded with the out of town cousins and aunt's, chatter prevailed. The racket sounding, like some strange music.

The kitchen was total madness, everyone seemed involved in making the vast "paella" for Christmas day, besides a ham, and a specially fed turkey. Grandma had been nourishing the poor animal for almost a month, to be stuffed with my family's special oyster stuffing. (Now I remember that was the reason I went into the phase of no poultry for about two years.)

Working with grandma in her kitchen was always Teresa my adoring Nanny, my mother, and my mother's two sister's Coco, and Maria Oliva, the visitors. Each of them will be chopping something or stirring a pot. All is cheerfulness and crossed opinions on how to cook this and spice that, everyone had something to say, I rejoice in the memory of it all, they were loud, opinionated ladies.

I clearly can see Abe, my cousin, as he tried to steal a big shrimp from the large paella pan, and my grandma slapping his hand, and giving him one of her freeze right there stares.

"Away from my kitchen, after what you did to the turkey the nerve, you have to understand throwing stones at it, makes the meat turkey hard."

Abe answers: "Yeah, but you killed it."

He then runs off. We all laugh so hard, as I do now at the recollection of such a long-ago incident.

Coming back from memory lane around seven thirty with my duties in the kitchen over I walk to my bedroom thinking how similar I am to these women who shaped so much the person I am today.

My mother taught me how beauty was not only in ones looks she had the flair to make everything around her as spectacular, as herself without even trying, it is as if she had a magic wand.

Grandma educated me on the impact of presence, the importance of being confident about our persona an expert at making grand entrances, this stout, tall, large lady with excellent features, would walk any store, restaurant, or party with an attitude of power, was always shown unconditional respect, and the best of everything.

Tia Pilar was the teacher of fine living, I inherited her love of books, magazines, antiques, but most important the art of appreciating being by yourself, and not caring to be different ever.

Aunt Maria Oliva was all for having fun, with people of all ages, she was the life of the party and the confidant of all the cousins.

From the only survivor Tia Coco, or as I used calling her "Tia Copetitos," a nickname I had made up for her in my teens, since her salon bouffant hairdos were never an in inch out of place. She taught me how to always look great in a day-to-day situation.

They all were so similar in their legacy of unmistakable style.

As I open my closet sighing from the recollection, I settle on my long checked black & white (sort of vintage 8-year-old Ralph Lauren) long wool strapless dress worn as a jumper with a black turtleneck.

With a long black pashmina I make one of my most significant and stunning turbans, and feeling great I take an overview in the mirror, and as if they could hear me, I say out loud:

"Yes ladies! You all helped make me unique, thank you and Merry Christmas."

Church

A few blocks from the house there is a beautiful small old church St. Luis Gonzaga, I love coming here for Christmas mass with dad the kids and Juanita, a sort of another Christmas ritual. Today giving thanks was an essential affair, I definitely needed God on my side.

After arriving from mass at nine P.M. my small immediate family gathers in the living room with the smell of pine tree, logs burning in the chimney. We start exchanging presents, on opening mine from my kids and father tears start rolling down my cheeks.

On my hands is a plane ticket to New York City for February, during fashion week already approved by my doctors.

I am excited and touched as Alex asks:

"Why do you cry, you should be happy?

For the first time the doubtful words come out from my lips:

"I do not know if I am going to make it"

So he stands up with his huge arms embraces my now skinny body, whispering: "Sure you will."

Alexis eyes well up with tears when she reaches to kiss me, my Dad takes his handkerchief from his pocket to clean his own misty eyes. Juanita with her present still unopened on her lap, just toughs it out.

Knowing now my trip down memory lane, had the reason of understanding how those women in my family left me the most precious gift called, resilience.

The emotional moment over. Lucia calls asking if I can set two more places on the table, they are coming for dinner, so now we are ten, including the only survivor of those incredible women my aunt Socorro, my ex-husband and Celia a nice on his side. I feel so happy to have so many joining us this Christmas.

Just after desert the doorbell starts ringing like for a party, people start arriving for after drinks, a procession of friends of all ages and gender there is a moment from eight we are almost twenty.

Love is all around. Even Santa Claus arrives unexpectedly, (a friend in disguise). Certain friends have been away for years, coming forward now in times of trouble.

A very Merry Christmas filled with the best medicine you can take, LOVE.

December 26, Chemo Day

The third chemo, just thinking about it makes me sick to my stomach, it helps having Lucia sit with me the whole four hours chatting nonstop trying her new makeup from Chanel. We need distraction from our woes and beauty is a good way to ignore reality.

Blond and blue eyed her skin looks even paler after all the stress from her brother's funeral only a couple of days before Christmas. Like when you are a teenager we sort of play with her new makeup encouraging her to try it out. The reddish lipstick, the pinkish blush, the blue eye shadow to enhance her eyes and boost up her grieving heart. A silly way to help her cope with the pain from her loss, and distract me from my reality, this is why we are friend's normalcy will be a bore.

There is no way you can give thanks to a friend who is roughing it out sitting were her late brother was treated for chemo. Arising no need to say anything aloud, just the being there is all it takes, this is friendship

The heaviness of the odor I have come to loath makes me feel a lot worse than the insertion of the needles in the catheter. Pondering on feeling the sickness to the stomach, the sting of a needle, the cold that reaches the bones, and leading to the heaviness of the unpleasant smell, all boils down to discomfort.

Still coping with all of the distress I grasp like a beggar for the hope of life. If anyone tries to shut the door on my face I will end up putting my foot forward and stopping them cold meeting them straight into their eyes, without saying the words it will be obvious, I will not give up the fight.

Chemotherapy, for me, was successful at minimizing the tumor's size. Fortunate to be given only for four more sessions after this one. The symptoms were a roller-coaster of nausea and discomfort, only for the best reason, of saving my life.

Home Alone

So Alex is flying to Mexico City, Alexis for the beach at Playa del Carmen, my Dad is going back to our hometown and Juanita is taking off to her own house in Aura, for New Years.

After the strain of yesterday's chemo, I wake up early to say goodbye to all assuring I will be alright, and go back to bed. I am staying all by myself, enough of everyone just being around seeing me throw up as soon as a certain smell triggers nausea.

Hearing my inside growl as if they have been turned upside down. Heaviness runs thru my body with a terrible need for sleep. Lacking strength, and feeling like a rag doll around noon time I finally push myself to the limit getting out of bed into the shower.

I fight with myself trying to look perkier dabbing a little makeup and a bit of lip-gloss, some mascara, and clean pjs. Even if it means I am going back to bed, I do everything to try and look my best it helps to feel less lousy.

Nausea wakes me from my deep sleep in the late afternoon I am soaked in sweat. Rushing to the bathroom with my stomach coming out from my mouth, I continue with the moist feeling invading my body.

The whole room is spinning around me, a wave of panic hits me at the same time as a chill runs all thru the last fiber of my being. Remembering I am all by myself, the house looms like a huge empty giant if I fall or scream no one will hear me. I mean no one.

About to slide down to the floor at any moment now, with no one to pick me up, my courageous idea of staying home alone, as if someone heard me yelling for help, the phone rings.

Stumbling to answer my friend Phil is on the line, my trembling voice gives me away, immediately he knows something is up. Finding out I am alone I can almost see him throw his silk pajamas and a collection of Cream de la Mer jars into his Louis Vuitton bag.

I just hear him say in a commanding voice:

"I am coming over and will stay the night, I'll be there in less than an hour."

Somehow the phone call makes me automatically feel better, even finding the strength for running a bath. Putting all kinds of bath salts, oils and foamy gels into the tub. On lowering my "still complete" body into the warm bubbly water, I can relate to those old Doris Day-Rock Hudson movies I used to watch as a child with my mother, a song comes to mind, so I start to sing:

"When I was a little girl I asked my mother what would I be? Will I be pretty? Will I be rich?

This is what she said to me:

"Qué sera, sera the future is not ours to see, what will be will be"

Remembering mother kind of puts my uneasy stomach and the fussiness in my head at ease, just for a few minutes I can relax my mind, touching my body every inch still in its place I keep on singing:

"What will be will be"

After coming out from the tub, I reach for a jar of rich almond body cream slowly covering every single inch of skin. Another needed ritual, massaging my breasts carefully, not in a sexual way but in a mental daily preparation a physical farewell to this part of me I really like. Even if my breasts are coming undone with the gravity of time, they are so mine, I will miss my right one dearly.

At this moment, I cannot ignore my appearance from the inside as from the outside they nourish each other. Taking some time to enhance my outer beauty as much as my inner attitude is predominately essential for survival.

I get myself into my clean leopard velour pajamas, with huge furry coat like robe, in dark chocolate again face cream, the gloss, the perfume, a pinch on the cheeks, wrapping on a rust colored turban around my head, checking with the mirror, and yes it's Me again.

As if a timer had been set I hear the doorbell. On opening the door I cannot sustain my laughter.

I find Phil on my doorstep with his logo Vuitton portfolio bag regally on his arm (stuffed like I thought with the la Mer face creams), wearing a Burberry camel trench coat and a big pashmina covered in paisleys all around his neck and shoulders. Underneath designer flannel pajamas and monogramed rust suede bed slippers, on his other arm is the Hugo Boss suit he will wear to a meeting next morning.

He will beat Florence Nightingale anytime, just seeing him makes my day, and I actually thank him for the love of just being there.

The Two Me's

B eing openly focused on the outside "Me" letting the other "Me" the one inside battle with the brooding or the feeling sorry "Me." Grasping my reality, of the two of us, and only I can separate them but can take neither for granted. Crucial since one can feed the other.

The 1939 painting by Frida Kahlo's the two Frida's to a certain point opened my eyes to my dilemma of playing out with the physical and mental pain of my two personas. She must have had days in which she was in scrutinizing pain from her polio and trolley accident, and she never let her guard down in relation to her image. She flourished with her outlandish ideas of fashion, making it her own. Setting apart her unique personal style, as a protective shield from her agony.

Like her I made my fashion according to the mood and the essence of the actual feeling of a determined moment as a way of avoiding fear, disguising it with different looks.

Having managed to create a system every morning for grooming takes almost two hours from crawling out of bed to doing some yoga, getting in the shower, dressing, and putting on makeup. Somehow it turns to be quite an exhausting affair since I am so detail-oriented on how to dress, which shoes look best and now, of course, the wig or turban I will pick for the mood of the day.

By the time I arrive for breakfast appetite has taken a leave of absence, food has sort of lost its true luster. I can even go on long absences without eating if I am not pushed to do so. Getting dressed is my go-to motivational activity, those two hours in which I shop inside my closet are the highlight of my day nothing else makes me happier.

Funny, one day dressed in a long vintage jersey wrap dress stamped in Pucci like multi-colored prints, under a furry coat and red leather round toe square heeled boots wearing the long brown wig with straight cut bangs a close acquaintance stops me:

"Hey, Rosina is it you?"

Laughter escapes me it all comes down how I am feeling on any given day. Either the Cher long red wig, the short blond bob, the brownish cut a la Ali McGraw in Love Story or the blond asymmetrical cut.

Mastering the art of creating exotic turbans for my head, all according to the clothes I will be wearing and the spirit of the day. Pashminas and scarfs of all sizes and prints have become another big part of my wardrobe.

Seeing how people react when I walk into a room wearing a big turban on my head, is like I am arriving from another planet, always bringing out a giggle or two. I am developing the expertise of moving people out of their comfort zones, which is a highly enjoyable feeling.

Getting dressed now is all about me, to please only me instead of others and to give me a purpose of individuality. Of course also to hide my almost baldhead in an amusing looking way.

The first time I walked with the long red wig into the office Sylvia, my assistant, said:

"Halo do you have an appointment"? On realizing it was just me, we both roared with laughter.

Clothes and accessories are key as always, and at this particular time turning into a substitute medicine especially for the mind. Forcing myself on being more creative as my evolving body goes thru the stages of change.

Playing with clothes for me has never only been for just covering my body. I thrive in the sense of pleasure and fun they provide even better if it means amusing others with my quirky sense of style.

Appreciation

J aime, my oncologist, warned me there would be a lot o hilarious suggestions about what to do or eat when you get the "Challenge." He was so right everyone seems to know about the last miracle cure. So I have been pretty obedient on the matter, shutting my ears to most of the well-intended recommendations.

At some point help is free for the taking, in some way one has to decide what suits us best. Too many opinions, in the end, will probably contradict one another. Excessive information, with a not so stable mind, can get pretty confusing.

So I listened quietly to all and at the end just did what the doctors ordered. Ok, I drank blessed water and had snake capsules. The first to purify my murky soul, the later to boost my skin. What would I not do for beauty's sake.

What most astonished me where the diet suggestions. After each chemo the food I would be able to eat had nothing to do with anything my taste buds would accept.

Surely it was like being pregnant again some things I would crave, and some would just make my stomach jump upside down like a jellybean. Awakening sensitivity in my taste buds, to the texture and consistency of food.

By far smell was the main key of discomfort automatically triggering me into the state of nausea. Provoking rhythmical noises inside my stomach, sounding exactly as a cappuccino coffee maker.

Since a very young age I have always been keen of certain smells, even before the "Challenge," walking into a house smelling of food has been an unpleasant affair.

Getting back to texture I could tolerate, were soft foods with no particular smell. My diet consisted of baked potatoes with the works, cream cheese, with bacon bits. Rejoicing on spoonful's of gelatin and the sensation of grainy cottage cheese pieces mixed with the sweetness of peaches. Grapefruit with hot tamarind dip or some other outlandish combination.

Never had I ever been picky with food, taught to eat everything on my plate. My only child status gave me no right of a tantrum when expressing disliking any particular food.

When one is healthy, we take many things like taste, surroundings, and most people for granted but having been warned, my life now appears as fragile as a crystal. Appreciating now every day unnoticed little things, like the smell of fresh cut grass, and the feel on my bare feet as I run thru large fields.

At night I am in awe of a dark sky lighted by tiny dots of stars, as if an initial life encounter, there but never noticed. Some nights, sitting mesmerized by a full moon's visit, getting lost in the beauty of it all.

My whole being feels enlarged and excited with this incredible newfound appreciation of my surroundings and the universe as a whole.

Becoming more sensitive to unnoticed people has a new meaning. The grocery boy, the doorman, the taxi driver, the street vendors, I really see them and listen to them with a more respectful attention.

Even learning to savor the taking of deeper breaths and feeling the air traveling thru my lungs, is a joyful alertness since it delivers the awareness of life.

Reconnecting

F riends have a way of losing track of each other, but tragedy has a funny way of re-uniting real friendships, of putting us out there to make a reconnection. The lost time is unimportant when you had a sincere relationship you just start back where you left it, and it truly works.

Every test we face has a positive side even one as devastating as the "Challenge". A most important message resonates in me, and it is the valuable gift of reconnecting with long lost friends and relatives.

A welcoming surprise was to find out how many people out there cared for me. In my daily running around I had lost them, getting entangled in work, immediate family, or just the monotony of day to day. Losing track of time, days turning into weeks, weeks into months, and sadly months into years.

Remembering my time in college, there were people I hung out day after day, a roommate who lived with me in my first apartment, or the ones I went out to party every single weekend even a long forgotten boyfriend, well they all have come forward.

One example will be my friendship with Alicia, who being from a little town in Mexico called Rio Verde, San Luis Potosi, married Gerard from Germany and has lived there for over forty years. Reuniting with her over the years is like when we saw each other every single day in our collage days. We have always been there for each other. The lasting bonds never to be broken, and now more than ever she is in my long distance support group.

All our lives we are creating connections with people, but at some point they break, the truth has nothing to do with not liking them anymore. The management of our time has become so complicated and guarded and filled with activities, we are cramming so much in a day it turns out in minutes of lost people.

At this moment of the year before hours for a new one to start, there is no greater love in my life than my two children, and my Dad. I must be grateful and not overlook the remarkable affection of all those who have come back into my life. They are enough to fill my old High School gym in Eagle Pass Texas.

New Year's

As the old year closes its doors to everything sad or evil, it feels like the New Year is opening them wide, permitting everything good walk in and take charge.

I realize that even with the heavy burden of getting the "Challenge" 2008 gave me a lot more than it took away from me, just by getting so much affection in return. So as we say in Mexico there is always something good that originates from the bad.

This special night maybe my mind is playing tricks on me, but at the four parties I attend, I feel people are more thankful for their lives than years before. Everyone seems nicer and happier, well maybe it is the bubbly, but it turns to be a great night.

The only night in the whole year it is ok to kiss a total stranger, and never again set eyes on him for the rest of our life. I am so thrilled cherishing the night and yes, I kiss and hug a lot of strangers.

My daughter Alexis is back from Playa, to host one of the best New Year's Eve affairs in town at the Habitat hotel where she is as I mentioned the PR manager, so here we wait for the clock to strike midnight.

The Hotel has a privileged view from the open pool bar, of mountains framing one important city area and on the other side you can spot a hanging long bridge, which materializes spectacularly even from afar.

Taking for granted the icy cold night, I am rejoicing in the moment, clad in a furry big white fox coat, under an A-line shift dress in emerald green embroidered flowers in gold threads with an oriental feel to it. Complimenting the look with long leather gloves, tights, and suede with lace booties all in black. A unique hat made of gold satin, with a 40's flair, topped with a long feather. A little net veil, covers half of my face providing mystery, mainly hiding my partial baldness.

Feeling beautiful tonight is of utmost importance a thing many women might not experience at this particular bald stage in their lives. Most would probably choose to be crawled up in bed wearing warm flannel red checked pajamas and thick grey socks, six days after a chemo. For me, this was hardly an option, life has to be mine, a pledge that I cannot break. Even if I have to dress it up a lot, and plastered it with makeup

January 2009

The New Year wakes me up a little after two o'clock, I force myself out of the comforts of my bed. My stomach again starts squeaking, picturing in my mind what foods I crave today. Settling oddly for raisin bran cereal, with a cup of coffee to be savored and enjoyed, since a week ago coffee was on the I cannot swallow list. After the chemo's, I now know I have to take baby steps with food.

Showering, after breakfast I put on a little makeup after an array of face creams. Never not even if I am staying home alone will I wear anything shabby, dirty, torn or the same pajama from last night. Especially today, New Year's Day a great occasion for my new turtleneck wool tunic with wide legged pants, a hooded brown wool cape, and the purple flat suede boots. A headband covers half of my baldness and over goes the capes hoody, I am ready to receive guest later in the evening.

Enjoying the chilly January day wrapped in a blanket I settle out on the chaise lounge outside in the patio delighted in the sun's warmth (never on my face, not recommended after chemo).

My first-year resolution is to give thanks, having now the occasion to cherish some alone time I get a wooden tray and set it with pens, stationery, and address book. I then start to write personal thank you notes to each and every one who has been there thru the ordeal of the "Challenge" to be sent with a stamp via regular mail.

As my pen slides thru the paper striking an emotional cord a tear or two will roll down without any warning. This exercise of doing it the old fashion way placed me in an unbelievable peace of mind, filled with love and gratitude for everyone.

Rediscovering this form of communication, which I highly recommend everyone, should try. A letter will be there forever, never to be deleted from anyone's inbox. All the love and care I been receiving could not go unnoticed expressing gratitude was the least I could do.

That first weekend of January after just recuperating from the chemo's aftermath I came down with this terrible cold putting me in bed with a heavy cough and high temperature. Attending one of my best friend's traditional birthday dinner became out of the question.

By Sunday I am not getting any better, even feeling worse than after chemo, my energy is at its lowest level, making it hard even to reach for the lip-gloss, dosing in and out from sleep.

Alex gets worried and calls Jaime, my oncologist who instructs him not to let me out of the house. Indicating that the weather is extremely cold, muddy and rainy, and stating he will come in a couple of hours to give me a shot.

Jaime arrives two hours later looking as handsome and stylish as ever, jeans tucked inside riding boots and a chunky sheepskin jacket, thick leather gloves and a long wool scarf around his neck. A priceless gesture to have my doctor come to the house on one of the coldest and stormiest evenings of the year, my heart flows with gratitude for him.

Next day I wake up to no more gloomy rain, the day is still chilly, but the sun is shining bright. I take a long hot shower reach for the face cream, and lip gloss a sign I am feeling better.

As I start dressing I put on some dark brown heavy tights and some cozy olive green wool pants with a thick ivory colored sweater and the hooded brown long blanket-like coat, my beaten up cowboy boots and go for a walk with myself. Recovering my health after being lost in the darkness of sickness the light of the sun on my face, as always is a joy of life.

Unexpected Kindness

B etween the tomatoes and the carrots in the grocery store, I get a big warm hug from a seventy-year-old lady, who I know to be the grandmother of Celia, a niece from my ex-husband's side who has become an important, part of my small family. I hear the lady say in a sincere, sweet tone of voice:

"Whenever you feel sick, sad or lonely, no matter what time of day or night I will come and take care of you, just feel free to call me."

Touched to the core, thinking how have I deserved this unconditional show of love, being cast my way, my eyes fill with tears as I hug her right back.

Compassion seems to come without the asking from many unexpected places without my trying to understand how this people I hardly know, would come and sincerely offer support in such a daunting time.

The issue is this "Challenge," has touched so many lives bonding strangers in a chain of support. I am not alone in my fight "My" war, is a "We" affair, in which, gender, age and social background become insignificant, arising an inherent necessity from people to offer help or an encouraging word of hope.

That same afternoon on unloading the groceries from the car, I spot the neighbors handy-man walking towards me, Don Carmelo hands me a bouquet of pink roses and says:

"Roses for your birthday and for fighting with dignity for life."

Tears flow without shame as I hug his tall bulky frame with gusto and fond appreciation for this man who has seen my kids grow from toddlers to the present day. An emblematic and respected fixture of our everyday life in our neighborhood. So unexpected is the love.

January 15 My Birthday

D ressing for this special evening starts with the selection of the dress, deciding on a black to the calf original Chinese one, Mandarin collar, slim cut to the body. Accessories of long pearl necklaces and black suede and lace booties.

In front of the mirror I arrange firmly the new blond straight bob cut wig, tilting my head from side to side, checking that the fit is perfect. Don't want a surprise of being left bald in the middle of the dancing floor. To finish the oriental mood, red lips and long black tips of eyeliner for the eyes. Ready for a night to celebrate.

After being so sick for almost a week, it is essential to feel pretty and sexy. Sickness has a way of attacking my essential feminine side, there is a relation of illness with drabness and un-sexiness. I fight so hard with this perception deleting it from my mind.

Fun and the celebration of life is the only topic on the agenda, leaving worries behind. I am in the edge of having a second chance, not knowing of the outcome after my scheduled operation in March.

Since early morning, calls, flowers, balloons, and presents arrive. Still being appreciated by friends is the best gift and the opportunity of being alive immersed in all this love, overwhelming but satisfying.

I have cherished many love stories in my life each one unique in its own way, three of them forever unforgettable. All individually different from the other placed in a special space at a particular time in my life.

Today dear friends have touched my heart, caressed it with tenderness and showered me with unconditional love, coming from the least unexpected places. Making me fall in love with love every single day.

The night's highlights are first a real monkey brought by my friends Leticia, Gabo and Dew as part of the entertainment making everyone roll over with laughter as he jumps from one friend to the other.

I have always been crazy about monkeys, but I am now sure I prefer them as a stuffed animal. For a moment this little creatures sad eyes, remind me he is a slave like myself, he to his keeper, and me to the "Challenge."

The other part of the present from this trio was a stuffed monkey. To this day he sits quietly like a guardian on a small trunk on the right side of my bed. He has turned out to be a great listener to whatever is going on in my confused state of mind, a discreet bystander, keeping to himself of whatever happens in my bedroom.

Another surprise is when I hear the loud sound of guitars and trumpets, and then ten Mariachis storm into the dining room crowded now with almost fifty people. My father sitting beside me is as startled as I am, tears, run down my cheeks when Alexis and Alex walk behind the band singing Las Mañanitas. When they hug me, feeling love is being in love.

Renegade

Two days after my birthday sitting in front of the mirror, observing the few wispy strands of hair barely covering my head, an attack of devastation strikes. The reflection is one of an aging lady, who is not how I want to look and less feel.

So I put on a pair of worn Levi's, and a gray hooded top to cover my skull, my trademark cowboy boots, long scarf around my neck, brown suede jacket, and walk the few blocks to the beauty parlor.

On arrival, it is as if I am walking on the set of Steel Magnolias, all of the women who work here are in their middle 60's. A strange sensation as always strikes me. They have been here for most of their lives. working like a family who neither of them is, sharing marriages, kids, and deaths, in a day-to-day apparent harmony.

I remember the place the same way since when I arrived for College in 1975. Neither one of them is the actual owner, in all my years coming here I have never seen her around, a mysterious silence falls whenever I have inquired so as a friend says:

"Better to be happy than to find out."

Dryers are big and yellow, curlers are pink and essential. A real beauty parlor where the reliable tools are permanents, Aqua Net spray, and sheer hairnets to hold tight little granny bobby-pin snail like curls.

I always joke I am their youngest client, the average ladies age ranges from the 70's to the 90's. Well suited chauffer's stand outside and wait in big fancy cars and nurses read magazines to pass the long hours of waiting on old complicated procedures in the art of getting their bosses pretty.

Beauty for these elderly women is a way of life. Age is irrelevant for them, since it is a high priority the appreciation of their image and a real devotion of their feminine self.

These ladies are the regulars. Faithfull clients over the years, scheduling appointments the same day of the month, for doing their nails, coloring, and cutting their hair. One day a week is booked of course for high stiff teased hairdos and manicure touch-ups.

For them, age and specific age-related illness are not stopping them so in no way can the "Challenge" prevent me from taking care of myself.

On opening the door I contemplate the scene, taking big long yoga-like breaths to give me the courage I walk up to the head stylist and ask her to shave my head. In unison everyone looks at each other with a sad expression on their faces.

Sensing my inner turmoil a petit white-haired eighty-year-old dressed meticulously, in a tweed black Chanel suit, and pearls gives me a motherly hug and her place on the waiting list.

As the few strands disappear, falling like feathers to the floor a wave of nostalgic feeling runs thru me. Goose bumps cover my whole body.

Around silence prevails, and all seem like in a dark trance, without uttering a word I start to see some teary eyes around. Knowing me only casually, these ladies have taken my pain as their own. Offering as we women do, an unconditional support.

My crazy mind starts working overtime, it is only a change of image: "goodbye to sex appeal, hallo renegade."

Out loud I repeat the famous words in Snow White:

"Mirror, mirror on the wall, who is the fairest of them all?" This breaks the tense moment and all start to laugh.

Before leaving I do a second take in front of one of the mirrors, not bad, exotic yes, patrician nose, big eyes, and full lips, if just my ears were a little smaller. When will we ever be satisfied with our looks?

An unexpected and shocking reflection, of the new "Me" and after a deep long gasp I walk out the door.

February 12th

New York, Fashion Week

After the chaos of leaving home, I am like a little kid filled with excitement. This trip, a consolation prize, a deserved freedom from blood tests, treatments, hospitals and nausea.

I will be on my own for five whole days a needed time to clear my mind and think. Excess love at times can get overwhelming. A required date with myself is imperative.

After finding the lump on that October night, the speed of things went nonstop my life crammed with unexpected developments that robbed me of time to be with "Me". Solitude is essential in preparation for the upcoming tough task of the mastectomy in March.

After coming out of La Guardia to grab a cab I am sight to be seen. Wrapped in a heavy warm circular sheep coat stamped in leopard prints from the 50's a big brown turban on my head, black turtle neck and black leather pants, with brown suede booties, you have to take a second glance and wonder about me.

Clothes whisper stories, so we must pay attention what we want to say about ourselves. For me sensing people watching me is an amusing enjoyment.

Savoring life as I slide inside the cab my excitement is at is peak. I have a silly grin on my face which only shows when you are in love, as I am with this enigmatic city.

The whole ride to the hotel I am in bliss, so after dropping my bags off, it is almost 4:00 P.M. Barely re-touching up my makeup. I then rush the two blocks to the tents at Bryant Park for my registration pass.

Catching my breath after hopping on the subway train to 21st Street to my friend's Mara's office. Just in time to pick up the invitations for the shows since Nini her assistant, leaves on the dot at 6.00 P.M.

Mara is a photographer who travels the world shooting the fashion collections, I am meeting her for lunch tomorrow. The shows started today and she's been at the tents since early morning snapping photographs of several shows.

Getting out from the subway on 42 street on my way back to my hotel, the heavy wind-chill literally gets me blown inside Sardis the famous theater restaurant. A couple of years have passed since coming here still the place remains the same as on my first visit in 1993. The famous caricatures of actors faces still deck the walls, so I walk to my left into the bar sheltering from the cold.

An intruder arriving at the "the regulars" hour, 6:30 P.M., the bartender John knows everyone by name and of course their drink of choice. Slowly I get involved in the conversation as their stories unfold.

Nick in his 70's an eccentric retired actor who at one time used to organize exotic trips to the Far East, a blue-eyed, tall, lean figure, and the moderator of the conversation.

Gina is a curvaceous Puerto Rican who talks with glee about turning 50 and is describing her upcoming birthday party in Vegas with all her girlfriends. Working for several years in the theater district coordinating wages and contracts for actors.

There is also Sal a chubby, friendly book editor, discussing with all the latest Broadway productions. After a few calls he seems to have gotten some tickets for the play called 39 Steps, and casually asks me to accompany him. I gladly accept, saying our goodbyes to the group and walk two doors down to where the theater stands.

After a very interesting show Sal walks me to the Paramount Hotel also steps from the theater. On finding the bar closed I invite him for a Pizza and a Samuel Adams just a door from the hotel, we then say our goodbyes and schedule a last drink with the regulars before going back home.

The Sardis regulars took me in that first night in the city with stories as disperse and funny as anything I would expect after the long months of dealing with the stress of this time bomb ticking inside me.

Waking up the next morning to one of those cold New York February days. My first option is to wear the wool stamped zebra coat under a black wool cat-suit with a full cut leg, my black booties and on my head a big red turban, with red leather gloves to match, and my black McQueen bowling bag, and of I, go out to brace the cold.

At nine o'clock as I walk out of the hotel to the few blocks to Bryant Park, I savor each step I take. Mingling between the hordes of people rushing off to work, an unknown entity, cherishing in the city's adrenaline. Still some people, do a double take, getting some smiles of approval and some roll their eyes in disbelief.

On walking inside the tents, I fit right in in the traditional sea of blacks worn as a uniform by most of the fashion community. Still, the subtle red touch and Zebra coat make me stand from the crowd of many more outlandish dressers.

We style creatures always trying to give our original proposal when immersed in this competitive and creative endeavor called fashion. An easy adventure is mixing, trends, colors, textures, and exotic furs. Sometimes we even run on the ridiculous, but in the end, praise and fun are what matter.

Fashion is for me the best freedom of expression a way of reinventing myself openly on a daily basis. Color is an enhancement partner. The construction of a garment is a form of playing with the lines of the body.

I thrive on watching what others express thru their clothes a fashion show of people's ideas even before a designer's presentation gives me a brighter outlook on what will be the next big trends.

Sitting in the coffee lounge savoring the needed morning dose with a blueberry muffin, I see a cheerful blond blue-eyed waving from the door as she walks towards me. Cristina is a newspaper correspondent from one of Mexico's most popular dailies. A fashion editor and mutual friend Chris from Monterrey hooked us up. So after cordialities, we start to plan our week ahead of shows and parties, becoming great friends in crime getting into every significant show of the moment.

At noontime I meet up with my friend Mara for lunch a few blocks from the tents at this incredible Italian restaurant, catching up on her work and travels. She is amazed to see me doing so well after the chemotherapy.

I jokingly say: "As long as my red turban does not fall on my pasta, or get it blown out of my head, I think I will be ok. Last night was a feat to keep it on."

She roars with laughter, and asks: "What about wearing a wig, is in it easier?"

I explain my problem: "Frankly, with this cold weather a wig by itself is not enough, so if I wear a muffler, turban, or a hat, when walking it starts to slide sideways, risking ending up bald in the middle of Times Square. I do not want it as a fashion statement."

Her laughter and mine seem to make the whole restaurant take notice of us, wanting to get in on the joke. We even get a complimentary dessert from the captain.

At night I meet up with my daughter's friend, funky Kari who has been living here for almost a year. When I see her arrive at the bar at Balthazar's one of my favorite places, in New York, I freeze just seeing her. In her late twenties, she is wearing a very short mini skirt with thick tights a close to the body distressed little suede jacket and Dr. Martin boots, no gloves and thankfully a thick scarf around her neck.

"Wow," I say hugging her. "Your hands are freezing."

The expected answer: "I lost my gloves on the subway."

Kari like Alexis, are free souls. Having lived together in the comfortable, warm life of Playa del Carmen, they assume too much wrapping up in thick clothes is getting into a restraining jacket. The truth is, being young they take the weather for granted, and I have become too sensitive to the cold.

So my alone time seems to end quite quickly between, Christina, Kari, and my friend Nat who works at Modeling Agency calls for scheduling a dinner party. My ex-assistant Edna living up on the Hamptons with her wonderful husband Mitch fixes me up on a blind date with Gilbert, the manager of a well-known French uptown restaurant.

So going on a date, you take extra care of what you will be wearing to make a good impression. For me now the essential accessory is what will go on my baldhead.

Developing my expertise at working with wool pashminas to construct big turbans on my head, I secure tonight's black one with a vintage crystal pin to hold it together. Complementing it with a black short sleeveless Sabrina like wool dress, tall over the knee suede boots, and over the elbow leather black gloves. The look is sealed with my dark brown mink to the hips jacket, tied with a wide black belt and my mink scarf to the neck.

So with a big boost of self-confidence, I jump into a cab uptown and take a deep breath and brace myself for adventure.

I recollect now on the date, not-really-a-date, forget a romantic attempt. To start, you cannot ask a girl out to the place where you work since interruptions by one person or the other are sure to occur. You also by no means invite your arriving client-friends to join you at your table, even less if you just saw them last week.

My conversation was more with Joshua a filmmaker. Gilbert did not sit still thru the whole dinner greeting clients and giving orders to the staff. My night was still an enjoyable affair with fantastic company, delicious food, and wine.

Recollection of the night will be more related to losing mysteriously my right-hand globe, and having the whole restaurant looking it up without success than ending up with a dreamy affair.

What I learnt a few days later from Gilbert himself over a brunch invitation at the uptown French Roast Cafe was an apology of sorts:

"I see you walking in looking great, and as you get closer I see the yellowish tint of your skin, and the turban covering your baldness, and I know you are sick. I freeze, acting foolish, and being selfish remembering someone close to me had just passed away from the "Challenge" a few months before."

Absorbed only in myself, with my trying to look as healthy as I possibly can, sometimes I forget how this "Challenge" has struck millions without pity. Leaving many with deep sadness and the fear of experiencing a loss all over again.

From this moment on we became friends and have seen each other almost every time I have come back to New York.

Me, Tired?

As I watch my reflection every morning before leaving the hotel I can't help but smile. In the twelve days I have been here I have played with four different coats, (I am great at packing) as many as ten head turbans of crazy proportions, and couple of boots.

Feeling every day happy and radiating such positive energy. Truly believing the whole of New York knows they have to tell me how great I look to make feel better.

So from Joey's happy face as I walk thru the front desk, compliments come from all sorts of people. A couple of lady's at this uptown amazing grocery store where I feel like a local, stop me and say: "We should dress like you every day you look so great."

Compliments abound, the guards at the tents offer one kind word every morning, and my Spanish friend Miguel who works in the security unit of the shows flirts daily with me, a real ego booster.

After much thought, and coming to the conclusion I was naïve at the moment, you can disguise the "Challenge" but not altogether hide it. Pictures from those days show the funny yellowish color on my skin as Gilbert mentioned.

People in general have a certain innate compassion when detecting a vulnerable situation in others. Acting respectful and applauding the effort and for me this support was all I needed.

I am a constant babbler an intruder in uninvited conversations with anyone I meet along my daily life, a bad habit inherited from my father. My mother who was the picture of poise and propriety like Emily Post herself will scold him on any occasion he started talking to an unknown bystander.

At a restaurant she would say: "Pepe why do you have to ask what the couple ordered from the menu, you do not know them?" Woman, you have to ask when things look delicious and more if you have never been to the restaurant before."

When on a road trip and we got a flat tire: "Pepe why on earth did you stop the driver from the trailer?" "Rosa, he will change my tire without myself getting dirty, just for a tip."

Waiting in a shopping center for us, Mom: "Who was the man you were so friendly with?" "Oh a guy I just met, who recommended a new great place to eat."

Learning since childhood talking to strangers was not all that bad, gives me first-hand information, on what is new in any given city I visit. This also helps on meeting people I would have never have met if I were proper and quiet. Second, besides embarrassing my children as my father did my mother, I have ended up with quite a group of new friends. And now they also do the same.

After relaying almost my whole life's story since my arrival to New York to Mark a new acquaintance I meet at a Gallery opening, he pop's a question I have had no time to consider: "Do you ever get tired?" Laughing I come up with the answer:

"Every night on arrival to my hotel I can feel every bone in my body aching from exhaustion. On taking off the turban and staring at my bald reflection in the mirror, I usually stop and wonder if I am sick at all since there is no real evident pain? And oh yes I get tired but life has to go on."

He gives out a big laugh, without missing to advise me to take it one step at a time. As I am coming back in a cab to the hotel way past midnight, I ponder to seriously consider Mark's suggestion to take it a little easy.

After a nice warm shower, I jump into bed cozying up in my velour animal print pajamas, still wondering about the evening. On reviewing tomorrow's schedule and before dozing off into dream world I see the date of my March operation in bold black letters. "To hell with resting, I am in New York now" I hear myself almost shout.

Every night I go to sleep around 1:00 A.M. if there was a party almost past 2:00 A.M. Next morning I am usually out of the hotel no later than 9:00 A.M. to meet Cristina at the tents, we take in the shows, and off to cocktails or dinner, before she leaves on a train back to Brooklyn.

There are some mornings I just cannot wake up for the first show, if it is not too important I can linger a little longer in bed. One sure way I am pushed out of from under the warm fluffy comforter is my coffee cravings, which helps me keep up with my long day.

I mix the shows with museums and the theater as soon as the gang from Mexico arrives on the fifth day, the activity gets even more hectic. Time now is a precious commodity and before the operation I relish in the emotion of just life.

One night was theater with the guys, off all showing on Broadway like a little kid Marcus picks Shrek. I am uncomfortably cold all thru the show, so he has to make it up the next day and takes me to the Metropolitan Museum of Art to my traditional visit to the Temple Dendur.

Next night dinner with the girls at Budhakan quite an emotional event. Waiting outside the restaurant, clad in my thick sheepskin stamped leopard coat a chocolate colored turban on my head, and dark brown suede boots. I hear Lourdes my Mexican celebrity friend, shouting from across the street.

Everyone's mouth seems to drop at the sight of her arresting presence, as she gets closer I stretch my arms, preventing one of her usual big bear hugs, knowing her playful and inquisitive ways in a jiffy she can pull my turban off, exposing my bowling bald like head, in no time.

Firmly warning her:

"Do not dare pull the turban off, I promise I will show you my baldness in the bathroom."

We are ushered to the head of the long communal table set in the main room where an important scene of the first Sex in the City movie was shot. Just after ordering drinks she cannot wait a minute longer. Off we go to the bathroom, and on unwrapping my turban instead of her expected nervous laughter tears roll down her cheeks and I get one of her biggest bear hugs ever.

Strangely facing every day my bald reflection I had stopped considering the tragedy effect. Now sharing my image with my friend it's like I have lifted a sort of protective armor guarding me as clothes do from my naked and exposed self.

How a piece of cloth piled on my head gives me such security, is as old as when the cave man donned furs to cover their bodies, as a way of protecting from the weather a way of shielding myself from the effects of the "Challenge."

Particularly at this moment more than ever my playing with fashion is not such a scattered brained idea. This way of thinking might also help others along the way. For all the craziness it implies and the selfishness of forgoing pain and desperation with vanity this is a way of keeping my self-worth and integrity in place.

I am coming to terms of what I think could be more respectful in the long run, for me. Making it very clear whatever the outcome for anyone else with any particular "Challenge" this is my offering a quirky way to confront it with dignity, just by making the effort of nourishing "your" image.

Central Park

I t is a cold rainy Sunday in February Fashion Week was just over on Friday. I am flying back home tomorrow after two exciting weeks in the city, I start to feel nostalgic.

Standing on the steps of the Museum of the City of New York, having just enjoyed a fabulous exhibit, a retrospective of Valentina's work, a designer from the 40's. I stop and take a deep breath amazed of the view of Central Park just in front of me. I start to brood, when will I be able to come back?

When I hear a voice bringing me out of my place of doom:

"You know Miss you look as pretty as a Russian dancer."

Compliments are one of the things I just love about this city.

"Well it is so very kind of you."

I answer totally enchanted by the gentleman's compliment we smile at each other as we booth rush off, but he has just made my day.

Of course, there is no way on earth this handsome elderly man can guess underneath all the wrappings of cloth, there is a bald headed lady, making the greatest effort no one can imagine just to be out there in this weather.

Dressed in a long black vintage wool skirt, from the 70's plastered with big sun like embroideries made of thick yarn threads in all kinds of bright colors with wool fringes around the hem.

Wearing my comfy new purple wedge suede platform boots, and my 80's dark brown mink jacket which falls below my hips. Over the coat is the knitted mink shawl looking like part of the jacket, held together by a 6-inch black wide belt. On my head, I have made a big turban like concoction with a black wool scarf, adorned with a 40's crystal color pin. So maybe this is what makes me look Russian, I guess?

Learning to accept compliments from where ever they are coming, openly reassuring my self-worth and appreciating my image with pride. On receiving flattery I will treasure it gladly, the "Challenge" cannot rob me the happiness this implies.

By far one of the best praises I got a night before was from a bouncer in one of the hottest clubs in New York at this time. Reservations were made but we were so many there was a big mix-up. With half of the group already inside, and seven of us standing outside in a long line in the cold, I see a big burly guy pointing at me almost screaming "Only her, just her".

Dressed in my white fox coat with a black over the knee suede black boots in a short sequence silver sweater dress, jet strangely what made me stand out from the crowd was the silver and black turban covering my bald head.

At this particular moment compliments are part of what the doctor ordered. Precisely on this trip, I have been collecting one by one in order to give me the much-needed courage I will need in March.

So as I am walking down museum row elated saying my good buy's first to the to the Guggenheim, the Cooper-Hewitt, and finally to the Met, reaching the bus stop almost in front of this magical building.

My cell startles me back to reality, it is Lourdes, my model friend. In her hurried style will ask, and answers herself, besides giving orders all in one sentence without stopping to catch a breath. "Where the hell are you, come to the Essex House we will go for lunch somewhere".

From in front of Central Park a part of the group from Mexico ends up in Greenwich Village in the Italian restaurant, Silvano's. Enjoying a late Sunday lunch of pasta and red wine, cherishing the company and my favorite city, New York.

Suddenly taking notice of the time, only an hour and a half left to hit the stores before closing time. Our last opportunity for binge-shopping, we head down to Lohman's on 7th Avenue down in Chelsea, ending up with an edited selection of garments I enjoy to this day.

St. Patrick's Cathedral

I have sort of some rituals on my last hours in New York City. I wake up very early for seven o'clock mass, at St. Patrick's Cathedral, after I am off for Belgian waffles at the Chelsea Square Dinner on 23^{dr} and 9th street, yes all the way down.

First let me say my meeting with God is cordial, and peaceful. No recriminations, or whys, a simple just take care of me, and let me live up to the trial you have sent me, and do not let me lose my whole breast, please!

The music from the organ sort of fills me with hope, connecting me with the majestic and imposing beauty of the Church. Every time I come here I feel protected by some sort of special force, as mass ends and the sign of the cross is administered, I feel like everything will be alright.

My breakfast at the dinner is like being with friends, they are a mix of nationalities from the Greek owner to the Mexican and Central American waiters. All hover and fuss over me some remembering me from past visits, keeping me company with witty conversation. No diet for me today as I dive into the plate of luscious Belgian waffles with thick ham on the side and lots of heavy maple syrup.

As I am walking out of the dinner where I once encountered the fashion photographer Richard Avedon, I glance across the street to Jerry's apartment who I used to date and stopped seeing a year ago. "Grumpy" as I am used calling him was not on my list this time around. Realizing that it mostly was due to my lack of courage, to have to relate to him the trial of my "Challenge," something I regret.

Bundle up in my weighty sheep leopard printed coat, underneath a brown jumpsuit with boots, and on my head a huge terracotta colored turban.

At 8.45 in the morning I might have looked a little overdressed, who cares when you feel so happy with the chit chat, the attention the comfort food and the coziness of the place. I would have lingered a little longer at the restaurant, but I have a plane to catch, and pick up my luggage at the hotel in Times Square.

Walking to the Subway on 23d and 8th relishing on the cold wind on my face, again sadly I say my good buys to the City.

Unpacking

A rriving back to my reality, now composed of work, family, doctors, hospitals, I realized how for granted had I taken the "Challenge" in this last twelve days, hardly giving a thought to the surgery one week away.

So as I am unpacking the suitcases with Juanita's help. I am not just re-organizing my clothes, with every garment I am stashing the memories of my trip inside drawers and into the closet. Every piece of clothing offers the time and the place of my visit, they became an exciting part of my every day throughout these two past weeks.

Again the striking sense of being two different persons altogether. One who enjoys the moment to the fullest, and the other is unable to grasp that this monster is secretly hiding under the layers of my skin. What this silent intruder does not know is soon he would be taken to trial.

March First

Tonight I have to face my demons. I stand with my original body in front of the mirror for the last time. A confrontation with just Me. Inside this brain, mixed emotions at my naked reflection.

An almost imaginary situation, the likeness is me, but to a degree unfamiliar. Difficult relating this person staring back, to the one who will be in surgery tomorrow. Questioning for the millionth time is this happening or is it just a bad dream?

Always have thought my breasts were too big, my hips too wide, a little proud of my flat stomach, and for my age not so much cellulite. I let out a big sigh. Now alone behind closed doors I am losing it, tears slowly roll down my cheeks.

Painfully realizing I do not want another body just this one with all its flaws and imperfections. I am happy with my resemblance wanting to store the memory forever in my brain before the mutilation process begins.

Slowly I said good-bye to my right breast, "hope all goes well and I do not lose you completely" I whisper as though it can hear me: "Thank you for being part of me all this time, thank you".

With the chemo the doctors reduced the tumor's size from 4.5 to 3.5, so there are big chances for saving the skin. For me, it has always been on the table, and all my doctors know what I want. Only my top surgeon has been adamant about it, and says he will know until he opens me up. I am in a limbo for tomorrow's outcome.

With all the turmoil going on in my head I decide not to see anyone before the surgery. Without warning my cousin, Paco arrives unexpectedly before nine. Gives me a bear hug, goes into the living room and sits his tall frame down on the edge of the 50's chaise lounge.

Somber looking lost for words babbling all sort of illogical whispers, and hands clenched, he is not his usual self. Always loud with funny stories one after the other, even his customary fridge ransacking is forgotten, as he lets spaces of silence come between us. I ache for the way he is hurting, accepting how comforting love can be and how silly I have been trying to shut it out.

Rosina Ramón

The anesthesiologist prescribed a relaxing pill for tonight. The effect is unsuccessful. I toss and turn all thru the night. Reality and dreams become a mingled affair. From here on, at night it will be hard to distinguish dreams from my thoughts, very hard.

The Surgery

At 6.45 in the morning, I am a nervous wreck. Arriving at the hospital I try not to show it for the sake of my immediate family, but I feel like I would come undone any minute now. Alex is preoccupied with all the paperwork, at the registration desk, as I am reading what seems to be an affidavit to sign, which heightens the already tense feeling, choking me.

The word death seems plastered all over the document, openly releasing the hospitals and doctors from responsibility if anything should go wrong. Anxiety is at its highest levels now. I want to throw my second pair (of many to come) of terry cloth slippers into the receptionist's face and run out, but looking down at my feet my leather high heel booties will be too uncomfortable even for a two block walk. What was I thinking when I put them, maybe asleep?

Alexis is taking care of my dad whose eyes by now seem forever watery. Every step he takes appears as he is carrying some heavy weight on his now slumped back.

As we arrive into the vast empty surgery ward, Juanita seems to be the toughest of us all, concentrating in picking up my things as she helps me get into an ugly mint colored robe. I am allowed a final hug and kiss to all of them. I see my father take his handkerchief from his pocket as the door closes and I go into the surgery room.

Being laid on this uncomfortable thin bed, I start to shiver from the cold and the tension of the moment. When the anesthesiologist starts prepping me up with sedatives, the stress lessens, and my limbs start to relax.

Final relief comes on seeing Dr. Canavati walking in with a warm smile of reassurance on his face. Accompanied by his nephew Dr. Mauricio, and Dr. Walberg, the plastic surgeon, they each briefly explain the procedure they will follow to my then numb self.

My mind is losing clarity as the tranquillizers start taking effect. Laying there with three men examining my exposed naked breasts. I dimly see Dr. Canavati black marker in hand as he draws lines where the incisions will be performed.

Again shivers run thru my body, suddenly the discussion of the operation starts to float like dark clouds inside my mind. Slowly I begin to lose the sound of their voices starting to float off into this white world of unconsciousness.

Recovery

Waking up in the recovery room, at already one in the afternoon, I am as cold as always. A nurse gets me all wrapped up in another blanket. Grasping her wrist I hear my desperate voice ask the dreaded question: "How is my breast?" I am not given to much information as to be expected, only that the temporary implant was installed. Giving God thanks, I drift off to sleep, awakening in my room by the noise of friends and relatives.

Alex has taken upon himself ordering everyone around, getting the room to a comfortable temperature, for me, but too hot for everyone else to be inside. I can see Alexis sweating, so I convince him I am ok as he starts nervously adjusting the thermostat.

Craving sleep, I will fall in and out of slumber, almost all day. I try to touch my breast to get an idea how my new body feels, meeting with dismay only the coarseness of bandages. I don't really want to look. Sleep is the best option now. There is the desire to stay safe in this place called the incoherent zone. Dozing off traveling with some heavy luggage, trying to decide at an intersection, which of its infinite roads to take. I run thru them back and forth undecided.

Awakened by doctor Canavati who has come to reassure me the surgery was a total success, my skin preserved and so was my nipple. I will later learn this is very unlikely to occur, a vital task left for the hands of doctor Walberg to work with.

As I had asked the temporary expansion was in place. Still, it will take some time to find out how much the skin would be able to hold. So without my knowing, this is the beginning of a long process of many surgeries to come.

Adjustments

The good news is the Challenge is out of my body lymph glands and all, with no trace of it spreading further. The problem will be first accommodating to different sensations like a continuous electro tingling waves under my arm. Second, on touch I have no feeling whatsoever on my new imitation breast. Third, and most worrisome I am left with adjusting to a new body, in the process of a peculiar transformation.

Rational thinking is impossible at the moment. I have been too spoiled and smothered by everyone. Tears seem are stuck somewhere inside my being. Time alone has not been an option, people come and go, and phones will not stop ringing. Grateful, not to be left on my own, and at the same time longing for a little solitude, for some crying time.

Overwhelming is the love, but the mind is unable to grasp the extent of what I have gone thru.

Arriving home after several nights in the hospital, pain forces me to my bed exhausted in search for comfort. The house becomes awfully quiet as if the stress has had an impact on all. Shutting the doors of their respective bedrooms the kids and Juanita deal quietly each with their own fears and doubts.

Laying helpless, hiding under the covers, hushing a crying rampage, tears fall freely, blurring, my vision. Courage runs hiding I guess in one of the closets leaving me paralyzed for what seems a long time.

When I finally stand to face my so-called friend the mirror, I decide to take it all a step at a time, fixing first my mind to adjust to my new body. All thru the first month, I will not even try to glimpse at my full reflection. I need time to first accept my new reality.

After the bandages come off, I take showers with closed eyes, even relying on Juanita's help with dressing me. I have to hear the closing of the clasps of the unsexy bras, before opening my eyes, and face at the odd unevenness of size and shape in relation to my other breast. What concerns me now, how the hell I would dress in the next few days?

Summer is around the corner a lot of my clothes will not be working with this type of contraptions since the bra straps are too thick for summer dressing the materials heavy, and filling in the blanks of space missing on my right side is now an everyday affair to adjust to.

Silence

S ilence has been a close friend since childhood, not something to fret or worry about. Being finally left alone after arriving from the hospital while Alex and Juanita go to the supermarket, I regret my desired for solitude.

Now silence has a loud sound to it. The "Challenge" may be out of my system, but a buzz clovers at my brain with a doubt that seems to haunt me.

Being left with only me and my thoughts of fear, that seem to get louder as I walk around the empty house. Accentuating this silence is the nagging idea that I forever will be on the "Challenge's" list and will never be able to let my guard down.

I will have to be in constant watch from now on of this creature ever entering my body again. For five years I will hold my breath every six months after a thorough check up.

Forever a sword will always be needed on hand to be able to fight any battle against this imposed slavery that looms around me.

Me

"You are so vain" the Carly Simon song, a fact in ME. I cannot let go. Being told I was free of the Challenge was a God sent blessing I could not stop giving thanks, but the demons of my vanity would not stop chasing ME.

Obsessing for options to look my best became a priority, dressing and undressing until something from my closet looks right, a time-consuming affair, and a way to escape my reality.

Blouses and dresses fly to the bed on piles, and the task of finding the right bra is an endless issue. For someone used to be organized and coordinated to whatever I will wear each day. Difficulty arises getting used to this new body which requires a little more thought and a lot more reassurance.

As self-consciousness sets in, I have to abide by what I teach in my modeling courses, beauty rests in the attitude one displays over our image. Practicing my theory, of liking Me overall, first. Competing with the only one facing the mirror, Me.

Then, as usual, I travel in time when the insecurities of my teen years and the trauma of being plump, short, and the size of my nose too big, blown out of proportion, by crazy ideas one has at such precarious age. Beauty appeared so out of my reach, silly how I thought of myself then.

Today I know as the Webster dictionary specifies beauty is in the eyes of the beholder, my translation:

"What is beautiful to me may not be beautiful to you, so in the end, everyone can be beautiful."

This is my dearest belief, one I have cherished close to my heart. Which at this point is perilously hanging on the edge of myself worth.

So now I ask: "How do I fall in love with Me all over again, lopsided boobs and all?"

"How do I face my mutilated reflection in the mirror without fainting?"

While everyone has thought of me to be so optimistic and strong thru out this whole ordeal, my doubts hunt me. Wearing a kind of armor in order not fall to pieces in front of people, I find the need to fetch the attitude essence out from hiding.

Evidently, it does not mean I will not experience days of uncertainties, hysterical tantrums, and rivers filled with tears, sitting "attitude" by force. Guiding it across this foggy rough road, and searching for assurance that I am still Me.

Facing People

Two weeks after my surgery I am giving a conference about fashion trends for spring, at a shopping mall. My first public appearance in front of a crowd in over a month.

Deciding to dress in my high waist skinny red leather skirt to the calf, a white blouse pleated on the front hides the difference of my uneven breasts. The tall to the knee vintage Karl Lagerfeld suede boots give me a needed height, and a black turban covers my baldness.

Certain to be making quite a striking effect on my fashion audience, I savor the moment. After the questions and answers, I can say I am happy with the outcome.

Stressed and being tired becomes irrelevant acknowledging only I, have to find the power to beat the pain and the weariness in order to keep my grip on life. Finding pain an inconvenience inside my body, during the day, light exposes me with no mercy to the world and if I permit the fear dusts to conquer me. I am at a loss.

Strangely as this may seem I believe profoundly that as much as I need medicine in order to beat sickness. Defying my comfort zone is essential, tackling dread, and pinning it to the ground until I allow the return of the next insecurity attack.

Nights, I am at my most vulnerable and fragile self, with only my thoughts in total obscurity. These last couples of weeks the pain has been sharp, painkillers are not much help, the heavy weight of my fake breast, and the trouble moving my right arm, often wake me up.

My bed has like six pillows to prop me in different ways. To reach the bathroom I stumble thru the darkness's and stillness, a long road, as if walking into an unknown mysterious forest. Convinced to be traveling within a bad nightmare, facing my too real reflection in the mirror and the uneven touch of my breasts. Endless the battle with Me and myself, spooking sleep away some nights till early dawn.

Dreams are confusing filled with some panic effect, a recurring theme is lying beside my mother in a green field. Emotions of happiness fill my body, a special comforting reassurance by the warmth of her embrace.

Suddenly out of nowhere safety turns to fright, as a black bird hovers over my head: "Mom, Mom, help." Screaming chocking on the words, waking up with the dryness of thirst and my body shaking. Needing like a kid, to leave my table lamp on all thru the night.

A day after this last nightmarish experience I am informed the next step is radiation. Merely half a way thru awaiting the end of the ordeal. The hard act of patience is teaching my mind to blank out and let me sleep at night.

The Mirror

As a month after the operation draws near I have not been able to see my whole naked body in front of the mirror. Breasts, are the principal symbol of femininity as a penis means masculinity, to a man. I guess no guy wants it chopped off, right?

Here rests the core of it all. The understanding I have not only lost a breast, my feminine self is deeply wounded. Mentioning this before, ok my breasts were already sagging and maybe too big but I liked them. I was very proud of them.

Recalling the impact of my body stages. Bullied from second to sixth grade for being fat, paved the road to dropping that weight in my teen years. Puberty was particularly gracious to me while my skinny friends developed into flat chested waifs, whom I envied. Finally coming to terms that my main perk was my body's curves, and to boys, sexy.

Standing on the threshold of uncertainty my fight with the mirror endures. Repeating in a whispering voice to myself I am in a state of mind preparation, conscious it is all in my head. Without success to convince the Rosina inside my head to face my reflection. Too dam scary. Sweating becomes familiar especially with confronting full mirrors threatening my composure, showing things I do not want to see or am not ready to accept.

Again I remember the mean old witch in Snow White she had her reason for fighting the mirror. "Mirror, mirror on the wall who is the fairest of them all." She hated the answer. I am terrified of it too.

Accepting dread of any kind can take a lot of time and yes tolerance. We are talking about mutilation to the body, which can send shivers down to anyone's spine, a disfigurement that attacks also the soul.

I was naive to comprehend this was just my second operation no way of guessing I would have to experience six more in order to get my body in a more alluring shape. Anxiety lurks around like a mean stalker, to be faced head on instead of letting it destroy myself value or breaking me into little irreparable pieces.

"Fear" is a feeling that I have put makeup on to disguise it, almost quiet during the day, but teasing constantly. At night this monster frequently hunts my dreams. A faceless character or like that bird always chasing me. Leaving me out of breath, with a heavy beating heart ready to explode. Logic tells me I am trying to escape the truth of what is the "Challenge".

So the mirrors have to stay on hold, at least for a while.

Red Hair

O ver the years friends and family have been amused at the way I dress, but now they understand it is my defense mechanism to face the fear monster. So comments on my way of dressing have become like a thing of the past even though sometimes I have caught one or two off-guard with a silly sort of smirk on their faces.

In 1993 Marc Jacobs was all into grunge, and there was another rage, the monastic trend. At the time I was taking a summer course in fashion, at FIT (The Fashion Institute of Technology), it was my first time in New York.

So going with the style of the moment I spent the hot month of July in the city, wearing long flowered print dresses with bell sleeves in chiffon like materials, lace up booties, or black and white converse tennis shoes and on my head this crochet kippah to decorate half of my head. I would walk the New York streets feeling like a flower child of the 60's, free and wild.

My hair by now is an inch long, dyed to a bright look at "Me" carrot red. For fun, I started playing with these handy crochet caps, which I still keep in different colors. Placing the kippah at the center of my very short hair tying it with long scarf around the temples letting it's tails fall freely down my shoulders. Complementing, my flimsy chiffon long romantic dresses. What in fashion language will be bohemian chic. Identifying myself particularly with the let's say a Romeo and Juliet trend, with the singular twist of cowboy boots.

Survival from this sickness did not only come by what the doctors prescribed. For me this playing around with fashion made me stand strong refuting as much as I could pessimism. Clothes, shoes and accessories, forever spiced my life like pepper on a stake. Keeping a journal on what I was wearing each day became the norm for measuring my mood swings, and debating with the demons hiding around in every corner of my brain.

Talking about the brain this complex apparatus inside our heads, which becomes a control machine for our movements, feelings and thoughts, has to be carefully programed and controlled at all times so it can work as an partner for survival.

So as my hair starts growing out of the short Betty Boo curly look in new red ringlets, morphing into the chin length wavy frizz of the 60's hippy movement. The metamorphosis of my body evolves, and so does my style of dressing, appreciating each one as they come along.

Baldness has been a liberating experience as if the loss of hair has been a grant of freedom, a rebellion to the establishment and to preconception of beauty, the closest to being naked to the world.

A clear tribute to all in my situation, our <u>baldness</u> was a sign of power and undeniable courage in facing the "Challenge" with <u>boldness</u>.

Holy Week

Going back home for the Easter holidays is a ritual, as I drive on the lonely highway by myself, with the stereo at a full blast. I am free with the doctors permission, to be enjoying the view of a blue sky. As when a little girl on the many trips with my parents, I start to guess on the form of those huge cushiony clouds above me. A bear? O no a bunny? Or, maybe a cat?

Long golden colored grass frame the sides of the road, on the horizon bluish shadowed mountains turn green, as I get closer to them. Landscapes, of vast peaceful spaces with only trees standing solemn in silence, embracing the sun.

Sensitiveness to nature is now a real enjoyment whatever the weather has to offer, sun, rain, cold or heat, they are a welcome feeling, on my body, they sort of whisper to me, hey! "You are alive". That is the nicest thing one can experience.

I love driving on this lonely roads the liberty of watching the colors of a given day change from, blues to burnt orange as the sun slowly hides behind the mountains. The sun and the moon, play hide and seek with each other, and the mountains act like the fairy god-mother, posing themselves as backdrops for the game.

My doctor almost prescribed this time alone as a needed medicine for the self and also to regain the confidence in the movement of my right arm. As much as I enjoy the drive I do not want to be alone on these winding and isolated roads at night, darkness invades the highway. Without no moon or stars your best bet from blackness is headlights from incoming or on going cars. Mountains can disappear in obscurity as if being swallowed into a vast abyss, like with the "Challenge" uncertainty prevails.

Arriving thankfully to my hometown before darkness sets in, the town feels as transformed as myself. My first visit since this intruder took hold of my body, which pricks every so often my brain with doubts.

Here I am in Piedras Negras border town with Eagle Pass Texas, the two cities have advanced a lot since my teen years. On the Mexican side new avenues, and plazas, on the American side, more banks, a larger shopping Mall a new High School campus, and finally a Community College.

I still like to drive to the old High School grounds and take long walks on the football field, trying to do this whenever I come down. Thirty odd years after graduation, and the memories of times where worries did not exist, and all you cared about was the boy you where madly in love, at the time, and what you would wear to the football game on Friday night.

Father is waiting for me sitting at the round wood kitchen table. For a moment I expect to hear my mother's excited chatter coming from their bedroom. A sharp stab of melancholy runs shivers thru my body just missing her.

For him it must be a difficult affair to be living in this stillness and silence when the absence of her presence appears to be crushing him every morning on his awaking to emptiness, on the next side of the bed but there is no way of uprooting him from his life.

After fixing him dinner he asks about his favorite subject my daughter Alexis. Since her birth she has been a special light in his existence and rejoices when one talks about her. Alex is not left out the conversation only their relationship is more a man-to-man one. Characterized by their similar sense of humor and their overall enjoyment of anything to do with food or any new electrical gadget shown on TV, or something peculiar found for a dollar at a flea-market.

When Alex was a toddler, my father would rejoice after all his friends mentioned, that his grandson was his splitting image. The boy he so badly expected me to be, he lost a lot of bets and cigars on my being born a girl.

Walking into my bedroom nostalgia strikes as I glimpse around the white brick bedroom. The also white colored crochet bedspread, handmade by Tia Pilar covers the bed adorned by aqua and green pillows to match the pistachio tinted rug.

The wood hope chest standing in front of the bed, with my mother's wedding dress inside, is framed by lace curtains hanging on the windows. Sitting on its top is a mantel clock from the 1850's that winds with a key, and when it strikes the time it offers a glorious chime.

Stopping to face my reflection on the oblong shaped mirror, which tops the vintage dressing table. Outlined by two antique bronze and crystal wall candelabras on each side. Sitting on the Louis XV coquette chair which for the first time I come to relate it's shape to a woman's sexy figure.

Wondering like I always do with antiques about their past lives. In this case, how many women's images where reflected onto this mirror, and what sort of lives did they lived? I will never have an answer, but as a child I made a lot of stories around all this old furniture.

As I am brushing my hair traveling thru melancholy, everything is so comforting and familiar, making me wish I had never moved, as if by staying here the "Challenge" would never had laid it's claws on me.

Cozying up on my bed I feel to drown in the too soft worn mattress, and on closing my eyes I can vividly picture my mother standing by the door's frame speaking to me, a coffee mug on her hand.

Her imaginary presence is all over the house, in the living room sitting on the delicate engraved medallion chair. Cooking, and chatting happily with Juanita in the kitchen, in her bedroom lying on the bed reading a book, or watching TV.

Smiling to myself at the memory, of herself perched on the vanity chair in front of the bathroom mirror, curlers under her balloon like astronaut portable hairdryer. Then touching up her high-up hairdo spraying it with vengeance, a can of Aqua Net in hand.

Needing her hurts so much, on opening the wall to wall closet in front of my bed, and unzipping an old garment bag, taking two of her favorite robes from inside which I hug to myself. Her smell still faintly lingers, sensing as if she is holding me in her arms.

My war against the mirror is blown out of proportion there are more mirrors than I recalled. I am careful dressing, closing my eyes during the day, and turning the lights off at night. The problem with the mirror has to do with facing my reality, the terrible dilemma of sexiness comes into question, beauty seems to be on hold, looks like my vanity is driving me crazy.

A week goes by fast visiting relatives, taking care of my father and going out with Larry (more on him on a next chapter). Besides training every afternoon a girl for a beauty pageant with walking and modeling runway techniques.

Some days I will cross the border to Eagle Pass Texas, for some window-shopping. An activity that used to be quite thrilling, spending hours browsing around, and trying on things. Now on arrival to the fitting rooms problems arise, first tackling the hard task of finding the right bra.

A flashback hits me, my mother and I were coaching my daughter Alexis who at age thirteen was getting her first bra at the JC Penney store at the local mall.

She was in such an awful mood not even letting us pronounce the word bra to the sales lady. In order to make the experience a swifter one I nicknamed bras, "mountain coverings" which made her even angrier, knowing that the teenage stage is a tough one, mom and myself just laughed it off.

Now I am wishing I had my mother helping me choose my mountain coverings.

There are not a lot of options for a person in my situation, besides it's quite difficult to try something on with your eyes closed relying on touch. At the moment my good boob drops a couple of inches above my waist. The sick one feels formless blob much like a pile of silly dough.

After trying bra after bra, I finally find the answer a smaller size lightly padded sport bra by Danskin which will reduce the good boob in size like a girdle and pull the sick one up making them seem almost even.

There is one drawback no beige or white, just blues and blacks, we are in the middle of spring and long prairie, strappy hippie dresses are in full fashion for summer, (a staple in my closet since College). After looking around for hours I select some light T-shirt cotton sweaters that tie conveniently in a knot at the front. I get them in several colors, they conceal the bra straps, and at least fake some cleavage.

The act of buying clothes now is a tiresome chore all on its own, carefully requiring a lot of thought and time to analyze the final look.

Here I come into the concept of beauty again, where positive attitude has to reign. This uneven feminine shape I am in, is triggering a level of high vulnerability. Striving to disguise this loss the best tool is my juggling with fashion.

Do I Cry?

People seem to wonder if I ever cry, of course I do. Crying, as it seems is freeing me from the chains inflicted by this inevitable sense of fear, cleaning and refreshing my shattered state of mind.

Since my arrival to my childhood home I am in an extended mourning stage, I've cried more than all thru the past months. After four years without my mother I feel her presence in every corner, needing comforting hugs, which are nowhere to be found, so I just cry.

I grieve for her absence, for my lack of courage in facing my naked body in front of the mirror, tricking my mind playing dress up just like when I was a little girl.

Flashes of memories of myself twirling around in mom's long aqua crochet dress embroidered with crystal beads on the low cut V-neck, falling of my shoulders several sizes too big for my then nine-year-old frame.

Happiness was simple then, the mirror and I had a great relationship not even my then plump self would interfere with my feeling pretty. I owned my beauty then, before the terrible uncertainty that caught up with me in my early teens.

Accidentally on my last day in my hometown, I see myself. Getting out of the shower as I am finishing drying my skin, somehow the towel ends on the floor. Face to face with my dreaded reflection, cold sweat runs down my forehead, glimpsing at the cut across my recuperating right boob, my nipple almost reaching my armpit. Biting my lips in surprise, I feel faint.

My image of this new body automatically hits my brain filling it with disbelief. Graving some courage and holding my breath I carefully analyze my likeness in what seems to be a second take, it is not a pretty sight to see. Catheter scar, dropped boob, and formless boob. Kneeling down on the floor bravery eludes me it is a lot to take in, and uncontrolled sobs rip thru my whole body.

All thru the week my Father appears like he is not even in the house, he has become quieter, only when I take him out for lunch or dinner he seems more cheerful, more talkative and with his old sense of humor back.

Thanks to his lack of hearing he does not take notice of my constant crying sessions, he is lost in his pain, of being without my mother whom he adored and coping with my "Challenge." I can see in his eyes it has been a too big a burden to handle.

We both try not to raise the subject as if it nothing is happening. Evasion has always been a part of our troubled relationship, "you do not ask I will not tell." Somehow I regret it so much now.

Coming Back

Tragedy is blown out of proportion by my mere thoughts, the uncertainty of what lies ahead is not clear I am in a limbo in understanding. Radiation will be the next step and the complexity of the procedure consisting of 25 sessions will be unraveling as I go along. Luckily I will be administered some oral source of chemotherapy, with the promise of no side effect.

Driving back home on the Thursday before Easter Sunday for a checkup with my reconstruction surgeon Dr. Walberg. A deep sigh escapes me remembering in the last six months, I recount all I have lost: my hair, finally, my period, the feeling in my right breast.

My negative thoughts, making me realize thru all the loss I have mostly acquired one really big thing the chance to stay alive.

Little did I know, as I was arriving from my trip, my friend Yogi had just lost the battle with her own Challenge. Having found out she was really sick after my operation, I took on calling her every other day, and I had promised to see her after my trip, big mistake.

Arriving from the doctor's appointment, I found a message on my answering machine, an answer to my call from two days before, one of her daughter's sadly leaves the news of her passing a week before. Falling to my knees on the floor, I start sobbing.

We had worked, and traveled together. Disagreed on many topics, along the way but we shared a lot of great laughs. She had the nag of calling me Mrs. Rosina in front of people, insisting I was older than her. Knowing well she had married while I was still in College, it was no use arguing the matter with her, it was just a lost battle.

She was pretty with delicate features white skin and black hair, rail thin since I met her in my 20's, she had been a great model back in the 70's when modeling in Monterrey was just starting, more than ten years before I started my agency.

Later, on she stablished a dancing studio, which I never understood why she shut down, since dancing had been her passion. She had that dancers grace in all her movements, to someone meeting her for the first time she must have appeared too choreographed, but immediately she will win anyone over with her very unique and spunky contagious laughter.

Yogi seemed to be constantly in a good mood, bragging proudly of her two daughters achievements' and of her ex-husband who I knew secretly she never stopped loving.

Without an official appointment death just shows up. Her absence leaves me in an abyss of pain, opening my eyes to my own weakness. Fragile "we" human beings are, confronting us to the slim line separating life from death, and how we have to cherish each living breath that is free for the taking.

Again the fear monster displays no respect with his usual bad manners of an intruder shaking my insecure self to its roots.

Days after I am scheduled now to my oncologist's office to program the radiation sessions. As Jaime my doctor patiently explains, his words do not help to appease the uneasiness. About to start the radiation therapy. With a 90-degree temperature on the outside and mourning the loss of my friend it was like a bulldozer was downloading a heavyweight on my heart.

On this particular day, I am a sight to be seen dressed in a stamped zebra balloon asymmetrical cut jumpsuit from H&M, and ballerina black flats, my two inch long curly red hair, is free of any bondage no scarf or wig on my head. Clearly if it weren't for the bright red lips that accentuates the whiteness of my pale skin, and my funky outfit I would plainly disappear as part of the white hospital walls.

Strange how we can take physical pain better than emotional pain. In the doctor's office I tilt my head on Alex's shoulder feeling the tears run down my cheeks as Jaime comforts me without success. I actually lose all my composure, breaking down for the first time in front of my son and doctor.

Awakening in the middle of the night, soaked in sweat, became a recurring affair, and tears would surprise me at one time, or another. Tears came without notice, making a mess of my makeup when I least expected. Standing at the line in the bank, while I was driving to the office, at the supermarket deciding what flavor of ice cream to pick, you name it, they came camouflaged as a sort of relief.

Sobbing which is more liberating had to be forced. I remember I went to the movies by myself several times to be able to cry. One of the movies was Nights in Rodarte I cried with big sobs together with Jessica Lane when

Richard Gere's character dies, sharing the pain with a character from a movie how weird is that? Strangely it made me feel a lot better.

Wondering why not reach for someone in my support group? I just could not do it in front of anyone else except for that day at the doctor's office. Teary eyes were all I could manage, but holler in the presence of others was out of the question, it was beyond me. Being caught inside my own anguish, I covered it by dressing quirky or putting lip-gloss on, so in a way it worked as time went by.

Radiation

Radiations are scheduled for 8:00 A. M. each morning. I wake up and put on some jogging pants with my red Converse tennis shoes, lipgloss, and pretend I am going for a run.

On my arrival to the hospital reality strikes, lying on this hard cold surface in a freezing room, boobs exposed to four technicians who fuss over me for twenty minutes. Debating seriously, about the precise alignment of my body.

This is how I come to get the only tattoo I will ever have. A tiny blue dot over my ribcage, to mark the exact spot for the radiation flash. Stamped for eternity to always remind me of the "Challenge".

After a fifteen-minute radiations procedure I drag myself back home and sleep till noontime. Jaime my doctor warned me I would be feeling tired and drowsy, I need sleep so much, as a source of escape from real life, and also to get rid of the burden of being so tired.

Moody feelings came in a combo, besides radiation México stood paralyzed by almost two weeks with an influenza alarm striking the nation. Even harder the international economy took a direct blow on all our business, and especially on my spirit, having nothing to do faced me with the reality of being sick, which I loathed.

My illness, was not a situation I willingly wanted to be in. Besides no one with a sane mind wants to hear a knock on the door open it and find the "Challenge" walk in and sit inside one's body.

Keeping busy has been a good medicine for ignoring self-pity. Facing a big grey elephant made of gloom in front of me is unacceptable. Being sure I was strong, coping with every blow head on.

This body in reality is comparable to a crystal structure, breakable in a whim. Confronting me to the mere fact of simply being human. Luckily I was defeating a battle, which so many have lost.

Hopelessness

What could have been funny skit for a TV program turned out to be a desolated affair. As I am finishing taking a shower somehow trying to put on my bra my arm gets entangled on one of the straps. Being my right arm still pretty stiff from the last operation, I am unable to move it with ease to my back, without pain. I start loudly calling for Juanita's help but no answer comes, it is one the loneliest moments in my ordeal.

Sitting down on the bathroom floor unable to move, tears start flowing from the sheer feeling of being helpless. I somehow crawl down to my bedroom, lying all tangled up on the rug, finally hearing Juanita's footsteps in the hallway. Seeing her walk inside the room I start bawling like a lost kid.

Finally, after getting me out of my bra entrapment, she fixes me one of her amazing teas, which helps me fall off into a tight sleep. Transporting me to one of my weird dreams, in which reality becomes part of the dream itself, like the Wizard of Oz or Alice in Wonderland, I lose myself in fairytale land.

After all the distress of the night before I am ready after almost seven months to take a hard look at my body. Without appointment I face the mirror.

The sight looks like a cartoon of sorts my good boob flopped down by gravity, my in reconstruction boob is upright but has a big cut across the top part going almost to my right under arm. A pleasant surprise is discovering my nipple looking to the north. so now instead of tears, I laugh at my now odd reflection. My nipple is a unique part of my feminine self, showing Dr. Canavati's great respect for my womanhood.

Strange, I had often squirmed when seeing people who were missing a part of their body, it gave me the shivers. Now I am one of them.

Tough realizing I am still whole even if a part of me is missing or damaged, "What matters is to be alive."

May 10ᵗʰ Mother's Day

A day which has never been the same since mother's passing almost five years to date, now the day turns out to be a nuisance squashing my heart. Every time I see someone with their mother, I am yes, very jealous.

I have missed her so much since this journey started, how comforting it would have been to awaken after each surgery and have her sitting on the sofa in front of my bed ready to give me support.

Almost hearing her voice, seeing her standing up tall and beautiful, holding my hand, or having her call me over the phone to see how I am feeling. Dreaming of her so often these past days, I think she is protectively watching over me.

The kids and I go for lunch to my cousins Celina's house with all her family, but still the day feels empty with a big void of past celebrations.

What difference does a year make I was oblivious dancing the night away at Edna's and Mitch's Jewish wedding in the Hamptons. I danced with the young, with the old with my lovely friend Mariel with the grooms father and the bride's mother, I danced with all the races of the world until I could hardly feel my feet.

I have treasured that day like a reminder of what joy feels like. Each day as I make the decision of what length or color of wig to wear I try to cherish the way I transform myself, and how having a joyful feeling beats teary days every time.

When pessimism strikes I only have to remember how those patients I see in my doctor's offices in wheelchairs, with their bonny frail bodies, eyes bulging from their sockets, with pale yellow skin. I have to give thanks to yes, God.

Shockingly realizing how I also have acquired such a peculiar hue during this ordeal. I am a con artist with makeup, mastering the ability of working with pink lip-gloss and blush, there is nothing like it to make me look and even feel youngish. Makeup aside, the wanting to survive is helping me win the battle against this "Challenge."

Still doubt is there, tinted by fear. What about all those who also fight and do not make it to the finish line? For sure it has to do with catching the "devil" by its tail at the right time, and sooner will always be better than later.

Mind & Body

My mind sometimes is alien to my body. Usually I am sure I look so great until my friend the mirror proves me wrong. Dressing always was so much fun but working with one flimsy boob falling down and one looking up to the stars is now quite an endeavor.

A daily matter of a balancing act, one boob needs support the other needs comfort since it still hurts and the arm cannot be raised up still. So every morning I play with the sport bras in a size smaller than mine to lift the floppy droopy one, but the tightness minimizes the size, the sick one just looks high but formless.

Being an expert in fashion styling I have learnt to play with pockets, ruffles, pleats, sequences long necklaces anything to camouflage, and now even out my so complicated boob image.

Abiding to old fashion standards the norm would be less is more but for the moment more is better. Deciding for a touch of stravaganza as a way of coping with the dilemma at hand. Color becomes a way of life, prints over prints collide happily with each other, to many eyes an incoherent scheme of combinations, to me a form of personal expression. Matchy-match is at the moment filled with boredom, I crave exaggeration.

Accessories are bold, lots of large wide bracelets, on booth of my wrists, enormous hoop earrings help frame my baldhead, or accentuate a turban. Booties and gladiator sandals in summer complement perfectly my long skirts, big weaved baskets substitute a leather bag. Decoration of myself is performed without boundaries or limitations, rules in my way of dress are banned, and it has definitely to do with being me.

May 15, Mexico City

The day of my 22nd radiation I wake up that morning with my head about to explode from a headache, unable to get out of bed, since even the light seems to worsen the throbbing on my temples. I cancel my appointment and feeling a little better in the afternoon I am off to meet with Jaime, my oncologist.

The bad news is my skin has started to get too sensitive from the burn of radiation, so I am granted two weeks of rest and heavy painkillers since I need to be in shape for a flight tomorrow to Mexico City. Confronted once again with one more of the discomforts in the process of survival.

The gratitude of being healthy comes after the pain in my body departs. Comparable to finding a pot of gold, filled with the energy to run, jump, laugh and fill my lungs with fresh air. The mere act of wellness is a symptom of life.

The "Challenge" an unwelcome intruder was minimizing my self-value, making me defenseless, jeopardizing my trip, which meant a needed boost to my deflated ego, besides putting my work on the line. So Juanita's magical teas to the rescue and with my doctor's prescription together they did the trick. Feeling afresh early next morning I fly to México City, setting my mind into a "feeling good mode," and my body responded to the message quickly.

Being hired to edit and style my friends, Lourdes and her partner Aba's clothing line for a fashion show was something I could not miss. Besides I had been already working for a week around the mood board missing the excitement of the work I love, was out of the question.

With about four inches now of red colored hair, wearing a camouflage short safari style shirtdress over linen wide olive green pants and white and gold cowboy boots, from the looks of people's faces at both airports I am quite a sight. Caring less at looking different, funky, or crazy, happiness is all around me.

On my second night in México city, I go out to dinner with a dear old friend, the closest to a date in this entire long road to recovery. Feeling amazing as I come down from my girlfriend's apartment, wearing high a waist ridding khaki pant tucked into brown suede boots, and a vintage cotton embroidered sequence blouse in burnt red, almost matching my hair color. Over my shoulders is my distressed leather Cavalli jacket.

Andy has the same sexy hippie look he had when I met him four years ago in the beautiful colonial town of Morelia. I could even swear he is wearing the same jeans when meeting him on the eve of New Years. He is in his early fifties but looks about ten years younger (like me we are excellent at hiding our real age) he still wears the Project Red pendant with the word "Arrived" which I gave him almost two years ago.

Morelia
(Four Years Before)

M orelia's main plaza is one of the most beautiful colonial plazas in
Mexico where people walk around the old Cathedral and lounge
around without any care in the world at one or the other traditional coffee
shops framed by tall Spanish style arches.

People gather around the clock, especially in the middle of the
afternoon, hearing the laughter and chatter as I walk thru the rows of
tables I am feeling quite the outsider as I perceive an interesting male
meticulously observing my every move.

Comfortably dressed in a long brown semi-circular knit skirt, V-neck
sweater with bell cut sleeves in a forest green shade, a long mustard tinted
scarf flies around my neck.

The sense of being watched is overwhelmingly flattering, my movements
are instinctively coordinated to entice my audience. Exaggerating every
step, in my snake burgundy colored boots, tipping down my wide-rimmed
suede hat as I flutter underneath my eyelashes, like a teen. Holding for
support to my fringed suede bag strapped across my chest, deliberately and
noisily clicking my silver bracelet's in a happy mood.

From out of the corner of my eyes, I spot a handsome longhaired
guy flirting openly with a kid's mischievous smile, his eyes twinkling
with a funny glee as I flirt back with him. Walking from his penetrating
gaze, I somehow know he has started following me. I start to intentionally
play hide and seek stepping inside a quaint little shop, where I end up
purchasing a short embroidered bolero jacket, as a way of buying my time.

On leaving the store we almost bump into each other, so I mockingly
say: "Hi are you looking for me?" And then we both start roaring with
laughter.

An unexpected and romantic encounter spending New Year's Eve
together, at marvelous 1700 old hacienda converted into one of the best
restaurants owned by my host in the city, called Las Mercedes. After
dinner, we bar hopped hand in hand till the sun started rising, like guilty
teenagers we tiptoed silently to my bedroom in my friend's house, giggling
happily with passionate gusto until falling asleep in each other's arms.

Awakening past noontime for a Mexican style brunch of chilaquiles, the best dish for a hangover. A mixture of tortilla chips, green or red sauce, chicken, cheese and heavy cream, toped this with sunny side up eggs on the side guacamole, and fried beans a good michelada beer concoction and ready to start the new year right.

For almost two days I leave my friends behind and Andy and I became inseparable showing me around the city, driving me to old churches and archeological sites, of course to the must visits of Pascuaró, and the Janitzio lakes, which are a sight to be seen.

Romance wears of when divided by distance if you do not commit wholly to building a relationship it evaporates as soon as it starts. Friendship, on the other hand, is a little more lenient affair you do not have to nourish it as often. After all the years we have kept the friendship without forgoing the flirting, and it has served us right and like with some of my special friends each time we see each other we just pick up where we left of.

My punkish short red hair gives Andy no clue about my ordeal with the "Challenge." After ordering wine at this cozy Italian restaurant I start relating my story, a shocked expression takes hold on his face.

For an expert in words he seems to lose his usual luster, chopping awkwardly sentences of comfort all throughout dinner. Andy, a successful film photographer, exciting is to hear him talk about his movie projects, is like experiencing the plot firsthand. Describing his undertakings in slow pauses of suspense, with explicit detail, of his intriguing schemes for lighting, which most of the time he has learnt from his own imagination. Winning over the year's diverse and significant recognition.

Tonight he becomes extra sensitive to my every need making me feel like I was the most beautiful girl in the room, at this point it was practically all I needed, to believe I looked great, even if it is was a little white lie. Compliments become essential to my appreciation, of my feminine self, they are needed like internal medicine to alleviate anxiety.

The Fashion Show

Working on the presentation of a collection is an amazing job. You start with fitting the models, editing the looks, coordinating the concepts, and organizing the order in which each piece of clothing will be shown on the runway.

Working for four days before the final presentation, almost nonstop, and going to bed at three or four in the morning, and getting up at eight was adrenaline to my body.

Back home I was always so sleepy. Now my body did not have time to feel tired, too much was going on. Being my friends well known celebrities the press was all over the event. I was just busy concentrating on every single detail. Coordinating accessories, and shoes for each look, and working with the makeup artists and the hair stylists, I was in my most happy element.

Weariness came after the applause and the excitement of success. It was no surprise I could hardly feel my feet, and every inch of my body started aching from plain fatigue. I had over done it I knew it. Facing the orderly chaos that is backstage after a show slumping into a chair with a champagne flute in hand I take it all in. The after photos, and what seems all of Mexico's press, cramming for interviews of my friends the designers, mixed with models taking selfie's shots before undressing.

Returning home the excitement and energy I had enjoyed for a week, took leave of absence. My body craved sleep even more than before. I started having lots of pain on my limbs; even my hands looked like being hit with arthritis. My fingers would unexpectedly fold and I had to use my other hand to put them back into position, I felt as a Pinocchio's of sorts.

On the doctor's office the next day he explained it was part of the after effects of the chemo. The treatment left remnants of its poisonous drug, hidden somewhere inside the body ready to claim presence at the time it saw fit.

I was dreading being told I would need another round of chemo, being extremely fortunate to be given it orally. Luckily radiations were suspended since the inside layers of the skin needed more repair time after the damaging burn.

Radiation is like being stuck in a microwave oven, so I was put on vitamin E to recuperate from the internal loss of moisture a pill I keep on taking every day, besides spreading oils and lotions all over my body. After a lot of effort my skin slowly recuperates, even after all the goopy stuff thrown inside this body.

Arriving from the doctor's office, I slump down on my king size bed, as my sight settles on a couple of engraved wooden boxes from India on the night table. I just love the work of delicately carved wood.

I take one box into my hands and start to think what if I could fill one to the rim with my regrets, anger, sadness, and fear but mostly with the pain and exhaustion I feel now. I want to shut these feelings tight inside never to let them free again. A tear escapes from my right eye, as it splashes onto the little box, lost forever.

The Cocktail

Arriving to a cocktail party at my cousins Abe's house, I feel all eyes are upon me as I walk the large colonial foyer to his welcoming outstretched arms. From the corner of my eye can clearly see some guests eying me and whispering between themselves, surely talking about my body being struck by the "Challenge," the least anyone needs in a difficult situation is pity.

Clothes maintain my confidence intact, let them talk. I am wearing very wide legged high waist linen pants in a sand hue. A loose t-shirt embroidered with mother of pearl shells, a gold linen circular jacket with bell cropped sleeves, and taupe colored high wedge suede sandals. My hair is now a mass of tinny strawberry red curls, which swing happily with each movement.

Feeling great I sit down with a large group and I am suddenly asked by a tactless lady "How do you do it? Keep up with the treatments, working, traveling, socializing and still have the energy and the same time to "try" to look amazing. I almost laugh at the "try part" detecting malice in her tone. As if stating whatever I was doing was really not working. Little does she know it's not an easy undertaking, to at least try?

Jealousy hits a nerve with some people, here she is a lady of means, in an important social gathering drained and drab looking in ripped jeans, excusing her looks with arguments of her multiple activities. Understanding by then that my attitude and self-assurance make her pretty uncomfortable. I almost yearn to be curled up in bed reading a good book instead wasting my precious time listening to her negative and senseless self.

For sure it is easier not to have to worry about wearing makeup, or think what to wear to camouflage my boobs, every time I go out. Dressing used to be effortless, now is a task to carefully map out and enjoy.

Many people may regard looking good as a waste of time, especially when sick, my appearance is crucial for feeling healthy. For me, an everyday affair, instantly my attitude transforms into positive vibes. Getting dressed, and putting a little makeup on even if I am not getting out of the house, triggers a defense mechanism of strength and confidence.

Having uniforms of long cozy skirts for booth summer and winter, and my cowboy beaten up boots give them a quirky feel. Long scarf's over blouses conceal the unevenness of my breasts, and strands of large wooden beads are another great option. Big chunky bracelets have always played an important part in my overall look, as essential as big tall turbans on my head. I wear enough trinkets to distract an army of spectators or maybe be confused with a fortuneteller.

Summer

M y on repair boob gets hard very hard sometimes because of the implant, and the effect caused by the radiation. An uncomfortable feeling of pain occurs when I try to raise my arm or lie on my right side, it is a reminder of the rocky road to health.

My boob sometimes with no warning will start to toughen up like a rock, especially if I wear an underwire bra. I have several times had to run to a bathroom wherever I may be to take the bra of. My solution has been taking the underwire from most of my bras, post mastectomy bras are so unattractive and impractical. This will become a sort of nagging thing as time evolves.

Looking attractive is a priority for the psychological impact on my idea of beauty. Shattered by the mutilation of my body, it has also been an assault on the mind.

I have a membership at this country club where most of the summer months I swim on a daily basis. Like an impatient child I am just waiting for the clock to strike six rush home and decide what swimsuit to wear with the coordinated attachments. An assortment of hats, baskets, pareos and flip-flops. My after pool wardrobe, is a mix of long cotton skirts with Mexican embroidered blouses bought in markets from Oaxaca to Merida.

The total pleasure of diving into the pool is invigorating, with just the water and Me. Moving my body with each stroke in rhythm with my brain I can't separate them. There is no pressure here, focusing only on my breathing, coordinating arms and legs, which feel longer with every stretch I simply let myself be free.

At the moment my pastime has become a little complicated. One day I dare wear a shiny gold maillot swimsuit, stuffed with two silicone boobs one cut smaller to even out the size. Taking the sun an easy task, hiding under a large black straw Pamela-hat and metallic flip-flops. Swimming in this sophisticated get up is risky matter.

For a while I just lay out reading with a large "Vampiro" on hand (a cocktail made of tequila, grapefruit juice and a Tabasco like red concoction), and enjoying the view of the mountains surrounding the club.

As the heat become unbearable, to cool off I brave myself and decide to jump in the water and give it a try. What I have been dreading happens. To my surprise instead of crying or being embarrassed, I have only the laughter option. While chasing one of my silicone boobs from drowning the other jumps out like a frog. I juggle splashing ridiculously like a child, until finding them. There very close by is God, with his camera rolling having the last laugh.

Re-discovering laughter has been a nice surprise, laughter has been there since the cave men appeared on the planet to signify happiness. Usually we take laughter for granted, we walk around without knowing that laughter therapy actually exists.

I was oblivious to this until I started seeing that my evolving body's transformation needed humor to heal. So on gray days laughs and touches of pink lip-gloss lighten the heavy load. As the poet E. E. Cummings noted:

"The most wasted day is a day without laughter"

August

August in Monterrey usually is the warmest month of the year, with the temporary implant my body seems to get even hotter. Triggering heat and often anxiety attacks confronting me with a yoyo like body temperature. Freezing and shivering in air conditioned rooms one moment and almost melting me down with sweat whenever I step outside.

The two forces of nature, heat and cold show no respect. The problem with heat it slows the thinking process of the mind making the overall activity of the body heavier as if in every step I have a brick strapped to my ankle.

If my life were not so full of people who love me, all of the discomforts I am experiencing will be a little tougher to cope with.

A strange sensation to explain it is like I am being smothered with a certain warmth liquid of love spilled from a wonderful crystal pitcher over the top of my head. Covering all of my body in this satin like sensation of softness, securing me from what may seem harm's way. Acknowledging all this love brings often an unexpected smile to my face.

Reconstruction

With a great gusto I welcome the September showers that seem to cool down not only the weather but also my overall self. Car windows rolled down to feel the brisk air hit my face. Alex is driving me at 6:00 A.M. in the morning we are in total silence going to the hospital. Today marks my first reconstruction surgery, and the 3rd operation.

The long streets are bare, but the light of early dawn sheds a bluish hue outlining the mountains in a breath-taking way. As mentioned before I have become more in tune with the appreciation of nature, and glad for the opportunity to be grateful for this.

Still I am speechless absorbing the sight but feeling numb the whole ride to the hospital. My brain is a blank paper without any written lines.

Clouding my mind, with senseless worries since last night, arriving home a total nervous wreck. After an overrated discussion over nothing with Juanita. Locking myself inside my bedroom, acting like a spoiled brat. Always uncertainty of the unknown equal's irrational behavior, striking at the dearest ones, around us.

Walking into the freezing hospital registration area with my son, and Juanita, perceiving clearly what nervousness does to one's brain. Permitting my hysteria to distort rationality. Forgetting to just ask again and again for a viable answer to the dreaded doubts that somehow overshadow my foolish incoherent thinking.

Surveys in México indicate only one out twenty of women stricken with breast "Challenge" undergo the process of reconstruction, a little inconceivable for me, why? Many will say for lack insurance, others will be either too scared to go from operation to operation. Or some may think what ever for like the priest I talked to months ago.

At the beginning of the "Challenge" I had many organizations that came up to me to offer their support, or invited me to group sessions, the reason I thanked them nicely, was in several conversation with them hardly any of them, many lady's off means had reconstructed.

For me it was crucial like breathing to be able to recuperate part of the loss of my feminine self, desiring to be attractive and sexy. Even if the whole world knew of my surgeries, and no permanent man in my life was in sight, it was first and foremost for "Me". Who will be the first that will face "Me" every single day in the Mirror.

Strangely enough, after this first surgery, I went back to the dating game. That is when tragedy takes a turn to comedy, while trying to squeeze men in my now complicated life.

Often commenting to my girlfriends that God must have a video camera following me around. And at night he sits with a popcorn bucket on his lap watching in a big Sony home theater at all the silly things happening to me, and roaring with laughter. Usually many have to do with romantic relationships.

Men & Boobs

F ear of how I would look to the eyes of any man was one of the toughest things I had to face up. As my body slowly transforms, the question of how I was going to be perceived by the male eye, became a dreaded question. Again the Witch in Snow White comes to mind.

Dating men is a problematic affair on its own, and the risk of being rejected often lingers in my brain, especially now. If they suddenly stop calling, my mind will surely relate it to my body.

My perception of myself after the first reconstruction was more or less, no significant change. To my eyes my good boob was still like when a long balloon loses air and then flops down. The reconstructed one starts to take a new and better shape, but, my nipple is looking less to the north only in funny sort of way like a blinking eye, not very sexy at all.

Having had lengthy discussions with my plastic surgeon on how I do not want to look. Understanding that to some extent most women want their boobs high up, personally, I think they look fake and ridiculous. In reality, it is all about the different perception of sexiness each of us ladies view of oneself, a very hard topic to agree on.

Bigger for me is not the best option, maybe since mine were naturally big, I am totally happy with a medium size. For many gals bigger are better in so many ways I guess? Can't stop the laughing, and then the memories:

Enrolled at age thirteen at the private Catholic Jr. High School in Eagle Pass Texas across my hometown. My overall plumpness started to melt down from my body, rearranging into a waist. My boobs expanding out from my training A cup bra to a C cup by ninth grade. A very insecure stage, and comparisons are unavoidable. Longing to be like the rest of my flat-chested friends. Little did I know, I was the dream girl of many of the boys.

"We are never happy with what is given to us girls that is the problem."

Fifteen days after the September surgery my recovery is impressive, my body seems to start to self-adjust to more convenient changes. There are still some natural discomforts, like the nagging electrifying feeling under my right armpit, and the heavy weight of my fake boob. Constantly tiptoeing around the mirror, too early for facing my new reflection.

Yes insecurity strikes hard!

Dating

S o in the course of the months of reconstruction starting in October when I met up after some months again with Larry, then in December with Keith, and the next year with Mario, and in between one or two dates to remember:

Texas
(Two Years Before)

I met Larry for the first time on a very warm July afternoon stopping at a rest area before entering the city of San Antonio, Texas. (Baby, a dear beautiful friend has fits of laughter about this meeting every time I tell the story. "Really, at a rest area, you are kidding?")

A must stop, after the two hour drive on crossing the border from my hometown of Piedras Negras, to the American side of Eagle Pass.

My father had a great appreciation for gourmet food, so when I was little girl, for at least one Sunday a month he would drive my mother and me to the big city. Our first stop would be Church, then lunch to a seafood place called Christie's, or buffet at the Gunther Hotel and after, window-shopping.

During the 60's stores where closed on Sundays, a constant that stung at my mother's desire for buying or at least browse around the stores, always complaining why we could not arrive a day before.

My first encounters with fashion were walking around holding my mother's hand, gazing at the window displays mesmerized as the clothes seemed to have their own special life.

I must have been around five, but I still can remember the color palate of those days, a mix of pastel shades, flower prints and polka dots in summer, grays, blacks, checks and furs in winter.

Our last outing will be to a movie at the Majestic Theater, with a treat, of popcorn or cotton candy. Sitting with my feet too short to reach the floor I was certain on looking up at the high ceiling the stars sketched all over the surface where truly real.

Now every time I look at the first star of the night I repeat faithfully, what my mother then taught me:

"Star bright, star light, I wish I may I wish I might, please grant me this wish tonight".

"Oh little star, I wish the "Challenge" is vanished forever from the face of the earth."

Too many years had passed since my coming to San Antonio, as often as I was used to. The city's expansion had been nonstop, too many new expressways and highways appeared to be rather confusing, never having a great sense of direction, I start to sweat. Before getting lost, I get down from the car at the rest area, to get specific location on how to get to my hotel by the North Star Mall shopping center.

Lilia, one of my best friends since Jr. High whose second wedding I am in town for, tries over the phone in vain to give me instructions. Feeling the gaze, a tall handsome green-eyed cowboy who is openly x-raying me top to bottom, and is looking to be in the best disposition to offer help (over time he has, described his vivid perception of our encounter).

"You were wearing hip hugging boot cut faded Levi's with a very flat stomach under a white muscle shirt showing full large firm breasts, and beaten up olive colored cowboy boots. Hardly no makeup, just lip gloss and blue eye mascara, strawberry blond pixie cut hair with touches of gold under a cowboy straw hat. A very sexy looking girl."

His description translates exactly how I was feeling about myself on that particular day. There are times in one's life that we feel so content, and good about our self that is out of the question something could go wrong, little did I know.

So this is how I met Larry, this tall rough man with crew cut hair, in tight jeans, Luke Casey cowboy boots and of course a Stetson cowboy hat, something never seen in my fashion book.

Over time we reached a point in our relationship in which we could talk and laugh about anything. Maybe his being twelve years younger than I had something to do with how comfortable and youthful I felt around him.

We started dating mostly when I went to my hometown, since I was traveling frequently back and forth from Monterrey to teach my modeling courses.

Experiencing always one funny incident after another. On our first date he took me star watching to a little ranch on the limits of the city. Walking hand in hand thru the fields I enjoyed the vast view of an infinite sky packed with stars. Strolling through the tall grass I did not realized on every step my long favorite prairie camouflage skirt was picking at its seems little miniature thorns. On arriving back home on taking off my cowboy boots, I started feeling the star shaped spikes cling to my skin, and to the pistachio colored rug in my childhood bedroom.

Funnier was after washing the skirt, the stubborn thorns became a nuisance, even after several months, every time I wore the skirt again, they hunted me for quite a while, making me laugh each time at the memory.

Hometown, October

Larry's witty sense of humor is one of his most flattering traits in the art of seduction. With his easiness of provoking laughs out of the dumbest situation. Very conscious how to melt you down with one look from those shimmering green eyes of his, a powerful and flirtatious advantage.

Arriving in my hometown for the last week of October to teach a modeling course, Larry took it upon himself to act as my shadow, all thru my stay. Picking me up after classes, enjoying coffee and stories with my father, as they waited for me to bake my mother's famous pineapple upside down cake.

With him simple things like grocery shopping, and driving around town on his pick-up truck while listening to his favorite country music took a new light.

Rediscovering myself forgotten things, like that hamburgers go great with chocolate milkshakes. That at 10:00 A.M. every morning the old Bakery in Eagle Pass, still cooks its second batch of fresh glazed doughnuts. Friday nights, is as always High School football night, with the band still playing the Hawaii Five-O theme.

On his visits to Monterrey he preferred going out to a bakery to eat as many cream puffs as he could muster, making it a hilarious affair. A funny character, moody, but straight forward still strangely tender and affectionate in a rough sort of way.

The most important thing with him is he was there for me, accepting all the ups and downs of the operations, enjoying to the full our time together always with too many laughs.

So Larry has stayed around popping in and out my life when our schedule allows us since meeting him at the "rest area" in 2007.

Year One

October 6th

C oming back from my hometown, I realized it has been a year of hospitals and treatments. Amazed at being a woman who can feel pretty nice about her over all self, even though the confidence part has to be put to a test on facing the mirror.

Being involved with fashion and beauty as an alternative treatment has been a distraction of sorts. Vanity is a blessed gift. Enjoying, without any resentment of the time I have to invest in making myself look and feel attractive.

A year at this point does not seem such a long time, but as I look into the mirror I see my changed reflection, my hair is now a la Mia Farrow only red and with miniature curls.

This new look is one I would have longed to have ages ago. My cheekbones look sort of hollow as I have lost some weight, but the skin has begun to rejuvenate miraculously. Seems all the sun block a night before every radiation, all the mother of pearl cream I have applied over my whole body for just $3.00 dollars a jar, and substituting honey for my facial soap have worked a sort magic.

Well I cannot deny having had at this time someone around to actually make me laugh, telling me how pretty I looked, helped a little. Even if we are not together the whole time because of the distance, we make the most of our days together.

One year ago today I discovered the lump on my right breast, and my life flew into a roller coaster of doctors, blood tests, scans and X rays. Coming in and out of hospitals, and then to the chemo treatments. This did not stop me from living, working or going out, in a way I forced myself to do it, bolstering my self-confidence.

My time spent in my hometown, with Larry at my side makes me feel feminine and sexy again, even if my new boob is not actually perfect and the difference with the other one quite visible. When someone accepts you the way you are it makes you feel whole. Beauty has also lot to do with being in good health, or just believing you are.

November

C oming out of the doctor's office with the news of the date for another operation, to be scheduled for the first days of December. My hair is a tad longer as red curls now frame my face. Having always dreamed of having curly hair, my idea of curls related to the romantic notion with the movement of such ringlets.

Picturing myself often running thru green fields in a long prairie dress, hair bouncing freely in the air. My actual straight hair felt at the time unassuming and bland. Always wanting the opposite of what we have, now I crave my straight hair badly. Hard to please a fashion mind.

So looking kind of funky and still quite sore from the last operation the other dating game started, a very detached ordeal, but an affair nonetheless, another push to flatter my ego.

I met Keith at a party, tall, tanned skin, curly black hair, deep expressive dark eyes with a rather large interesting nose, since my nose is no small matter this will become a joke of sorts every time we kissed.

Watching him walk confidently toward where I was sitting. Getting down on his knees, addressing me with an old familiarity. Having many friends in common, but never meeting before. Instantly flirting with me, the type of guy, who touches some part of your body as he speaks paying attention to my every single movement. Eyes engrossed as if I was the only girl in the room.

His sexy demeanor draws me instantly toward him, and then as I turn around catch him doing the same to the next girl who just walked in. Being just out of the operation and with the holidays around the corner, I paid attention only to what felt was happening between us and bite the bait, without a blink.

Everything was going great, spending after Christmas dinner together, but after a couple months go by I find the gigolo trait, clearly plastered all over him and decide to keep him at arm's length. Since at this particular moment I am very sensitive yearning for some kind of grounded relationship it is very easy to confuse what I am actually feeling.

Seeing him occasionally, I felt I was not ready for any full disclosure of my body, but eventually one thing leads to another, until boom one day understanding I cannot be in any relationship by parts. Being guarded, I did not want to seem needy as I was at the time. Learning by now men want exactly that, to feel needed. At this crucial time it was of most importance to stand in my own two feet.

Love has to a certain degree escaped me of lately

losing its way from me, cheating me, threatening my senses, and playing games on my emotional stability.

The "Challenge" makes one susceptible, and it is so easy to misjudge how real are the feeling towards any member of the opposite sex, because of the desire to be accepted, with all my liabilities.

Opting for toughness, as a shield to hide my deep rooted mindset of fear and insecurities, shutting the door to openness, big mistake.

In all, "Love" can be substituted by friendship in a way everything comes down to companionship. Having someone to really count on, is what is of the most importance. Happy to say Keith and I are still friends and incidentally introducing me to several female friends I cherish.

Beautiful Ladies

T he idea of beauty is engraved in our subconscious from early age. We are jugged accepted or rejected according to how pretty we are born. We strive from then on to accommodate to the category we have been placed under. Starting the competition with beauties who are actually alien to our own reality.

Forgetting that the only image we can compete with is the one facing us in front of the mirror, and it is only in our power to transform it into the special beauty due to us.

Imagine how I felt after working with beauty all my life, then this "Challenge" strikes shattering my whole being to the depth of my most precious inner self. Turning out to be so out of tune with my body, as the process of transformation evolved. Facing me with the dilemma of loss, a loss so intimate in my inner and outer persona, aching to the very core of my existence. Fighting the mirror in the process of acceptance of a different beauty.

When we become sick the need of survival is our principal goal, illness makes us aware the little control we have over the complicated apparatus of poison under our skin, and we somehow are dumped not only to feeling rotten but also externalizing that pain on the outside adopting drabness as a dress code, but for me this was not an option.

I grew up in a household where beauty was a sort of mantra, in all of its glory and not only in looks but in ones surroundings. Having to do not only with the right dress, or the shoe or bag, but also the way a pillow was strategically placed on the sofa, or on which vase and precise angle the flower arrangement will be set on the table.

Decoration of the body had a lot to do with the decoration of the space, I was taught how to create beauty in the flesh seem like it belonged to me. Constructing my surroundings with comfort and the right esthetics at the same time making myself look amazing.

My teachers are long ago gone, my mother Rosa Maria, her mother grandma Coco, and my great aunt her sister, aunt Pilar the core backbone in my upbringing on beauty.

Remembering things vividly, my mother dressing for my uncles wedding in the early 60's in a leaf green taffeta draped dress with matching shoes, and bag. Making her appear taller than she was, with a cone shaped hat of different green hues of chiffon roses piled upwards. This outlined her beautiful patrician features, with that tint of ivory translucent skin making her look breathtaking. Always as a kid, I was in total awe of mother's beauty. Feeling in my young years quite the ugly plump duckling.

Seeing my grandmother get dressed was like being immersed in one of those Botero's paintings. She was tall, heavy of built with large breasts, and thick arms, not an easy task for Teresa, her petit maid (my nanny) closing all the clasps to her large bustier and girdle. This undergarments, always the basics of her everyday wear no matter the weather.

Grandma had been a widow since before I was born, and that would not keep her from wearing her engagement ring, wedding band and her long string of pearls on a daily basis. Looking always stylish, I never ever heard her complain about all those uncomfortable trappings. Even in the characteristically hot days of summer in our hometown, she underwent discomfort all for the sake of beauty.

My great aunt lived a life of travel and leisurely reading, to the background of classical music. Finding her at any given day, with perfectly manicured nails in bright lacquer red. Flawlessly permed blondish white colored hair held by a five cent net, her light powdered skin accentuated by bright red lips matching her nails.

Dressing in cool cotton shirtdresses in summer and tweed suits with fur collars during the winter. When visiting her, I will find her always ready for receiving company, and for serving you coffee. I have no recollection of finding her dressed in an old bath robe, or a shabby dress, not even at an early hour.

She was like thirteen years older than my grandma, but in contrast her built was narrow and slim, a body I inherited from her.

So with so much vanity all around me it was easy to use it as a refuge. My decision was not an easy affair. Occasionally there were days that my optimistic self-went to hide inside the closet, and I will have to battle it out, sitting it by force in front of my dresser. Urgently convincing it to let me be pretty, and confident again.

There were days that the mirror was not friendly at all, as much as I would try there was a ghostly reflection of myself staring back at me. Some days as I am doing my makeup a clownish reflection stares back at me. Even starting playing games in which I truly made myself presume I looked pretty, when feeling lousy and lost.

Sleep is an alternative escape, when the anxiety attack of insecurity chased me around my bedroom. Sleep if I will permit, let a day turn into night, losing days in the process. Inadvisable, here I am fighting for life and permit my vulnerability to drown me in the shadows of the night, robbing me of the sun and the blue sky.

An enemy is only ready to strike, if we only let him, as much anguish I might feel pushing down on my chest during the darkness. Comfort came in the middle of the night with tall glasses of chocolate Quick and Oreo cookies.

Always the noise during daylight, protects and distracts me from what is going on inside my head, a clearer vision is more at hand. Breathing better during the day, safeguarded from my own self. My worst adversary is my lonely and gloomy thoughts that I try to paint with a makeup brush.

December

To a great degree I owe my amazing recovery to this, by nourishing my attitude and to the fact I have a great team of doctors unconditionally by my side.

On the first days of the month Alexis my daughter calls from Mexico city with the bad news that the captain of my team Dr. Canavati passed away from heart failure, only two weeks before removing my catheter, I become more than devastated. Here was the man that had saved my life less than a year before, now surprised by death.

We are puppets our strings running a fine line that can snap at any given moment.

Talking a week before with his eldest son and my daughter's friend, who had reassured me his father was getting better, and now being surprised by heart attack. Losing him felt as if I had lost my most trusted ally.

Sadness takes over me, vulnerability knocking the door on hopelessness, this was not only my doctor but a man with a wife and kids. A wife he himself had saved from the "Challenge" two sons a daughter, and grandchildren. For me it was too much, really too much to take in.

Walking into mass for his funeral service, I could not stop the tears smearing my mascara. When paying my condolences to his wife, who I had never I met before. On telling her my name as we hugged, crying she said:

"He saved us booth and now he is gone".

Monday December the 7th

O nly a couple more hours till my 4th operation, always nervousness strikes so I take to reading a John Grishman novel to escape my mess up thoughts. How will I come out this time around? Will the retrieving of the catheter leave a big scar? Not good for strapless dresses. Wondering, will this time around the size of one boob and the other even out? On that thought I would say hold it a bit since there will be a few more operations to go.

"What do you want perfection?" Some people have asked along the way, usually hearing:

"You look great as you are".

Conforming is not my style, deciding it is not only about looking great, but feeling whole, that is what I yearn to accomplish. Reconstruction is for me not about only the aspect of beauty. Is teaching the mind to appreciate this new person, who is undergoing the process of transformation.

As usual we leave the house to the hospital in the early dawn, and Alex's, driving puts me in a bad mood he seems to speed more while I am around, as though he has an excuse to gripe about my constant nagging. Juanita sits in the back seat without making a sound, perceiving my overall nervousness. All boils down to a bad night's sleep and to the stress of the OPERATION.

Analyzing the word operation means opening, in this case my body will be cut, exposed, invaded in its privacy, and manipulated. While I will be traveling in the unconscious world of whiteness. Memory is lost no recollection or dream will be recorded it is like skipping around in time.

So as I face my doctors in the operating room, a nostalgic feeling for the one missing. His absence touching everyone. Dr. Canavati was the life of the party, bouncing happily around with his horse loud voice and grey long hair setting everyone at ease with his cheerful mood and disposition.

Dr. Mauricio, his nephew looks somber and withdrawn, taking now his uncles place, reassuring me that everything will run smoothly. Doctor Walberg my plastic surgeon also arrives with comforting words. The night before he mapped my breasts with a Script marker on where the incisions will be performed. This morning my reflection on the mirror, was my body as a walking blackboard.

As usual, I am freezing. I can never stop being so uncomfortably cold inside hospitals. The nurses try to make me feel better with some more layers of pristine white sheets, which hardly helps everyone works to be kind, soothing me with needed reassurance.

Hearing vaguely the anesthesiologist thoroughly explains the procedure as I am being poked with needles, then in no time I have drifted to the white strange world of the unknown.

Time is lost, memories erased, I wake up already in my room and the first thing I do is dab some lip-gloss on my parched lips. I know now by Juanita's face that Alex took my cell phone with him to school, so when people start calling to see how I am doing Alex tells them:

"Great she is bitching that I left her without her cell phone".

I really feel quite well, I am dispatched home the next day and put to my bed for a couple of days.

When you are out of the office even if you planned ahead, everything gets kind of hectic so I start to work from my bed on a casting call for a catalog shoot over twenty models, are hired, around ten kids are scheduled to be at 4:00 pm in a park for the first take. Thirty minutes after, the sun gets sort of tired and goes off to sleep letting a cloud do its deed.

Monterrey's weather, without warning, starts getting awfully cold, the sky turns gray, and rain starts pouring non-stop in the middle of the shoot. As all hell breaks loose, waiting for the weather to give us an insight on how it will act. I start to juggle the rescheduling of models, quite an affair. Off they go to a studio shoot as a more practical solution, you cannot mess with Mr. Weather.

Needing one foot in my real life, is essential in order not to get lost in self-pity, so even in bed I will keep myself busy. Friends can visit for a while but at the end of the day, I am living just with myself. Knowing exactly how tired I am, or where the pain is sharper. As much as all the odds are against me, trying to fight with all my being for normalcy is the best option.

Consideration for all those around me is a must, absorbed in my inner pain, I have taken for granted the suffering of my love ones. Let's face it, when sick we all can be very selfish, hurting mostly the ones closer to us with neediness, sometimes overlooking what inner chaos they are also experiencing.

The thing is sort of tricky, ourselves being always two of us. The inside you and the outside you. Only we know the real anguish or the pain or the craziness going on inside our mind and body.

Love ones around us cannot really know, even when sharing about our self or open up to them we all have a very private "persona" totally hidden in a dark corner of our brain. With a life of unique parts that make the whole of who we ARE but most who we are afraid to become with all our mess-up feelings.

The Holidays

The holidays start as usual with the cousin's reunion only four days after my operation a day before their mother's birthday, on December 12th.

Tia Coco is my mother's only surviving sibling, at seventy-nine, the resemblance to my mother now striking, it pains me to look at her without giving a sigh.

I arrive wearing a dress from the 60's which belonged to my mother. A long circular cut jersey number, high neckline, and a tight bodice that embraces the waist. The skinny sleeves make my arms appear longer, and the red and silver pattern, resembles a Cavalli print, looking great with the white fox coat.

I feel spectacular, and everyone seems to hover over me telling me how wonderful I look. Family support makes you feel better even if it is not the whole truth, little white lies always help. I love them for it.

Every year, it seems we are more at the dinner table Frank one of my cousin Celina's sons is now married to Brandy.

Lauren my cousins Abe's daughter has a new boyfriend, and so the family grows, my father missed this dinner canceling at the last minute, and Alexi's plane was unable to land due to bad weather, sending the plane back to Mexico City so they were sorely missed this time around.

Arriving after three in the morning to my house, took a toll on me the next day unable to get up from bed all during the day. Finally Alex forced me out from under the covers, in the late afternoon. I throw on a pair of jeans a thick knitted sweater, my cowboy boots a jean padded pea coat a rabbit scarf and hat. A gift I got last night from striking redhead Esther, my cousin Abe's wife.

So almost by force we will have our ritual of getting the tree, with Juanita and one of Alex's most hell raising friend Luis-Mi. He will stay overnight after partying the night away, and missing his morning flight to Tijuana, so we include him in our shopping experience.

As we walk around the tree fair I remember how happy my mother was, the last Christmas before her passing, helping me decide on which three to pick and the hard time we had convincing her we had to go back to the house. I also miss dad and Alexis who were always more interested in the chocolate and churros than on picking a tree.

Like last year I will conduct the trimming of the three from the living room couch, and let the smell of pine fill my lungs.

Dressed in a long wool grey turtleneck dress and thick grey sweater with my purple suede boots I sit unfolding each decoration covered by tissue paper, savoring in the memory attached to each one. Very special is the music horse bought when Alexis was a year old, how far away that seems.

Of great sentimental value, are the two ornaments which mother bought for Alexis and Alex with their birth date inscribed on each sphere for their first Christmas. After my mom died, I rescued her blond angel with a bouffant hairdo, more like a doll from the 60's, not your traditional angel but so much like the way mom and her two sisters wore their hair in those days.

All the memories that fill this three also are the hope for a better year.

As my mother before me I try to make Christmas as magical as I can for everyone. Father and Alexis arrive one day before the big celebration, so the house is all ready to greet them.

Even though it may be just in my mind, but getting the house decorated is a big ordeal, but one I highly enjoy, a way to keep my mind from the stress of this last operation. The Christmas spirit takes residence in my being even more so than last year. You see I have been given a second chance a way to anew the past and make today if not perfect better.

Sighing, I hold on the palm of my hand a crystal house trimming which can be opened from its rooftop, unlocking the lid I stick in a little piece of folded paper with my dreams and gratitude scribbled inside.

Every year I think the tree is even more beautiful than the year before, dominating the living room. Deciding in which branch my little house will hang, I sit like a child in awe, as the aroma continues to filter thru my lungs. Enjoying this particular moment of hope.

As friends and family come and go thru the holidays the pain of the operation lingers at the back of my worries, I am too entertained with an upcoming New Year trip to the magical Mexican town called San Miguel the Allende the storm seems to be finally over.

San Miguel de Allende

New Year 2010

The idea of coming to San Miguel for the New Year started by my dear traveling companion, Pepe. Around three years ago, he convinced our friend from New York Natalie about the magic of San Miguel de Allende in the heart of Mexico. Taking her to Rizzoli's bookstore to show her a book of the Magical town and Natalie just fell in love.

On several of our trips to New York, the topic was occasionally brought upon the dinner table, until hands-on Natalie took charge. For over six months, she worked first on getting a fun group together and second taking it upon herself to search for houses. E-mailing us of the options at hand, scheduling an itinerary for arrivals and departures, she was so set on making it work, surpassing our expectations.

In between all her planning, I went through two surgeries, the last at the beginning of December, so I needed badly a different New Year's ending. knowing very well that more surgeries were still to come.

After packing my long prairie skirts, a pair of jeans, a suede jacket, a couple of bulky sweaters, and of course, my forever cowboy boots a must for San Miguel's cobblestone streets. Jumping into my friend Joan's SUV, we hit the road for a five-hour drive accompanied by Pepe and lots of laughs.

Natalie was the first one to arrive at Casa la Espiga, taking the master bedroom. A well-deserved prize for all of her hard work.

Coming in from Monterrey, a couple of hours after her, as she opened the door greeting us, we were overwhelmed with all the little details the property had to offer.

Houses here were built mostly at the beginning of the 1800's. Always a surprise as you walk past its massive high wood front doors just stepping from the sidewalks' brim, possessing unique enchantment, the outside intertwined with the inside, as you walk into cozy open living room patios, dining areas, and tranquilizing fountains around colorful bugambilia trees. Real fireplaces adorn each room adding warmth and special lighting, to the usual dark, thick, cold walls and very high ceilings. The weather is usually warm during the day, and you can even take the sun on the rooftops terraces with a great view of the many church copulas that abound in the city.

Nights are chilly, great for sitting in front of a fireplace with a tequila shot at hand, and a crochet blanket on your lap to the crack of fire logs.

A house immersed in a colonial world of times past. Antiques are mixed, much like my own house with Mexican artifacts.

Walls exhibit a lot of old religious paintings and carved wooden saints as if waiting for prayer. A filled atmosphere of peace and tranquility where reading is the best way to pass your day, making television in such a setting seem inappropriate and entirely out of place.

Settling myself in what is supposed to be the Ghost room, we always have stories like this in old Mexican towns. Charming is the little upstairs library, besides having a window overlooking the street, built especially for serenades and lovers whispers.

Luckily the cute Ghost never bothered to show his face or make strange icky sounds, so I am sure he must have liked me or felt sympathy for me.

Pepe and Joan went for Morocco decorated apartment, great for two bachelors on the town. An almost separate building with its living area and two bedrooms.

This Magical town's life revolves around a central plaza where an excellent option is always to stroll to one of the quaint little restaurants or cafes surrounding it.

Artists galleries are all around, as unique jewelry and clothing boutiques, of very creative Mexican designers. Finding the exclusive pieces of pottery, and linen, either at a posh store or at the colorful central market.

My friend Anna arrived at dawn the next day with three big suitcases. Being the bubbly person that she is, I had some trouble trying to make her sustain her excitement and wake everyone up.

After moving with difficulty all her luggage into my room, as she starts to unpack, I cannot sustain my laughter. Her shoes, and clothes are more suited for Las Vegas than the laidback affair that is San Miguel.

Ana: I say, "Cobblestones, streets are not suitable for stilettos."

Back into her suitcase, go the Louboutin's and Manolo's settling for the rest of the week with some pretty beaten up Converse sneakers.

Phil, my dear crazy friend, arrives that evening from Mexico City, with his set of Louis Vuitton luggage, more suitable for a Ritz Hotel.

Being the hilarious character that he is, immediately chooses to be the assistant cook to the actual cook Josefina, like all of us he finds a true enjoyment in cooking but must of all on eating.

New Year's morning with Natalie's help, we start setting the main dining table with all the house had to offer pottery dishes, colored crystal glasses, and actual silverware. Bright fuccia napkins mixed with green table mats and bugambilia flower arrangements cut from the patio's trees set the final touch for our celebratory dinner.

A very at home feeling as every little detail we could think of was at hand to make everything look breathtaking.

Josefina prepared one of the best Mole (chicken in a thick sauce of different chilies, peanuts, chocolates and spices). Complemented by a cactus salad with shrimp, vinaigrette dressing, and sides of guacamole, rice, and beans. A Mexican menu I designed in honor of our American friend.

After dinner, we all strolled down two blocks to the central plaza, the heart of the town where everyone gathers to watch the fireworks and count the minutes to midnight. Dancing and singing with great gusto to Mariachi bands until the early morning.

That week was like walking into a new life, one solely dedicated to appreciating and thanking God for the pleasure of the moment. I was learning to survive the "Challenge," incorporating recuperation into the normalcy of my daylily life.

So awakening to a New Year, I hung all of my worries to dry out in the sun on the rooftop of Casa La Espiga.

Josefina prepared one of the best Mole (chicken in a thick sauce of different chilies, peanuts, and chocolates). Complemented by a cactus salad with shrimp, vinaigrette dressing, and sides of guacamole, rice, and beans. A Mexican dinner in honor of our American friend.

After dinner we all strolled down two blocks to the central plaza, the heart of the town where everyone gathers to watch the fireworks and count the minutes to midnight. Dancing and singing with great gusto to Mariachi bands until the early dawn.

That week was like walking into a new life one solely dedicated to appreciating everything around me. So awakening to a New Year I hung all of my worries to dry out in the sun, on the rooftop of Casa La Espiga.

Facing the site of the many crosses on top of the cupolas of all of the churches around the town. I thanking God dearly for this week, and this time, enjoying friends who have shown me such unconditional support.

Rosina Ramón

Learning to survive the "Challenge," incorporating recuperation with survival into the normalcy of life. I start keeping track in an orderly accurate way of only the good things around me. Looking for the pleasure of the moment, and merely savoring life.

January

Loss

Two days before my birthday I get a call from my father, his ninety year old sister has just passed away.

Driving home for the funeral in the middle of the afternoon. Slowly watching the sun setting behind the mountains. Viewing the spectacular transformations the color yellow undergoes in a matter of minutes. Painting the land with a rainbow of all of its different hues, ending in a bright orange light, before darkness strikes.

The empty roads give me time to think, so I wonder how my aunt felt about her life before she stopped remembering, what day it was or who she was. Alzheimer is the cancer of the brain erasing our most precious gift, memories. Recollections of sadness and happiness are the motor of a life well lived.

Without memories we lose our time on this earth a very heartbreaking process, for both patient and family. Mother went thru the same deleting stage in her last months, even forgetting who I was. This for me was a hard burden to accept, how could she forget me her only child, for whom she had fought for three years to conceive. Who sheltered me with exaggeration from harm's way. All of a sudden my face was erased from her memory bank, and when standing by her side, I was a stranger, even losing my pet name from her "Picoreta" (her made up word for teaser). So this sort of "Challenge" has a different disguise, as a blank book with not even a line on its pages.

Larry arrives at the funeral house at almost the same time I am getting out of the car, it is always nice to see him, enjoying his company very much. We go inside the funeral parlor encountering several raised eyebrows. Hushed whispers and raised eyebrows around us. The cowboy and the fashion girl, and of course our twelve-year age difference; halo small town.

I am spotting my father sitting beside Yoli, the youngest and only remaining sister, looking booth disoriented from their loss. A family of ten brothers and sisters amounts to only the two of them left with their sorrow and loneliness.

My father looking like he has aged years in only a couple of weeks without seeing him. Clearly drained from the grief of the ordeal as he stands up with difficulty to give me a hug. He appears to be carrying a big heavy burden, quiet as usual hiding in his own lonely world.

After mass and lunch at my cousin's house I clearly acknowledge that my father has become weary. Finally convincing him on going home, so he can rest from the strain of the day.

As I enter my parent's house I feel like I always do I want to run inside and look for my mother, the house is very quiet, as the maid has left for the evening.

How lonely it feels without my mother, it is so touching to view my father in this vast silence, without the constant chatter between them, missing her constant nagging for perfection of order. Funnily now he has become a mirror of her whims, no clothes on the floor, no baby powder all over the bathroom and now even drying the crystal shower door as was her rule after every shower. He has controlled his chaos in her honor.

Another thing he has strangely managed is punctuality. Mother will start around noon time calling every coffee shop in town asking if he was there with some of his groups, so he would arrive in time for lunch. Little did she know all the owners where sworn to secrecy to keep quiet. She never would find him but it was his cue to cut the chit chat short and rush home.

After he goes to sleep me and Larry go out to get one of the best clamato's you can buy, sold at a little drive thru joint. All the stress requires the reward of really needing one. I am dressed all in black, leather pants, turtleneck, and warm circular wool cape held with a very wide belt and black suede booties we go off to his little ranch on the outskirts of town to gaze up at the stars and talk till after midnight.

Since my mother's passing I have tried to reason with my father to rent or sell the house move in with Alex and me to Monterrey, but the uprooting is something he cannot really take into consideration.

Next day as I pull out the car from the driveway I perceive his weariness on his short plump frame as he is waving from the kitchen's back door with his teary yellowish eyes and his memories, at least he has that to keep him company.

Driving back from my hometown at noon, facing the almost empty road ahead, I feel a sort of anguish squeezing at my heart, on having left my dad looking so sad, I am dismayed that I cannot lighten this pain he is hauling around.

January 15th

T hree days after the funeral I fly to Mexico City for a meeting on the day of my birthday and merrier times.

Sometimes you sort of want to escape a birthday, like the year just slipped by. Staying at Lourdes's house this is not an option, there is no way the day might go unnoticed. What should have been a little dinner with her roomy, my other dear friend Lucia, and her husband, turns out to a whole restaurant filled with almost two hundred unknown people finding out it is my birthday.

So champagne flutes galore, birthday cake and like ten waiters singing Happy Birthday. Partying like it was New Year's, understanding now that a birthday is really a time to rejoice on being alive. Each day now I am liberating myself more and more from the "Challenge" something I have to celebrate every single day.

February 11th,

New York, Fashion Week

An utterly beautiful view as New York meets me covered in snow as I can see from the window of my plane arriving at JFK airport.

My excitement takes the better part of me after a whole year of coping with treatments and operations. I am so happy to be back, almost jumping inside the cab like a kid who gets a bag of candy. The moment gets a grey cloud of sadness over it, when on turning my phone, and finding the news of designer Alexander McQueen's suicide. The great creative talent of a design wizard is now history.

Arriving at my hotel drop my bags and like always rush to Bryant Park for my credentials where the only thing you hear is about McQueen's death, and the farewell to this venue. This will be the last time the shows will be held here, next year it will be at Lincoln Center. Then as usual I take the subway to Mara's office to pick up the invites.

After all, is taken care, I am to meet Pepe, my photographer friend, from Monterrey who is waiting for me in Soho, at Balthazar's.

Walking in thru the swinging doors, I spot him at the bar with some friends. Since is his habit he complements on the way I am dressed, black wool long to the body turtle neck dress, a gold chain belt from the 60's hangs around the hips, black booties with thick heels and a red curly sheep coat.

I had promised I would never get another coat ever, but last year I had stumbled upon the coat in a little store around the block called Foravi and was unable to keep my hands off from it, besides it was like my pre-operation gift at the time and for now my fashion statement for this trip.

What can I say about walking into this French like bistro, like Paris in New York, always packed with interesting people. Six years ago I met Mara, in a warm July afternoon, at this same spot, right in front of the bar. I was having a beer and waiting for Alex, my son who was browsing around in his favorite Old Navy store.

Mara talked about being a runway photographer who follows the collection circuit. I told her about my modeling agency, and my work as a fashion consultant. I mentioned I was coming back in February for Fashion Week, she offered to get me invitations for some shows, and our friendship started.

Mara is a New Yorker of Italian decent, she is lively easy going and is married to a marvelous man. Their lives are so complimented that you are almost envious when she mentions his name, and on meeting him, I could sense his total admiration and love just by the way his eyes met hers.

Sometimes thru chance encounters, we fall into others' lives, and an irrelevant conversation may set you to be friends forever. Then you may think of the missed friendships along the way, people we casually encountered and will never see again for the rest of our lives. Strange, a moments decision who to keep track off and who is left to be lost.

Of I am a different person from last year my hair is now short a la Mia Farrow but red and curly a la Betty Boob, sort of matching with the red coat. Mostly my way of thinking has changed, it seems this "Challenge" has given me a certain new outlook on the way I have come to appreciate everything around me. Also becoming more considerate with others since so many have been giving me their time and support.

Jerry is on this trip, on my making amends list, so after an hour goes by he arrives to take me to dinner at nice Japanese restaurant close by. Updating ourselves after a year and a half pause, we catch up with the ups and downs of our lives. Grumpy, is from now on in my to do list every time I am in New York.

This town is very close to my heart, every day I am here I give thanks for just being allowed to be back. The distraction of shows, parties and catching up with friends is a tool I will use as a preparation of the road that lies ahead, my 5th operation.

The different perspectives, Alexander McQueen, left life because he couldn't cope with the pressure around him, the terrible tricks played in an unstable mind. The contradiction; I cannot stop fighting to live life the best way as I possibly can.

March 26th

A sort of rehearsed drill which starts at dawn as Alex speeds to the hospital thru empty streets. Arriving at the motions of registering collecting my package which include my 5th pair of hospital's terry cloth logo slippers and enough free parking tickets for two months. Getting on the elevator to the surgery floor, everything is sort of familiar, even the nurses are starting to call me by my name. I felt like Miss Popularity!

So on to the 5th step of reconstruction. At first you visualize the procedure to recovery as easy. What I did not know that to everything there is a long process done step by step.

For many, it may look like a vain affair. For me, the alignment of my boobs, has to do with what I am feeling inside my head. Related with my shattered femininity, whatever I can do to buster that up I would do.

There is always for me a close tie that the way I look is how in the end will feel. Like what is in the exterior will project automatically internal distress, programed by the way my brain sees me in front of the mirror. Reconstruction is just a tool, that in the end will help my brain tell my body, I am getting better. Even if this is not the end of the procedure. Trying always to keep on looking for ways to make this bad experience a positive affair.

April-July

E aster Sunday is spent in Piedras, thanking God, who has blessed me with so much strength, after each surgery. A process confronting me with several things like: stress, exhaustion, pain and uncertainty. In order to cope with all of the above, I had to learn to give thanks.

Some days I gave thanks after seeing a blue sky, after being cuddled with blankets by a nurse when telling her I was cold. I gave thanks at the smiles of a stranger, who complimented how nice I looked.

Most of all I give thanks for my loved ones, for my son and daughter's baby steps at success in the middle of the turmoil that has touched their lives.

Today a special gratefulness on seeing Dad chirpier than usual with Larry at his side, watching a football game in the TV room sharing a beer. To seal the Holiday With Juanita's help, we bake glazed ham, mashed potatoes, and Mom's recipe for green bean casserole, with curly French onions. Murmuring under my breath, and I give thanks.

The day before I had taken my dad across to Eagle Pass, to fix his ear-piece and install a new battery. Our conversations over the phone were getting lost in communication. I would ask loudly:

"How was the domino game last night?" He would answer: "The tool shed is coming just fine."

I had to laugh, glad to have won one little battle.

The weekend over, I say good bye to my men in my hometown and with Juanita we go back to Monterrey. Life goes on, as usual, before the summer months, shows, photo shoots, events, checkups, and tests, then in July a fantastic trip to San Francisco.

Alex, my son, was taking an architecture course at the University of San Francisco for a whole month. I had planned with Mariel a dear friend and ex-model in her early 20's to visit Alex in the last week of his course. Mariel is a beautiful girl with long ash blond hair, milky white skin, intriguing light brown eyes, a real head turner.

This was our second trip together, she says she has more fun with me than people her own age because usually a funny adventure always happens.

Like any good mother, I had nagged Alex about renting a place, two months in advance. Apparently, two weeks before his departure he had nowhere to stay. In my mother hen controlling sate I went onto Craig's list. On my usual haste to get things done, instead of renting a studio I set him up for only a futon, yes a futon for one.

A house managed by a computer geek in his 20's, with like six rooms and like five more geeks renting, the other rooms it was like a boarding place for students not like the studio I had viewed from the photo on the Internet.

Alex on his arrival knew I would be in shock with a futon only drama. Convincing the owner on fixing the problem, by making him buy two waterbeds since the actual price had not been cheap.

Certain I would make a big fuss, my son had not told me about my big mistake. He knew he would end up with no place to stay, and surely he would have to miss classes, in the tedious process of finding a new place. Silence was his best option, aware he would be in school on our arrival. Knowing I would come up with a solution to my own mess by the time we met, and would not have to face the hurricane until it was over.

Getting down from the cab we are faced with what looks like an endless walk up of steep stairs. Catching our breaths on pulling two huge suitcases we finally arrive to the room with a lot of cons, but a fantastic view of the city.

The futon ordeal, was one thing. To me worst, was no closet in sight. Laying my eyes on the scared skinny young owner who was speechless, and on grabbing Mariel's arm, I say:

"There is no way I am going to walk down those stairs again with our suitcases and look for another place. I have an idea let's go and buy ourselves a clothing rack and hangers. Who cares if we have to sleep on water beds, what is really more important is where the clothes should hang".

"A deal" Mariel answers laughing.

San Francisco is a town of friendly people, dancing salsa on Sunday afternoons, great restaurants, fabulous museums and the best vintage shopping you can find.

San Francisco's weather gets kind of cold in the afternoon, so my suede and jean jacket came in handy with long prairie skirts and my dear cowboy beat-up boots.

One chilly afternoon we ended in Castro Street the gay district where you get to meet the most fascinating people ever and find incredible little shops. We are strolling down the street while encountering two handsome guys walking holding hands wearing to our astonishment tinny bikini bottoms and nothing else.

I cannot contain myself and ask them if we can take a picture, so the end results are of two girls wrapped up with jackets and scarfs with a couple of almost naked guys. We cannot stop the laughter when we see the actual take. One of the guys without our noticing pulled up a sort of flap that was covering his delicate parts. Well thanks to Photoshop not visible now in the picture, so there goes one more adventure.

Every trip that came along turned out to be a mental preparation for the following operation. My life since the beginning of the "Challenge" was organized around when the next operation will be scheduled.

August-September

As the month draws to an end, another operation is in order the 6th. This is the first surgery that I am not afraid of looking at my reflection in the mirror, maybe I am getting the hang of it.

My right boob has stopped being the deflated balloon that it was. I now have come out with a teenager's boob that actually looks very cute. Of course, the procedure is for aligning the size of the sick boob, who is at a loss in its shape, but getting there.

I am almost entirely alone this time around, it is too much hassle to drag people to the hospital for the sixth time. Only a night stay and for what now seems a simple procedure. Still, the calls came, and some of my closest friends dropped by for a visit.

Laying on the hospital bed that night, I started to realize, this is not the last surgery. I am actually taking in the doctor's explanation and understanding the process. Finding out the skin takes time to heal itself.

My sick boob is needing more skin to fill up to the good one's size in specific places. Under my arm the skin is thin, to close to the bone, and an uncomfortable sensation causes a painful electric shock.

So after really getting this inside my head, I think of all the people that have not had this opportunity. Realizing how lucky in the end I have been to be recuperating my femininity and health.

Year Two

October, 6th

Two years now since the "Challenge" stroke its fearsome blow. I am being asked by the local Televisa station to talk about my trial, in a special program. This exposure allows me to reach out to a lot of women facing this hard jolt on the heart, and body.

On my arrival to the TV station where I had worked years before coordinating two successful beauty pageants in which two girls I trained represented Mexico in Miss Universe in 1997 and 1998. As I am walking down the hallway arm in arm with my son Alex, fond memories flash through.

Honoring the color of the movement I am wearing a light powder pink suede skirt with a cotton crochet sweater also in pink, and wine colored snakeskin boots. My hair is still reddish almost to my chin, I get a lot of compliments from everyone, which is an ego booster. Being on TV is something I have managed pretty well over the years, so I feel entirely at ease with appearing on the show.

The host, is a pretty and proper looking girl with perfectly chiseled features. On starting the interview I see her jaw almost drop at my answers:

"Surviving the challenge for me has to do with an attitude based on the principle of beauty," no matter how sick I have felt I always forced myself to reach for the lip gloss." For a moment she fumbles with her notes like lost on how to go about to the next question, which she practically does not ask, as I go on:

"I just want every woman watching or experiencing the "Challenge," not to give up to despair, beauty gives you a leeway of courage to face what you dread with more power, it is like when you go for a job interview you dress the part, empowering you to succeed."

"So yes I played with wigs of different lengths and colors, crazy turbans on my head, beating my insecurities with my love for fashion."

"Working on feeling beautiful even when feeling lousy, it was enough medicine for body and soul." "I cannot ever forget that."

"Another important note, do not let anyone tell you, no matter "Who," you do not need to reconstruct, if you have the chance, do not waste the opportunity."

"Your obligation is to look good first only for yourself, not for anyone else. Because you only have one body, this is the one who will face you every morning in front of the mirror, and this body is the one to care for, with unconditional love."

When the interview was over, I saw a teary-eyed or two as my son hugs me, saying: "Mom I am so proud of you, I love you."

On the other hand the host and some executives around where in a state of shock. I had in between lines touched without pity the Macho nerve, something unexpected to them. Too bad it was live. I rejoiced in my power, and prayed it woke some women up.

Sadly neither my dad nor Alexis were in town, my daughter had just moved to Mexico City to live. Yes, they too would have also been very proud of me!

November

Los Cabos Baja California

O ne of my most awakening and moving experience was when Lourdes my dear model-celebrity friend calls from Mexico, inviting me to Los Cabos. I am in Los Angeles buying clothes for a boutique store when I get her call.

"Hey I want to give you an advanced Birthday present, want to go to Los Cabos, I have plane tickets for four and a suite at Las Ventana's"

Without any hesitation I say yes, oblivious to why she was going. I just knew she had been hired to be the presenter at some event. So without much information a week after arriving from LA I am on the first flight out on a Friday morning to Los Cabos, for the first time in my life, with her sister Viv as my companion.

Viv who more times than others is wrongly mistaken for her older famous and gorgeous sister, is the mother of four, ages from 2 to 13, with an athletic built and always a gregarious sense of humor. Our second time around traveling together Viv is again my roomy, on her sister's invitation.

We are picked up at the airport by someone from the mayor's office. With humor we roll our eyes at each other, enjoying all the considerations of borrowed stardom, and the tranquilizing view of the sea on our way to the hotel.

On arrival to Las Ventana's one of Cabos most incredible hotels, we cannot help our excitement at the sight of the place. Greeted with a tropical drink by the manager, we start to relish on being treated in such a unique way and cannot stop our nervous laughter at all the fuss around us.

We just can't wait, how we will be treated, when Lourdes the real celebrity arrives with Aba, her partner.

So as we walk inside the hacienda-style rooms in our luxury suite, we are in awe with the details of it all, and the spectacular view of the sea from our private veranda. Viv is enjoying the freedom of being kid-free for a couple of days, and I can escape my constant upkeep of tests and more tests, surely a breath of fancy fresh air to enjoy at our ease.

As soon as Lourdes and Aba arrive, our pace changes, there is a dinner engagement with the organizers of the event.

Aba always in a perky sunny mood that matches her good looks big dark cat eyes light tanned skin an Angelina Jolie kind of mouth a figure to die for, and the flattest abs you can find anywhere.

So after the dinner, we go to one of the trendiest bars in town to meet Paola Compean who is a "Challenge" survivor like myself, and the organizer of the event Lourdes was hired to host on Sunday.

Paola a pretty vivacious blue-eyed blond and a cherished member of the Los Cabos society takes it upon herself organizing this memorable event, in order to raise awareness about the "Challenge."

Dawning finally on me why Lourdes brought me in the first place, personally I can relate to the cause. Feeling very flattered to be considered to offer my testimony.

Sunday morning the magnitude of it all astonishes me, arriving to an almost pink and white beach filled with around 3,500 men woman and children. We all get our pink t-shirt, and after testimonials, we form the largest EVER human "PINK RIBBON" on the beach.

On the same tone as the Televisa interview, I relate my story getting a lot of applause and many bear hugs.

In the end, like all the others, I am a "tiny but valuable dot" on the panoramic photograph.

A very heart moving and tearful event engraved forever inside my heart and mind. Thanks to Lourdes, one of the most significant birthdays presents to cherish, always.

December

The tall, thin model strolls down the runway, in chiffon printed skirt in storm like colors of degraded greys, worn with a big chunky knitted brick colored sweater, flat distressed silver boots, and a soft to the hip suede trench in onyx.

As she walks to the beat of the DJ's mix, she tilts her black fedora hat as she crosses with a handsome male model. He is wearing a tartan jacket in grays' and browns, brick hue turtle neck, dark brown pants, brown-reddish leather boots, and a messenger bag to match, strapped across his lean and firm chest.

The runway concept changes into reds, as the music mix turns into a Christmassy tune. The large impressive three instantly flashes multicolored lights, as all twenty models stroll out on the runway for the last time, and the press starts shooting the big Christmas scene.

A sigh escapes me as the models fill the backstage with the usual big commotion, and the media follows them for more photos and an extensive interview I usually give over the fashion trends of the show.

A good work year drawing to a close, looking back to a lot of real life-changing experiences as meaningful as Cabo was, also speaking to 4,000 women at a convention, about how I have been beating the "Challenge" thru fashion and merely trying to look pretty.

The most heartbreaking experience was a talk I delivered at a women's prison, where I made the connection to the "Challenge" with the deprivation of freedom, stating:

"With the imposition of a positive attitude, and dabbing some lip gloss on, I have chased the fear demons lurking inside my head sabotaging my true liberty, if given the chance. Each of you have the power to enhance your outer beauty even in the darkest moments of solitude and despair, and on facing the mirror you will feel so much better about yourselves."

"We all only need a ray of hope, you gave us one, thank you." Wrote one of the inmates to me.

January

Mexico City

A famous Mexican rock band called Moderato is the background of the rock-inspired collection I styled for my friends, Lourdes & Aba's line.

The collection is made up of imitation long leather train skirts with embroidered t-shirts, short dresses with insert leather details and distressed chunky style boots with fishnets.

A long feather earring adorns only one ear lobe of each model, skinny leather-like pants tucked inside tall knee boots, are worn with white shirts tails sticking out under vests embroidered in sequences. Silver chain necklaces engraved with skull heads hang long around the model's necks.

A week and a half of work ending with an uproar of applause just fifteen minutes after the show started that is the way of fashion shows.

I wake up late the next day too tired to get up from bed every bone of my body aches, the after stress effect. Pulling the shutters up marveling at Mexico's skyline from my window, tall buildings framed by a blue sky and big white clouds announcing lovely weather. The spectacular view from my friends guest room draws a melancholic tear down my cheek.

At almost eleven o'clock the house is still quiet, the night before took a strain on us all. I tiptoe quietly, knowing that as soon as I walk into the bathroom the six Pomeranians, my friend's sort of children will awake everyone in the apartment with a chorus of barks. Only three hours before leaving to the airport, and just enough time to have breakfast with my daughter.

Besides work my trip to the city was also an emotional one. Alexis my daughter after living three years in Playa del Carmen on the Riviera Maya had moved for a few months back to Monterrey to work in the Habitat hotel chain that had transferred her to Mexico managing the Public Relations of three of its hip hotels in the city.

Two days before the show, over beer and tacos, Alexis announced she would be moving to India for a year, to work with Sarah, a jewelry designer I had introduced her to in New York, something really unexpected. With all that was going on with the show, I did not have time to fully digest it all until now. The night before after the runway between the shows excitement and dancing to the famous band my daughter simply stated it was a done deal. India as her next stop, in only two weeks.

As I am closing my suitcase my phone rings Alexis brilliant face flashes on the screen, a sign she is coming up on the elevator to the apartment, my little girl no more. Quite an emotional moment as I hug her not wanting to let her go.

Almost on the verge of tears, I drop myself on the airplane seat. On closing my eyes my mind reels a million thoughts a minute crushing at my heart. My kids are adults now with their dreams to catch, facing their lives on their own terms. Saying goodbye is not an easy task.

Alex having missed the Australia opportunity on finding out of my "Challenge" is taking an internship in Stuttgart Germany at the Lava firm of Architecture Design, for nine months and will be leaving at the beginning of March.

These two last years, the "Challenge" had been my priority. Neglecting my children and what they were feeling. Being so thoroughly engrossed in myself, first on the hard stage of acceptance of the "Challenge," then in the process of banishing it from my body. Their departure is sort of freeing them from the pressure this devil has plainly put them under.

Having also neglected my father who has over time become more secluded. Sometimes sitting for long periods just dosing in and off to sleep. Silence for him has been his only way out. Missing his sunny disposition and the way he will just relish going to a bar or a coffee with friends, or bully us around with his sense of humor.

Alexis leaving for India was very hard on him. Since her birth, he had fallen instantly in love with her, giving in to her every whim. Her sudden decision did not give her time to fly back and forth say a proper goodbye. Adding an extra dose of sadness that he sort of carried like another significant burden.

Arriving back home I get immersed into another emotional whirlwind. Alex excitement over his trip to Germany is contagious. Juanita and I help him pack, and he then unpacks as are his ways, almost at the last minute. In the end, it seems he is just traveling with five pairs of jeans, and like thirty briefs and twenty pairs of socks. Men!

When the day comes, to see him go after my long hugs and sticky kisses, my father and Juanita drive back with me in silence from the airport. Each with their own nostalgic thoughts.

Rosina Ramón

On opening the door the house looms large and quiet. Only children are prepared for empty spaces, I was taught to be creative with my time. Loneliness was never an issue to be felt.

Now for the first time in my life, the emptiness seems hard to fill, my two kids are gone chasing their own rainbows, facing me with a new reality. Vacant rooms and silence that I start filling with music and flowers.

My days become engrossed in work, and the never-ending tests and exams as part of a watchful eye on any monster that may be looming around the corner.

March

Monterrey

Light, pale, breezy dresses play against the model's body as they stroll down an imaginary runway on the floor of the Habitat's hotel pool bar. Clad with big chunky Swarovski necklaces and thick cuffs, designer Alejandro's Carlyn's clothes look dreamy. As a sequence of bias-cut gowns appear each one more glamorous than the other, at the end the designer walks out, and cameras start flashing.

The cocktail starts, as we are hanging the clothes packing the jewelry, collecting the shoes in a very crowded stairway that served as a tiny dressing room for almost twenty people.

There is a thing about a venue, it may look great, but usually were never conceived for fashion shows. Over time I have learnt to accommodate to uncomfortable spaces and the crazy weather of a backstage.

Arriving home after midnight I find a message on my night table it is from the doctor's office, May the 6th next operation, a sigh escapes me as I tumble down to bed fully clothed, falling asleep even with my gladiator sandals on.

April

G oing to Los Angeles the week before Easter Sunday was a last minute deal, it was my third trip to Los Angeles since November consulting a boutique owner.

A sort of mix up on the last shipment had been detained at customs and I had to go back for some express last minute purchases. I was skeptical in the beginning since it was the first Easter week I was not spending in Piedras with my father since my mom's passing. Luckily my job is my total passion, searching trends, finding new designers, simply selecting the clothes. Packing my bags I jumped at the opportunity.

Having discovered not just the fashion choices in the city but the great restaurants, amazing museums LA is an easy town everything is very clean and organized. Only it cannot ever grow on me as the cramped and crowded New York, a city that makes my just being there feel more alive.

Flying back to Monterrey four days before Easter Sunday, I still pondered with the idea of driving to my hometown for the weekend to visit dad. The thought that stopped me, was in less than ten days I was scheduled for another operation. Facing me with the need for some restful couple of days.

There are a bunch of maybes or what ifs, when we take a road in our lives that was not planed, and spending the weekend with old friends faced me with an unexpected encounter.

Mario had been a friend for many years, we had in different times of our lives been together at diverse gatherings with our respective others.

Once, years ago at a party at my house my then twelve year old daughter had caught him making out with his then girlfriend in the tiny guest bathroom. Every time we ran across each other, I reminded him of the incident, becoming our private joke.

Meeting up with him, since my last birthday party last January. Suddenly in front of all our mutual and longtime friends he started openly flirting with me. What looked to be a joke, and after my 7th operation and trip he already had scheduled, another dating game started.

May

W riting is an exercise of freeing the mind of my own imposed burdens and fears. A way to make sense of the pain of having my body mutilated in one of my most womanly places "MY BREAST'S".

Realizing it is not only about me. This is a disease that connects me to others who have suffered one way or the other thru this "Challenge", and my quest is to offer hope with my using the tools of beauty for the survival of the soul.

It's very hard to understand but it is like I gained a subscription to this strange club. Here the language of chemo and radiation may mean nothing to others, but is a big deal to me and to many women experiencing this nightmarish trip.

Just the talk about puking after chemo or facing my bald head in the mirror, all feels better thru this companionship of sorts. Bonding me immediately with some of my special kind. Background or income is irrelevant since there are many of us hovering around, partners in sickness.

I have strived on finding consolation for me and want to share the knowledge of the power our feminine gender provides thru the misjudged cult of vanity. I have learned, to be right.

So May the 6th was what I thought my last reconstructive operation, #7th, funny coincidence I had found my lump on October 6th 2008 I was now after almost three years on what looked like my last narcissist trip.

For the first time my son was not here to drive me to the hospital. Alex was still in Stuttgart, Germany and Alexis my daughter in Jaipur, India. As it has been usual in my case someone from the support group always volunteers. Rebel a dear friend offered to take me this time around, and of course Juanita came along for the ride.

I went into surgery around 9:00 AM and woke up well past noon to find my room filled with flowers. On my door Rebel had hung a roll up poster stating the kind of friends we have been over the years, a touching gesture.

After she rushes off to work, programmed as the changing of the guards Viv, Lourdes sister arrives and takes charge. Viv's young daughter, brings me a little bracelet with the word "FORTITUDE," engraved. Attached to it a small pamphlet explains the meaning:

"Clears the path to obstacles, opens new and better beginnings, with strength and courage in pain and adversity; invincible."

The description summarizes my outlook at this long road to survival and to the claiming of my right to regain some normalcy in my body. Another mantra comes into mind:

"Don't stop, don't quit and don't give up."

Having to learn that recuperating needs the art of patience and the investment of time. Also has a bit to do with my stubbornness of simply wanting to never stop liking me.

On the left side, on my good breast, a smaller implant was installed to even my two baby's out, although the size will never be precisely the same. The change was evident, and now I could enjoy something fundamental to us girls, cleavage.

Cleavage did not seem something to brood about along the way of my many surgeries, it was never on my mind, or dreams.

Then around three weeks after my surgery on the first day, I dare wear a low cut, V-neck fitted t-shirt with skinny jeans, a surprising flattering reflection of a well-formed womanly body with cleavage. An image on the mirror that would never give away the visit of the "Challenge."

The ultimate result to feeling again sexy, after so long, thanks to God, and of course to Dr. Walberg.

Dating-Game

M ario calls letting me know he is back in town. Having my doubts about dating him, let's say he is not my type. Whatever my type is? Being picky in the men department at this particular time, and age was in a way a little hilarious.

Excuses started floating around my crazy mind: He is too short, too tanned, and then I will remember his bewitching expressive eyes. Gazing at me, in a mischievous sexy way, and his easiness with word management, in the end an enchanting flirt. So I gave in.

Over the years I had turned down dates with short men, since in the family being tall was usually the norm to aspire. Not very tall myself but with heels I was pretty taller than Mario. The funny thing, I came to realize I felt totally at ease with me towering over him, it was sort of empowering.

The relationship started just two weeks after my seventh operation. So the beginning of summer has me trapped in a girdle over my knees for every single day for almost six weeks not what you would expect to be a sexy attire. Imagining me like Houdini trying to get out of something with like almost thirty hooks and two zippers, and flirt at the same time, a little comical and entertaining.

Truth be told, you do not really know someone as when you date him, so I realized I hardly knew him. First of all, he had become a vegetarian, and had stopped drinking for some time. Our first dates were like being with a fussy little kid once you sat with him over the dinner table.

Feeling at ease around him, was not enough even though his sense of humor was enticing so in truth, we thought we could skip stages, not understanding what we were getting into.

Romantic relationships vary in more ways than one they can be lasting or a passing fling, simple preferences like liking your coffee black or with a touch of milk can become a significant dilemma as in this case when one is vegan, and the other is not, a war of the tastes can inevitably erupt.

This is just a glimpse of how complex "us" as human beings are or tend to be. When you take up with someone new or someone you thought knowing, you "two" have to start to accommodate each other into the spaces, and likes of your lives.

A total logistical endeavor has to strategically be put into place so no one steps into each other's shadow. A lot of concessions have to be made on both parts so each one has to be willing to make it work. The investment has to be on equal terms

Even though my life at the time was full of work with modeling and fashion courses, and since the end of the year, I had a fashion segment every Tuesday on a local TV station. Besides a heavy social agenda, but still, the house loomed larger than ever with my son and my daughter abroad. Juanita was off to her hometown every other week tending to her sick brother.

My father came and went from Monterrey to our hometown, leaving me alone for many days. So it seemed right for the time being to let myself go and give it a try at a new relationship with an old but younger friend.

Over the course of my life I have greatly enjoyed the arts and of course artists, so let's say Mario a dedicated and successful artist in his own right, became the third of his trade in my curriculum of boyfriends over the years.

One thing I had experienced about artists is the complex trait over their self-worth usually being a little self-centered, to the incapacity of sharing any type of light.

Over the years I had also made a name for myself in fashion in our community and the toll of sharing the spotlight was too much for the relationship to flourish.

Something I later realized, was nagging at him from the beginning. Adding to the trial, my father suddenly passing away, and myself getting into a terrible needy stage. This was enough for him to run away like Speedy Gonzalez.

June-July

F ather arrived after my surgery staying a couple of weeks, roaming around the house like carrying a more substantial burden than usual. I understand it all too clearly now. He did not know how to say goodbye and I was too selfish to see it.

After Sunday lunch he started complaining of stomach pains, so I drove him to the hospital, and after a check up the doctor confirmed, nothing was amiss and that he was just in great shape for his, eighty-six years.

A couple of days later, over breakfast, he firmly stated he was going back home, that day. Nothing I said could change his mind or wait for Juanita to arrive from her hometown to accompany him to Piedras. I tried to reason with him, to no avail.

We talked every single day after his departure, and I found him in better spirits than when he was at my house.

His rituals reestablished: Domino on Tuesdays with the boys at the club, breakfast on Wednesdays with my cousin Ricardo and two longtime friends the brothers Raul and Frank, Fridays was dinner with the remaining group of couples, mom and him befriended even before their marriage. Saturday's coffee at the McDonalds in Eagle Pass and Sunday lunch with whoever called him up. His life was very structured after my mom's passing, hard to uproot him from that.

After a week and a half had passed, I got a call from cousin Ricardo, with whom he was closest to saying dad was very sick. That was on Wednesday July the first.

That evening as I am making the preparations for going to my hometown Alfonso, another of the cousin's calls from the house saying dad was doing much better after being checked and prescribed by the doctor, assuring me not to worry.

On hearing dad's voice I felt assured he is recuperating. Before hanging up he says, "I love you" I answer back "I love you too."

Needing at least a day to hire a driver, road insecurity at this particular moment was at its peak, not easy to get any one on board. Driving by myself, like I was used to, is out of the question. Highways were being burglarized by the different drug cartels, and driving at night, unthinkable.

Dad and I talked several times on Thursday, July the second, sounding livelier, even describing in detail his lunch of liver and onions with Worchester sauce and rice knowing I will say "yuk".

Talking to him again the next morning and after hearing him tell me he had a hearty breakfast of his beloved waffles. I assured him I would be there the next day. Waiting for a driver was complicating everything, and driving to my hometown in Piedras Negras takes almost five hours.

In the middle of the afternoon a nagging feeling makes me call him again, trying several times but getting no answer.

Worried I call Ricardo, my cousin, who unable to even contact dad's housekeeper in a haste walks the two blocks to our house. On his arrival it was too late, a heart attack surprised him sitting in the den watching Television.

Receiving the call, that Friday July the third at around five, waves of devastation stabbing deeply right into my heart. Alone at my house in Monterrey, desolation disables my logic button, and officially I become an orphan.

Being left by my own devices since my daughter was off in India and my son in Germany, I am facing my dad's death without them. I guess I could not have done it all without the help of my whole group of cousins and some unconditional friends.

First calling my cousin Abe who is off on business somewhere in Tijuana, stunned, but offering needed comfort, and immediately arranging for me to be taken to my hometown, to organize the funeral.

Unable to think straight and in total shock. I start dropping clothes into a suitcase, taking them out and putting them back in again, like in a trance. Pacing the hallway, as with mother's passing, tears go into hiding, it is too sudden, too painful, too alone, and too empty.

Less than two hours after Esther, Abe's wife arrives with a driver, facing sadness together she becomes my rock during this ordeal. What worries me most is reaching the kids, but I am unable to do so before we start on the long drive ahead to my hometown.

Alex was traveling for the weekend to Portugal, Alexis, in India the time difference on three continents complicating things. Sensing the sorrow this will cause them, unconditionally I adopt the burden for us tree.

First I finally reach my daughter in India who cannot stop sobbing wanting to come down for the funeral. A completely absurd idea, impossible she would be able to arrive for the funeral to be held the next day. In Mexico, a burial it is usually done the day after.

Way past midnight already in fathers den where a few hours before he had sat watching TV. Feeling the loneliness of death around me, I finally reached Alex in Portugal.

Distance is tough on a family's tragedy, all the love is there in the heart of everyone, but what we humans crave most is the touch, and the comfort of an embrace. My children's and I had to deal individually with our sadness, healing slowly as time saw fit.

After mass we arrive at the cemetery to the family plot were my mother and her parent's rest. I knew father always wanted to lie beside her. Mother's grave was already opened, as if waiting to embrace him, on his decent into the earth with her.

Unable to shed any tears which were stuck somewhere inside. My heart beating fast as I recognize the lavender casket and on top of it the dry remains of a rose. One I had placed almost six years ago.

My father was cremated, to this day I do not know how I came to that decision or if it was what he would have wanted. We never talked about it, bracing the subject had seemed always hard. Realizing at the moment, an unwise choice not to face the only inevitable departure that is death.

An unknown hand placed the wooden urn on top of mother's casket, and over it, I firmly settled six red roses two for each of my parents from my small family of three.

Then a silly thought hit me why had I never even asked father why he had picked the color lavender for mom's coffin. I could not ever remember seeing her wearing or liking that color. Even trivial things will be left without an answer now too late to find out, very late.

I have tried so hard to unravel my messed up feelings over my father's passing, as if an empty void was left on the long hallway of life. Here I was recuperating from the "Challenge's" blow, himself being healthy, and now unexpectedly gone. Processing the hard reality, not to "ever" see him again, and the chance to say a proper goodbye, a heavy metal load squashing my heart.

Emptiness

On arrival to the house after the funeral, I stepped into every room hoping without success for a final glimpse of "Him" Left around me was only emptiness, memories, and heavy silence, broken by faraway imaginary voices that resonated around me.

On closing my eyes it was like hearing them, they are talking in the kitchen fighting over petty everyday things. My dad a very early riser will brew a coffee pot and then will walk shuffling his slippers with two cups on each hand almost filled to the brim with lots of milk. One mug for him and one for my mother, I can clearly hear her voice:

"Pepe be careful not to spill the coffee all over the floor."

I vividly see my mother propped up in bed savoring the brew, simultaneously turning the TV on to watch the news, my father sitting on his side of the bed, both with feet crossed one on top of the other. Like a mirrored reflection of each other, living together for 53 years.

Friends came and went that day. Esther who had accompanied me all thru the event and calmed me down with her faith and her fabulous enigmatic presence. Even her helpful suggestion of myself wearing a white eyelet dress for the service turned out to be a more comforting idea. The light, that white gives, was a powerful booster of energy and even a commodity for the July heat.

Esther was the best representative for the clan of older cousins that could not make it. Having to go back to Monterrey, it was decided that my other cousin Paco will be sending someone to pick me up in a couple of days.

My life is filled with cousins and friends as I mentioned in my thank you speech at the burial:

"I have unconditional cousins and amazing, reliable friends."

From both of my parents side family came, most of my out of town cousins were here, in the end all had to go back to their hometowns, and the ones living here returned to their lives.

Except for one of the youngest Alfonso who is a sort of little brother, stayed after midnight. At the same time, Ana and Alberto two friends who live two hours in a nearby town decided to keep me company for that first night and of course unconditional Larry, who had been staying at bay all during the services.

The next morning I said my goodbyes to Ana and Albert, and had to ask Larry to leave me by myself that second night. Needing time to arrange my thoughts, facing the empty house, and also to confront the reality of loss.

So that night, all alone I peeked thru the rooms, accompanied by the music playing from vinyl records on the stereo from the 60's. To this day I can describe each corner of the house, since it had been like this for years. Sooner or later I would have to decide what to do with all, thinking of that moment overwhelmed me.

Many may decide to just shut the door, throw the key and walk away. Why bother about old pieces of furniture, and objects. To a certain degree these "things" are part of my essence, ingrained in my general aesthetics.

Mother cared deeply about the way her house looked, she treated it as sort of a dollhouse. Everything had a unique story, told to me many times. Preparing myself to undertake now the task of caring for the possessions of her love.

So I took a pencil and a yellow pad making a list of what was precious to them, and to me. Walking from the entrance hall to every single room, I found the spaces in my house back in Monterrey for furniture lamps, tables, and all type of pieces until everything sort of blended in happily.

This exercise was at the same time heartbreaking, as healing. Every object has a memory every room has a past, the images vivid as my parent's presence felt close. Shutting my eyes I could see them clearly embracing me. Then as always without knocking a flood of tears escaped freely. Realizing the hard truth I am all alone now.

As dawn draws near, I make a pot of coffee and sit on my father's spot on the back porch surrounded by large imposing trees. An enormous pine I had one day planted after school when I was twelve, stands now solemn. The grass and weeds have not been cut in a quite a while, and crickets squeak, as darkness turns to light. Silence is broken as the day awakes to the usual sounds of a new life.

Out from behind a bush I suddenly see it, the old turtle that has lived on the backyard for many years has come to pay her condolences. I am not really alone anymore.

The Last Farewell

A round noon that day, I call my cousin Mercedes, first for the company
since my alone time had ended, she is tall and broad of built a constant
reminder of grandma's in face and body.

What you love most about her is her sarcastic wit and the powerful
influence she has overall her six other siblings including handsome Alfonso.
Ordering them all around, since she was left in charge by her mother to
run their state. She can be warm and friendly, but like a general has the
upper hand at controlling even her older brothers.

Knowing how reliable she can be she drove me around town settling
the loose ends left after a funeral. Giving her a list of things I would want
them to later have when the movers came, which at the time I had no
definite date.

On arrival as we walked into the house, Juanita my surrogate mother
had arrived from her own trial with the passing of her brother. I was so
relieved to see her, and more tears were shed in her arms.

When you rely over time on someone, things need not be asked.
Juanita had already started packing some objects she was sure my mother
would not want me to leave behind not even at this early stage. She knew
her too well.

So after a week, as agreed with my cousin Paco, a driver comes to
fetch us, to take us back to Monterrey. Taking a last glimpse around each
room, and standing by my dad's desk in the den, placing my hands on
the back of his chair, and closing my eyes, I imagine hugging him tightly.
Locking my memories after shutting the door, in tears I flee the house to
the waiting car.

As we drive back thru mountains that have been sliced in half to
accommodate for the new super hi-ways my thoughts are on my childhood
trips and the non-stop chatter between my parents that would rock me to
sleep.

The next day after our arrival a mass was held in honor of my father
where all the cousins and friends came to pay their respects. Mario is
nowhere in sight. We had talked the day of my father's passing, and

calling me several times while in my hometown, but my perceptive self-felt something to be amiss.

On a faraway bench, I spotted Anna Isabel a tall, beautiful model that works at the agency sitting with her mother, a bouquet of gardenias on her lap. At the end of mass, and everyone comes for the final hugs she hands me the bouquet ordered by my son Alex. Precisely at that moment the void of my kids absence, strikes a hole into my heart. Tears flow in automatic mode.

Mario finally materializes, after two days from my arrival back into town, and the relationship sort of carries a normal course. I did not have the strength of facing him with any sort of recriminations or asking for needed support which I felt him incapable to give, and after a month or two we parted ways.

Needing Stage

A little over a month after my father's passing, I wake up in the middle of the night with great anguish pushing on my agitated beating heart. In my dream, someone is chasing me in my parent's backyard. My chiffon long dress slit to shreds, feeling being pulled down by a powerful force.

Sleep left me till like early dawn suddenly, I knew. I had to go back home and dismantle the house, so first thing next morning I started to organize the move.

There was no use on putting it off. The house was at the moment an easy target for burglars. The country was in turmoil of a high delinquency rate. Border towns were at a higher risk, recently with the alarming drug wars. I could not inflict the responsibility of the house on any of my cousins. I had to take charge also of selling it, there was no other way to go about it.

Walking into my parent's house, one month after my father's funeral, a devastating sense of desolation runs thru the center of my body. Expecting to see him there, nostalgia hits hard, as I pace into each room only to find emptiness.

Juanita starts turning the air conditioner since the heat is unbearable for it is early August. Settling down like guests in the large living room, making up our minds on where to start. For over an hour she tells her stories while working with my parents, usually one anecdote funnier than the other.

Relating to her my parent's fabulous New Year's party held in this very room when they were younger. People came and went till all hours of the night and food was served like it was a Luby's cafeteria, pleasant memories always warm the heart.

Then as if on cue before shedding any more tears, the doorbell rings us back to the present, her daughter in-law and her two teenage sons arrived with the packing essentials.

For two whole days, we packed almost nonstop, my parents life into boxes.

The last night over pizza and wine with Mercedes, and two of her daughters, we laugh so hard as Larry is relating stories of ghosts and haunted houses. Gladly I would welcome any of my parents, walking in on us at the center of their activities their kitchen, left almost untouched to this day.

On closing the door to an almost empty house, it seems virtually stripped of all its memories. Rooms loom large, and like with the Challenge a part of me erased, and only partially mended. Never will my body be as it once was, as this house it is all in the past.

Rearranging

Exhausted, we reached Monterrey hours before the moving team. My organization skills had come in handy. I had made a sketch copy for all to follow on the arrangement of where each piece of furniture belonged. A specific map, that made it a great time saver when the movers finally arrived.

I had no problem mixing pieces from one house to the other. When you love antiques and quirky things you can bring yourself to building little warmth to different areas, if you are open to no formal protocol, elements morph comfortably together.

My idea of creating charming spaces with unusual artifacts once belonging to family members of different generations is my way of decorating. Mother used to say:

"Rosina, it seems like you are just waiting for someone to die to add something old, and make a room look new in your house."

I laugh at the memory of her comment and know she must be happy with what I am doing now with her precious things.

For over two months, I worked rearranging the furniture to the exact space I wanted each piece to fit. My house is an eclectic blend of times past, Mexican artifacts and modern paintings. Very much like the way I dress, mixing things that may never match but are just me, and my peculiar style. A tossed salad of sorts.

The hard realization in the aftermath of my father's passing was that a chapter of my life was over. Objects became for me this anchor to the past, a consolation prize. Reminding, how loved I had been by this two people responsible for giving me life.

I will wrestle at nights with a feeling of abandoning the house that had been my parent's shelter now standing alone and currently empty. On closing my eyes before falling asleep, I walked thru each room as if when I was a child. Vivid with memories, almost hearing whispers of conversations and practically perceiving the characteristic smell that becomes ingrained in the life of a house.

Rearranging old objects in the end was like starting a new life for all.

I became certain, that after all the spirit never indeed abandons an inhabited space or its things, and imagined my parent's still are around me.

Divided

A lexis living in India had made us even closer than when living in Mexico City. Skyping practically every single day, and more after father's passing, we urgently needed time to heal together.

Alex in Germany was not an exception we would be on constant contact. With the time differences in three continents I would talk to Alexis way past midnight and with Alex in the middle of the day.

My schedules were coordinated around their waking hours. I stopped needing sleep, for my priority that long summer was the feeling of companionship, and healing as a family.

I then started a sort of count down on the calendar just waiting for their arrival in December.

September

Cecubi

The Tecnologico de Monterrey, my sons Alma Matter, was summoned during a semester with presenting a viable project in a class called Cathedra Blanca, imparted by the well-known Mexican architect Agustin Landa Vertiz.

The task was to propose to the government a community center in the middle of one of the worst underprivileged gang-troubled areas in the heart of the city.

Nine students worked with the architect on the original layouts when finally authorized by the Governor. Supervising the construction one of the nine students was Alex, my son.

The Cecubi as it is known is 7,000 square feet of a recreational center of sports, the arts, technology, movie theaters and homemaking facilities. Built for a population immersed in crime, shedding this type of complex a ray of hope, keeping people away from corruption.

So it is fitting to say how proud I was when I was invited by the class's group to receive in the representation of my son an official recognition from the Governor.

Excited for his great accomplishment at this early stage of his career. I could not sustain a teary eye. My dad who had been with us at the traditional ceremony for the constructions kick off, was sadly not here to see the finished building. He would have been so proud of his grandson. I clearly could picture him around his friends, endlessly bragging about Alex for months to come.

Then as always I stop and think how many mothers that have lost this battle with the "Challenge" have also lost the chance of seeing their kid's success? I rejoiced in this moment with an immense pride, and gave thanks, to God.

Year Three

October, 6th

T oday marks three years after first finding the lump on my right breast. Looking back after all the pain and anguish experienced, over the "Challenge." At the moment writing about it, is as if I am talking about a different person outside of me.

I see the photos with my bald-head and look very much like an out of space creature. Never had I noticed myself to be that pale and the size of my features appear that large, well I know my nose, and my ears are not small, but they looked huge in my bald days. Figuring out that looking oddly different was a unique beauty, with a twist, that was just mine.

Now, I cannot be happier about how I am feeling. As I stare at my reflection in the mirror, there is a considerable resemblance to my university years only blonder. I am parting my hair in the middle again, a strangely youngish effect, it is not only in my mind I see the now pictures and I look fresher. Who cares, it is my own beauty now.

Three years ago, I started living under the mantra of vanity by fooling myself at believing I was just looking fine. With all the colored wigs, scarfs around my head, and tubes of lip-gloss, that helped me arrive at where I am today.

Now clean with no traces of the "Challenge," it is true that I am still in treatment and that I have to get checked up every six months. Of course, regular checkups should be on everyone's list, and popping a pill every single day is not a very hard task, it is like washing my teeth, I just to do it. For beauty's sake.

Friendships

New York

I meet up with Mara again in New York after almost a year and a half from our last encounter. The operations and other trips made me unable to attend fashion week this year.

Real friendships are the ones that stand the blank spaces of time. For over two hours over lunch at a nice restaurant in Chelsea we had a sincere review of our happiness and troubles during the year. Some relationships are nurtured more on quality than the actual time you spend with someone.

Lucia, my dear friend, invited me on this trip with her daughter Cozz. Lucia I mentioned, is ten years younger, acting always like a mother hen, something ingrained in her nature, and not worth fighting about. She made sure the whole weekend, I did not get stranded on the subway, or go dancing like a Coyote Ugly girl at some bar when not at her side, it was very amusing.

While in New York, I instantly get this vast amount of energy, that even fifteen-year-old Cozz is left tired after days filled with shopping and sightseeing. Essentially the purpose of the trip was me the stylist, helping her buy a new wardrobe. A great present from her parents and for me a big break after a tough couple of months after my father's passing.

My arrival into the city was three hours behind schedule, due to the first surprising early snow. After dinner, as we walk down Times Square snowflakes keep on falling over our heads, and a marvelous feeling of brightness surrounds us; it is magical.

The euphoria of being in Time Square accompanied by the marvelous work of nature. A feeling of happiness takes hold of us at the sight. The camaraderie of the moment, and the sense of just being alive to be able to experience the snow, and the lights, we all feel utterly lucky.

This is a moment so special, wishing I could meet with God, and give him a bear hug.

So here I am in New York for the first time during Halloween, walking in between the famous parade on Bleecker Street to my friends Natalie's apartment, people are everywhere making it hard to walk, everyone is in disguise I am not the exception.

With a feather hat and a long red wig, in an Yves Saint Laurent vintage wrap around dress with strings that connect to ruffles at the sleeves. A very Morticia Adams look, wishing with no success to look more like Cher. Only, Natalie's Medusa is a hard competition.

Pepe my photographer buddy also in town, arrives for dinner dressed like a sort of Ronald McDonald and his friend like a kind of rapper with an enormous Afro wig.

Fabrizio Natalie's fiancé is in a gladiator costume made with a mini skirt from Natalie's closet from Dolce & Gabanna's last year's summer collection worn with tall gladiator sandals and of course a crown of olive leaves over his temples. Agreeing to wear this get up proves he is unconditionally in Love for her, and ready not to back down on marrying her in May.

So off we go after drinks and dinner again into the streets of people screaming excitedly trick or trick, young and old merged in plain fun. Taking pictures with total strangers dressed in incredible costumes, you feel you are in a freaky horror movie. A total delight of just living life again as a child. I guess that has been the lesson all along after the "Challenge", the real enjoyment of being silly, and have a long hard laugh is of utmost importance.

Maybe it is my love for this city that even taking long breaths of cold air is such a lively feeling, cherishing every instant that I am here.

Halloween in New York is almost a national holiday from the early morning you see people walking in the most creative costumes to the office, with portfolio's in hand. The parade of craziness continues all thru the day until way past midnight. Waking up the next day to a city that had too much, drinks and party, a rehearsal prelude to New Year's Eve.

December 22

Christmas

Alex is calling me from Holland the day of his arrival. His plane connection coming from Germany canceled due to the weather. Thinking first he is playing a big joke on me, and sadly I realize it is true.

I will have to postpone his welcoming party for the next day, e-mails and calls to make, food to store, but mostly hold the feeling of excitement that is nagging at my heart ready to explode.

A month ago after New York, I flew to Mexico City to greet Alexis. She decided to cut short her stay in India and the meeting was filled with all she had missed during the months after her brief visit in the end of August. I was so relieved to see her since she had caught a strange disease of the skin on her last week's traveling around the colorful country.

I had always related the infection to a picture she had posted in murky waters almost hugging a colossal hippopotamus. We mother's with this sixth sense are hardly ever wrong, but as always being brushed off as lunatics, is the norm. Thankfully after doctors prescribed antibiotics, the infection had subsided arriving back in Mexico in one piece.

One more day of anxiously waiting for Alex's arrival after his call, feeling longer than the nine months of his absence. The weather is a mess all over the world on this precise day, besides being a critical traveling date only two days before Christmas Eve.

So after many more delays and a party going on already at my house a friend and I drive to the airport after midnight to fetch him.

My heart almost stops racing until I see his tall and now very lean frame walk out to pick his luggage. Breaching security, I run to hug him as I hear the guard's voice:

"Mam, you cannot go in," I turn to him with a steely like stare, and briskly say, "nine months without seeing my son who is going to stop me"? He can't do much, I am already in my son's arms.

There is a thing about Christmas that eventually takes hold of us. A nostalgic feeling that marks the failures and successes. The last days of the year seem like a warning on how well or not we managed our time.

Tough realizing, that the actions and events of previous months are what we have to brood or rejoice about as the three light shine on us. Regrets are set inside a drawer and the key is thrown away, shedding a tear for love lost and for our loved ones who surprised us with their final parting.

Still the feeling that at any moment we might hear their voice when the phone rings or see them standing as we open the door to a knock that sounds much like theirs. Only the deep stab in our heart from the empty chair at the Christmas dinner table, and longing for the need of at least one more day.

New Year 2011

A rriving with Alex to Cancun for New Year's, I had forgotten that the color of the sea here was aqua blue just like one of the 100 colors in my Crayola box when I was a kid. The sea, together with the sun fills my being with such positive energy, a sort of mesmerizing impact on my senses. Amazing and infinity beauty.

Walking for a week every single morning wondering where the sea begins or where it ends. Pondering that in life we know where it all begins, but like the sea, we do not know where or when it ends.

On some of my walks Alex is by my side chatting excitedly about his life in Germany and his trips around Europe. My father comes up often in our long conversations, and the sting of his absence touches us.

When alone I am immersed in the beauty and the privilege of this view, free for me to take. Closing my eyes and listening to the swaying sound of waves. Reaching after almost four years at a stage of waking up to a new life every day. The "Challenge" is left in my memories as the painful unraveling of a long film in which I played a leading role, surviving like the heroine.

One of my large rimed hats shields me from the sun, the thin blue and white batik dress that matches my bathing suit is almost soaked by tingling splashes of water. On each step I register the silky feeling of sand on my toes. Melancholy strikes with a lot of mixed emotions that have been bundled up inside me, then the tears flow by.

A spectator on the outside wondering, did this happen to me? I only have to look at my reflection in any mirror to know how real it was.

As much as the magic of Christmas conquers my soul, there is the void left by the absence of my father's presence. Wishing to go back a year and change so many things and give him so much more than I gave him. Never will I feel like it was enough, or maybe I did not try harder to make life easier for him.

Being both of us genuinely stubborn beings, me trying to convince him to leave his hometown and move in with us, without success. Coming to the awareness that at eighty six he was fighting for his independence as much as trying to stay clear of all that was happening to my body. His keeping himself at bay helped him not to have to face the fact of my fight with the "Challenge".

So as much as I may regret not having him near I can now understand the terrible anguish, he must have gone thru when he came for a visit. The utterly feeling of helplessness of having his hands tied without being able to do anything to relieve my pain.

Avoidance seems to be a way out for a lot of people, especially for men. Their way of thinking that by not facing the facts the truth will probably disappear and take care by itself.

Life may go on, confronting us with the wound of the loss, always dividing our life in a before and after phase. Today will never bring back yesterday we will only have the memories to cherish, that is only thing we have left.

Playa del Carmen

New Year's Eve

S o after the fireworks on the beach of Playa del Carmen and the traditional waiting for daybreak, I sit on the sand with Alex and a couple of his friends, after seven in the morning. Brushing of the sand of my long off white linen dress, donning on the ethnic embroidered camel hooded cape, that seems to have been the talk of the night, I walk barefooted and elated to the apartment two blocks ahead.

Alex stays, at the party that is still going on, DJ music at full blast. We could not meet up with Alexis, my daughter, she had no way of getting on the bus from Tulum with Tita her dog and practically her daughter. We cannot understand how they don't allow dogs on buses.

The discrimination of Tita for Alexis was a shock. For me a missed opportunity for seeing my daughter, but Tita is her priority, there are more photos of Tita on her Facebook page than of her brother or myself. Boyfriends have always had to accommodate themselves to Tita's needs, one even babysat for a couple of months while she was in India.

Everywhere she has worked Tita is almost in between the lines of her contracts, arriving many days with her to the office, to parties, and of course trips to the Riviera Maya, where she was born. Alexis always says Tita misses the sand.

I say she did a great job raising Tita, since she has the manners of a great dame, so much better than the way I raised Alexis, still I missed giving her a New Year's hug.

January

I was introduced to Eugene a very nice looking guy thru a business acquaintance. Eugene originally from Spain, is the manager of an international marketing firm. We start dating casually, a guy with a great sense of humor, with not a dull moment around him.

His easygoing nature becomes a perfect companion to my dear friend Mariel's wedding, enchanting everyone with his laid-back demeanor. A natural at spicing everything up with his quick wit, at the same time making everyone supper at ease, as if all were long ago acquaintances.

There is always an unusual detail about "the" men I date, as my luck has it. With Eugene, I was having tons o fun, long intense conversations, but no romance. I just knew something was awry, his charm camouflaging a bugging feeling.

Then one chilly night at the end of January as God must have been bored with the horrible weather he himself had triggered, decided to have a laugh on me.

Eugene's call comes as I am getting ready for friend's birthday party. His voice is a bit anxious stating the urgency to see me. Still, in my ignorance, I try to convince him to accompany a friend and myself to the party, he declines, insisting he has to see me.

Shortly the doorbell sounds louder than usual, in a hurry on opening the door, instead of shock, I let out a nervous laughter. Understanding immediately that this revelation is no funny matter for the person facing me, and that he mustered a lot of courage to be standing in front of me.

Staring back into my eyes, is a plump, green eyed lady, in her late 40's with a heavy sadness about her. Wearing black platform shoes, patterned stockings, a too tight satin black skirt, a tweed jacket with a Chanel like weave, and an iconic style Margaret Thatcher bow-tie blouse. Carmen, Eugene's altered female ego is on my doorstep.

A joke is being played on me, a guy I am dating is a travesty? I clearly can hear God munching on popcorn, chuckling, and whispering:

"You did not see this one coming?"

Almost speechless, unable to laugh or cry, the best option is to ask him for a much-needed drink. Getting the bottle and glasses I try to

213

calm my agitated state of mind. I see his hands trembling as he fights nervously unscrewing the wine bottle. This disclosure must have been a tough decision to confront me with such a big secret.

For a while I listen, to his years of hiding from the shame of being different, and having no one to turn to, except for his sister. Strangely now, I have made the list to share his burden.

Why was I chosen? I will never know. What I do know is all of us have a load we must carry in one way or the other, and is up to only us to live with it or ignore it. So I ask him:

"I choose to face the Challenge, are you willing to face this and lead an open happy life?"

The answer is interrupted by the doorbell as I am pouring our first glass of wine. My friend Marcela a petite "sexy moreana" with a perfect pear shape figure, dark expressive eyes, and long black straight hair, arrives to pick me up for the party. As she walks into the warm living room on seeing my visitor, she takes off her coat as if the heat is too much to bear, throws it on a sofa, it carelessly ending on the floor. With a startled face, nodding her head at my offering of a wine glass. Suddenly, on recuperating from her disbelief, stammers a raspy sounding:

"Hi, so nice to meet you".

With silly conversation, I try to sooth the awkward moment, so I keep on babbling trivialities, until we finish the wine and Carmen announces she (or he) will be living for a club and we air kiss her (or him) goodbye.

As I close the door behind her (him) Marcela bursts into nervous laughter, and says "I really feel like I am in a movie" yes I say "God's movie, and we are the stars of his movie, and prince charming is not even a prince" we laugh until tears come out.

Carmen is now a good friend to gossip about the latest fashion and makeup trends. Eyebrows are raised when dressed in drag we meet at a bar or at coffee shop. Inclusiveness of gender acceptance is something to keep on fighting for all over the world.

This type of segregation still to this day has him or her pondering to answer my question. Without facing up to a true identity, and the freedom of happiness.

February

Waking up at early dawn, even with the central heating on I can feel it is a cold day outside, so dragging myself out of the warm comforter I splash my face with yes freezing water to open my eyes from the heaviness of sleep.

I turn on the shower, and as I strip my clothes off, I see the reflection of my sharpie marked body on the wall mirror. Rapidly I turn the shower off remembering that soap and water would erase the marks for this 8th and hopefully my last reconstruction operation.

I pull up some black stirrup pants a massive cream-colored knitted chunky sweater and black suede booties. On my way of wakening Alex I reach in one of the closets for the fuzzy white and black zebra stamped coat, black beret, and a long red scarf. I pick up my overnight bag, and on opening the front door I feel the icy wind on my face.

Getting inside the car after throwing the bag on the back seat I close my eyes enjoying some minutes by myself before Alex drives me to the hospital.

A sort of familiar drill that has been going on for three years, my body has not entirely healed from all the implicit intrusions. This operation specifically will again target filling in some blanks. From where ever it can be found fat will be sucked then injected back into places like on my underarm, where my skin is very thin close to the bone, and almost transparent.

Again the same drill check in at the hospital reception. Sign those dreaded papers with tiny print, which after reading them for the eight-time still give me goose bumps all over my body. From the sheer thought of anything going wrong, it is sort of signing your life away. I take a deep breath sign, and pick up another pair of terry cloth slippers and hope for the best.

A chilly breeze wakes me up from Snow Whites world everything went according to schedule, no use fretting anymore about anything I am alive and it looks like we are almost at the end of the alignment process.

Many people keep asking, why to go to all this hassle, with so many operations. First it all started with just wanting to look like myself again, then the adjustments had to be made since discomfort and pain became part of the scene.

Then I was faced with this hard truth about only one out of twenty women in Mexico have breast reconstruction after a mastectomy, and I feel that there is a hidden macho agenda, as much as a lack of good insurance.

Again, a flashback hits me, remembering that encounter with the priest at the beginning of my ordeal. Now it seems crazier than before that he could be so naïve to think that I did not have to care of how my body looks. Only me facing the mirror it was utterly ridiculous and depreciating advice. I do not recommend anyone to take to heart.

I will always be a believer you have only one body, and you are responsible for it since your birth and anything that harms it also affects your inner self we cannot separate them.

Now as I see my reflection in the mirror I know it is far from perfect, or like my body used to be, but I feel pretty good about it, and for me, it is of the utmost importance. I will always have respect for this body, perfect or not.

Having made peace with myself, I no longer dread the reflection in the mirror anymore, and I wish anyone that has gone thru this would feel this way.

March-April

Piedras Negras

Almost ten months from my father's passing, we go back to my hometown to meet up with some clients interested in buying the house.

Emptiness takes a toll on the property, tall weeds are almost blocking the view from the outside. Finding people to clean is a priority, opening the front door loneliness strikes, hitting me straight to the heart.

Alex first visit after coming back from Germany, his eyes fill with tears for a moment. Aching for him when seeing him walk into my father's den, as if expecting to find him sitting at his desk, which is the only piece of furniture still in this room. Surrounded by total silence we embrace feeling the loss that becomes more real being here.

Without furniture the house seems larger than I can remember. Work has to be done, floors are covered with dust, bathrooms with mildew, only the two bedrooms, and the kitchen look like they are expecting guests, us.

There is something in cleaning an abandoned house when you have so few elements to work with, tidiness becomes crucial, besides I could not be in Mothers house and skip some serious cleaning. She actually considered Mr. Clean a rock star, I laugh at the thought.

So between two hired boys for the patio Alex and Juanita, we left the house, as mother would have fancied, but the buyers didn't show for the appointment. To a certain point, I was deeply relieved. My childhood house is my anchor to the past, I have been having a severe problem with letting it go.

The window in my childhood bedroom has only thin lace curtains. As I fall asleep, I am rocked by the dancing of the tree leaves outside on the porch, outlined by the light of my neighbors back patio. Sensing someone is watching me, waking up startled to just a dream.

The first night, back home in Monterrey, while dozing off to dreamland, my bed faces the hallways door, in a dozing stage I clearly see the window in front of me. Lace curtains floating, losing myself to where exactly I am, and the feeling of being watched prevails. As if the two houses morphed from a place 500 miles away into just one. My parent's presence a constant for me, and a protective shield from the "Challenge."

Old Friendship

Alicia my friend from my college days, originally from San Luis Potosi, Mexico, has lived in Germany for over forty years with her husband and kids. After her finding out about my "Challenge" reconnecting, was a needed affair. The void inflicted by the separation of the location of our daily lives never had tarnished our relationship, since our College days.

Burdened by the strain on inheriting both our childhood homes with the trappings of entangled feelings stashed away in a somber little corner. Our reunion served as a healing process from our parent's loss, and the in-between's of "just" life.

Understanding this over our daily bottle of red wine in the course of four endless nights comes down to the distinct tests we have faced in all our years living in different countries with so many, unlike customs and traditions.

She has battled with a diversity of thought, and strictness of the German culture, and the big scare which was a heart attack suffered by her adoring husband. Alienated by her siblings as an outcast after her parents death, the culprit of all, distance.

We arrived at a conclusion we have to confront our trials in the best possible way, she has done it by painting and dancing rumba. I have done it thru my love of fashion, yoga and cooking.

Strange to find out that the anguish of my parent's empty house, which usually wakes me up at night, also wakes her up far away in Holzminden, Germany.

Arriving both at the conclusion that our houses will sell when the opportunity arises. Knowing that each of us has been responsible for stalling our chances of selling. Considering our sentimental attachments, which has us tied down to our past, simply afraid of not meeting up to our parents expectations.

Being able to have this conversation with Alicia that magical weekend, after almost ten years of not seeing each other in the flesh. Picking up on our lives as if space and time had not mattered.

The feeling of being able to bear down our deepest woes and insecurities, and re-discovering our rare and special friendship, one that we cannot ever stop treasuring.

May

Mexico City

Alexis is by now very settled in Mexico City working in a marketing firm, and now in partnership with a restaurant group, she calls me up about the opening of her hip restaurant in la Colonia Roma the heart of a new wave of eateries and clubs in the city.

There will be a particular party for the opening of Romita Comedor, and my daughter is organizing the whole event and seems pressured with press and celebrity's arrival.

Lourdes and Aba call me to invite me to stay at their house if I decide to fly to Mexico. I am swamped with work and can't seem to be able to skip out of town for a few days.

Phil my friend calls and gives specific orders, get organized:

"There is no way you are going to miss your, daughters big night I have booked you a ticket already, so you fly in two days."

Having no other alternative, I agree only deciding it will be a surprise for my daughter and no one must tell her anything.

Lourdes driver, with his usual welcoming disposition is there to pick me up at the airport, outlining that I will have enough time to rest and get ready for the evening.

On our arrival to this fantastic restored French colonial house in one of Mexico's first fancy neighborhoods from the beginning of 1900, the now trendy Colonia La Condesa.

After like what felt more than 100 steps on a very steep stair and trying to control the trailing strings of my asymmetrical olive green parachute style dress. Catching my breath, we arrive at a crowded sort of garden room with high ceilings and beautiful stainless steel glass windows.

The place is a work of art, I start to get sentimental as I get to experience with great pride my daughter's success, the event is a hit, a scene filled with art and fashion people, and overflowing with paparazzi.

After finally spotting her in the middle of a big crowd. Looking great in one of her signature black long gauzy dresses, a turban of black flowers and feathers on her head. Surprised, she hugs me excited taking me around the room to be introduced to her friends and partners. Giving thanks, on acknowledging I am here because God wanted me to live this with her. Motherly love strikes me hard I am out of control with happiness.

June

Tecnológico de Monterrey Graduation

Overwhelmed by mixed feelings on seeing Alex, my son walking with a characteristic attitude of accomplishment. Straight in posture, formal in manner, and yes, strikingly tall and handsome.

Sometimes I think he resembles a lot like my father, but traces of my mother linger. Siblings tend to be quite different, Alex has light blondish brown hair and translucent white skin. Alexis has dark brown hair and light almond skin. He has a square, angular jawline where my daughter's face is more oval-shaped.

Alexis resembles more to myself when in my teen years, only with more delicate features and of course, a smaller nose. Their likeness mirrors in the warmth of their brown-yellowish eyes, just like my father's.

Dad would be delighted to be here today. He has been in Alex's thoughts, since awakening this morning, and now, of course, in his heart.

Considering all this in the middle of Alex's graduation ceremony. Alexis missed it, because of work and could not make it from Mexico City. My ex-husband, Alejandro, is sitting on my left side, and Juanita is on my right. My heart is beating so fast, almost popping out from the sheer excitement of being so proud.

Almost choking with trapped tears, controlling them slightly in front of nearly two thousand people. We are here with a son coming out of College with high recommendations from his teachers, and the Lava firm he interned in Stuttgart Germany.

Lucky me, God, let me have the chance to rejoice to see all my hard work of putting my son thru school with all the ups and downs this enabled. As Alex walks back to his seat, diploma raised high on his arm. Our eyes meet, and clearly he is saying, thank you.

I then repeat, to God thank you, thank you, as tears roll down my cheeks.

July

Piedras Negras, Mexico

Even without the furniture, the house seems pretty and cozy. The vast emptiness as I walk in the long hallway has nothing to do with furniture or decorations. The absence of its inhabitants is the harsh void.

As usual, flashback of memories. When I was around nine, I used to be scared about walking in this long hall at night. The darkness seemed to hide some unfriendly creatures who, at one point, will jump from out of this blackness and attack me without warning.

Walking into my childhood's bedroom, I stare at the three big wooden sliding closet doors, recalling how I would think in my little messed up child's head that at night some strange monster was hiding inside also ready to pop up as soon as the lights went out.

As my parents slept, I would sit on a couch between our rooms, whimpering quietly with a feeling of dread. After much deliberation, I would finally end up on my parent's bed.

I had not thought of that episode of my life until today a hot July night arriving at what used to be my parent's house. Fear can actually inflict on the brain, anxiety similar to when I was told: "You have the Challenge."

How do you beat this dread that creeps unwillingly into our lives without explanation? On one of many nights in the hospital by myself, I experienced this type of fear. Familiar but alien until now that I can find it's origin.

Now the fear is back, a tree of more than twenty meters high in the backyard is being towed down because it was overflowing with termite. After proudly standing for over a hundred years in the same spot, it will have to go down, too devastating.

I feel Larry's arms around me, guessing what I am going thru. It is as if with tearing down the three I am being uprooted from my parent's house. Strange that we had to bring the three-down almost a year after my father's passing, as if the three knew his large branches were not needed anymore, to give his shade to my father's bedroom.

On looking to sell the house I can only think how dare I do this to my parents, and the thought who will live a new life here, will these people meet their expectations? I was left by myself with a lot of hard questions to answer.

Really how hard it is to let go, eventually, I will have to let go, and holding to the memories is a way for me to keep them alive, at least in my heart and thoughts. So one day, I expect to find someone who appreciates the old place and makes a nice life inside it as we did.

I have pictured a young family with kids who can run around the backyard and can build a pink dollhouse like the one I used to have. I remember trying to sit Celina, my cousin, to drink tea with me in a ladylike manner. Hardly it never worked, she preferred the swings and getting dirty, she had brothers as her teachers that being why.

Over the years, I never gave a thought to the importance of the house when they were alive. Now that they are gone, my sentimentality has taken hold of me. Every time I come down, I am at peace with myself and relish at being here sleeping in my little girl's bedroom feeling safe, loved, and protected from the "Challenge" hitting me again.

Larry calls me crazy and laughs at me because when walking at one time or another inside the house, I announce my arrival to them, "Mom, Dad, I am home." That silly action makes me so happy that it would not surprise me. They will answer back.

I have told Larry I was very happy in this house I do not have sad memories living here, problems came and went no big deal until their passing.

Love Notes

Maybe my biggest tragedy was when at 15 I fell madly in love with my first handsome blond, blue-eyed American boyfriend Brad. My parents did not approve our relationship since he was a senior and I was an eighth-grader.

So an old fashion romance of correspondence emerged between us since Jr. High. Writing love notes, every single day, relaying on a couple of friends as our mailmen. This went on through my High School years, and after graduation I was sent to school in Monterrey and the love was lost.

After my mom's passing, I found those notes stashed away at the back of a drawer in my bedroom's closet. Folded neatly inside wooden boxes of the popular men's scent from the 70's English Leather.

Confirming with this my mother always knew of those notes, never throwing them away. They were stashed together with photographs and letters of her Spanish boyfriend. Meeting him when traveling with my grandfather to Spain when visiting his sisters during her late teens.

Once she related to me the story of how Pablo had arrived in America, a graduated doctor one month shy before my parent's wedding.

In those letters, I had the core facts of the romance that spanned over the five years of her travels back and forth to Spain. She had been madly in love, almost to the point of staying with him in one of her last trips, but he was still a student with nothing to offer her.

My grandparents had not been very supportive of the relationship, so it was a relief to them when she decided to marry my father a then successful businessman. The story sort of repeated itself with Brad and myself.

Fate plays tricks on us, I lost Brad with great sorrow as my mother lost Pablo. Still, I keep my letters and hers as a reminder of our first love.

Becoming her accomplice, never showing my father her box of letters. How could I? She was the love of his life.

The River

Piedras Negras, Mexico

I have become very keen on color. I guess it is because of the merchandising courses I teach for stores?

I had not realized that a golf course has the greenest and healthiest grass. From a certain distance, it degrades from one lighter grasshopper green to darker emerald green or the other way around depending on my dear friend the sun.

The different hues of blues the Rio Grande's water vary on the specific time of day where the sun hits the water. Light is the enhancer of actual color, without light we will only have darkness, and a colorless world.

This sort of new form of perception only comes with a new found gratefulness of all that surrounds me. Every day we wake up rushing to our programed and strictly choreographed day, not even looking up at the sky.

Sadly I had not paid close attention until that first morning, I went for a jog on the new running path two blocks from the house. Overlooking the Rio Grande, which separates the two border cities Eagle Pass Texas, and Piedras Negras Coahuila.

I have fallen so much in awe of the view which for years I took for granted. On the American side, the Fourth Duncan Club, sparse green acres of a golf course, on the Mexican land, the two bridges that connect the cities and the old railroad tracks are quite a sight to behold, of two uninteresting towns that now sort of draw me, to stay and value them.

Recalling that for three years in my early teens I crossed the bridge to school every single day. A bus will pick me up around six in the morning. Dressed in the required navy blue uniform of pleated skirt and cardigan with a white button-up shirt white knee socks and penny loafers I dragged my sleepy deprived self to one of the cold green leather upholstered seats.

Usually, at three o'clock, during the summer days, with friends we would walk back from the Catholic Jr. High School to the bridge, after buying a ten cent red ice Popsicle and paying a nickel for the toll.

Fridays used to be a special day, for boy watching. We all rolled up or skirts from the waist, making it shorter and un-tucking the white shirt to cover the bulge. Dabbing strawberry lip-gloss on our mouths, made us all feel sexy.

Walking into the Rexall pharmacy for a burger and fries, and for dessert a glassed doughnut with vanilla ice cream. I was thirteen, so I cannot comprehend how, with that type of diet, I started to lose my baby fat, or maybe it was the long walks on the bridge.

On the winter days, it would be a little tougher we would walk all bundle up in heavy jackets gloves, scarfs, and cozy knitted caps, trying to hitchhike with whoever took pity of three frozen girls, Rose Lee, Angie and myself.

In those days, the bridge looked like it was an endless runway. Now I realize it is a pretty short walk for the crossing. The perception of space minimizes as the years' pass, and what seemed once huge becomes smaller.

Relating this to the tumor when I first found the lump it felt immense, to the touch, as the chemo attacked it reducing the size, and then diminished by the operation, to a certain degree it takes time to change a perception.

Silent Watchers

A round me, there is always something to bring out a laugh. I have made it my routine every time I go back to my hometown to jog over the riverbank every morning around seven-thirty, and enjoy the amazing view.

An exercise that frees me of tension that builds up on my right side where the "Challenge" struck helping with my stiff arm. Mostly my whole body rejoices at the beautiful sight of the river filling me up with a profound peace and energy.

Usually, the weather this time of year is scorching hot, the sun comes out very early, so my outfit is a sight to be taken into consideration. Intriguing to a great degree for the eyes of border patrol officers across the river, on the American side.

As if in unison every single morning I can spot like four of them lining up with binoculars on hand. I guess trying to figure out what to make up of a gal running in white tennis shoes, cowboy hat, camouflage shorts, and an old grey tank t-shirt. A smile escapes me every time I see them. Inevitably they must start missing me when, after a week, I usually return home and disappear for a couple of months. Dawning on me that in all the days, months, and years of my fight with the "Challenge" my playing with beauty, had really worked.

You don't have four border patrol officers waiting for a crazy dressed girl to throw herself down the river? They actually thought I looked attractive or at least weird. Then rapidly I flashed back to the compliments of the elderly man in New York in front of Central Park, and the ladies at the Uptown supermarket, the fruit vendor at the street stand, or the boy who wash's my car, my list could go on and on. Funky or appealing I hit a cord, to be taken into account, and be appreciated, on how nice I looked.

How many times have we ignored the allure of ourselves, minimizing our looks and self-worth, tiptoeing around our insecurities.

I had long time before acknowledged the act of a compliment as a lifter of spirits, related to how I was feeling or looking. Sometimes in an ordinary day and thru the unraveling of the "Challenge," I lost sight of how important they are to the core of one's self.

Sincere compliments are felt. I should never have no objection where "they" come from, it is for me to grab, with a big thanks of acceptance. Being shy about being told I looked beautiful, at any given time, was now my right to cherish even in the lousiest moments of my being sick or lost. This was a revelation for me, as it should be for all.

Here I come to another basic truth to be flattered by anyone, I trek back to my attitude, over my image. Convinced that beauty has never been about my height, or how wide my hips are or how big is my nose, beauty is the whole of me, tall, short, thin, or plump it is mine. I am simply unique.

Respecting all the imperfections of my initial body, and fighting the anguish on facing the mirror, with now my new body.

Love

As time slips from our control events happen, life fades as my parents did years ago. Still more defiant is to come to terms with the void of loss. Left only with the memories and the objects, which serve as reminders of what once was, simply my roots. As is the foundation of who I am, engrained by those ladies who taught me resilience and the appreciation of my own beauty.

Something as fragile as a cut crystal chandelier from the 1800's proudly hanging from my dining room ceiling, after having lighted so many lives. Some I can account for like when it hung at my father's parents' house when a child, and in my teens after grandmas death in my parent's dining room.

Now, as I sit marveling at its magnificence in my own home, I wonder what about before crossing the ocean from France on whose ceiling was it hung and whose lives did it fill with light?

That is something I will never know, what seems vivid to me at the moment is that in the end it is all about the light, it is all about the hope of seeing a gleaming ray at the end of any obscure and robust experience.

The importance appreciating who we are, and in the end is all about that special respect we owe to ourselves in any situation as hard as it may seem.

I have been a lucky one, to see a new brightness after the "Challenge." Experiencing loss in so many ways, understanding over the years, only the light of love has been and will always be there to keep me going.

Silly of me, fretting over the importance of my looks, and even with all the unevenness of my now imperfect body, I can face now the mirror and Love Me, even more.

Of course with the help of some lip-gloss on.

Rosina Ramón

A Last Thought on a New Challenge

April 2020

Four months before the new year, forced out of my comfort zone after being told that I needed a hysterectomy. A strange, uncertain lump had no clear identity and was dangling without any proper credentials inside my body.

I started to go through life like in slow motion with my breast cancer background, as in a black and white movie. I was facing the probability for a second time, with a not welcome encounter with Mrs. Death. I even made lists of things I would like to leave for friends and love ones if the outcome turned bleak. Objects of fond importance to me from a specific time in my life with no more value only to myself.

Grateful after successful surgery, I was dismissed with a free pass for life and another chance for a new beginning. How Lucky is that? Following doctors' orders, I was to stay put for at least a month confined at home.

As I am recovering, something grey hangs over the air like a sticky gloomy cloud following me around the house, as visitors come and go, like a warning with no name tag.

After Christmas, I was allowed back into the world to enjoy the festivities, decorate the house, and stroll the city streets filled with lights.

On New Year's, I organized one of my most fabulous parties in a long time that felt like a United Nations reunion, or as my son, Alex, dubbed it a cruise around the world without leaving home with guests from all nationalities.

The year appeared to be full of new ventures, and like always, we expect the best and never fear the worst, but something was not quite right. I figured it was because of the coldest and greyest days of the year.

After my Birthday in the middle of January, I was taken to bed for almost two weeks with bronchitis. I couldn't believe it, again to seclusion. Struggling to get back to health and organizing the year's work calendar of events, I finally accomplished it in the last days of the month. I took a long weekend off to attend Alexis' son Kenzo's, my first grandson's two year Birthday Party in Cozumel.

Looking back at this trip, I remember the strange buzz around me. For the first time in my life, I did not strike my usual impertinent conversations with one stranger or another. I went into the plane as in a sheltered bubble, without minding the usual stares, dressed in a linen coat from the 50's in camel and white, turtle neck to match, taupe linen pants, comfy suede nude espadrilles, a large straw hat in hand, and a zebra printed bag.

Feeling detached and disconnected from others, I walk to the baggage claim to pick my bag and hurry for the bus to Playa del Carmen. On arrival, I walk in a floating sensation the two blocks from the station to board the ferry for Cozumel.

Looking back, this is when things become scary. As the ferry starts moving, the weather becomes chilly. Forceful rain rocks the vessel sideways as if almost ready to flip us overboard. Wrapping a scarf around my head to shelter from the splashing water coming from the surrounding windows, no protection from the thick plastic curtains which flow with an unknown power sticking to the roof of the ceiling. I started wondering if Mrs. D was again taunting me.

The half-hour ride felt like never-ending until I spot the Cozumel lights. Finally, the ferry begins adjusting to a normal rhythm, realizing I am soaking wet, mascara smudged, and trembling slowly, regaining my composure before walking into firm ground.

Kenzo's celebration was like a farewell party to normalcy as we have known it to be. Having a chance of enjoying the company of Ryan's his dad's incredible family, and time with my daughter. Now on remembering those days of white sand, sunny skies, and infinite blue waves of cold water, I yearn for more time of such beauty and companionship.

We do not appreciate the view until it is snatched abruptly from us. Arriving back to Monterrey on March the 4th, eeriness prevails as we all require a temperature test after onboarding the plane.

The next day I am coordinating the clothes for a photo shoot, and since my concentration is at its peak, my uneasiness disappears. Selecting the music for a bridal fashion show the next day perks my spirits, and I completely forget my nagging feelings.

On the 14th, after the fashion show of fabulous designer wedding dresses, our worlds came crashing down. Lockdown officially started.

We had heard of an epidemic hitting the city of Wuhan oceans away in China, a couple of months before. Of course, we took it for granted ignoring even the communication gadgets blinking at our fingertips.

After China, Korea, and several cruise ships became infected with the deadly Corona Virus, there was no way to stop it.

Italy's devastation started on the eve of the last shows of fashion week; being the designer Giorgio Armani the first to take action, opting for a presentation, free of press and guests, in general. Considering all in fashion an eccentric measure of overreaction.

Fashion people continued their pilgrimage to Paris were kissy kisses and hugs prevailed. The shows continued on schedule until many started to become aware of the matter's seriousness and some left to their respective countries in haste. Hitting France, London, and other parts of Europe badly, but Italy and Spain were the most affected.

Instead of rapid action in all of North America, our governments sat on their asses as the Corona Virus arrived, conquering with a giant fist, first the U.S. and with a vengeance, my favorite city in the world, New York.

The virus then started spreading around our continent without a control plan from our leaders.

As I see it, "We" are now faced with World War III, without a single shot fired, so different that our great-grandparent's days. Lunatics disguised as leaders, threatening lives without any well-based plan of action.

A distinct reality, accessing the little power we humans possess over an unknown disease. With no trace or face invisible, a type of unique cancer ready to strike by the minute. And hitting hard it has and without pity. Thousands are losing lives, and the toll rises.

How do you treat such an enemy? If the weapons are not there to fight with, and our leaders' minds are more worried about the economy and their self-inflated egos. Abiding by blindness and to their cabinet of "YES MEN."

Aside from our leaders' peculiarity, there is so much good coming out of this darkness on such trying times. Alliances are being integrated health workers in charge, as transportation personnel like firefighters and police officers. Supermarket vendors work day and night, stocking their isles with provisions for all; restaurants and fast food delivery are now a norm all over.

"Stay at Home" is now an international anthem in North America established more by its community than by leadership. As people, we are coming together more than ever by acts of kindness and compassion, which are the new form of needed collaboration.

Coping With a New Way Life

A fter enjoying freedom, being locked down inside my home, day-to-day living has taken some significant unfamiliar adjustments to grasp.

Waking up to days of solitude and silence has obliged me to embrace a new normal, accepting this as a new friend instead of losing my head.

Days turned into weeks and then months, adjusting the hours as spaces for introspection for what we aspire in our future, taking a stern look at how I had lived in the past. Very much like the rabbit in Alice in Wonderland, hurrying in an unknown direction.

For me, exasperation or depression was out of the question, having above all to appreciate my self-worth. It was crucial even to permit feeling lost. Re-invention became my only answer.

Before it all happened, I had started to believe I was the main character in a feature film. My reality was as strange as it began to appear on an imaginary screen in front of me. In the back of my mind hunting me, all thru the months before the lockdown. As incoherent as this surreal movie became, the truth materialized, facing me with the dilemma of not being able to hug my loved ones or sit with them for Sunday dinner, secluded and protected from this virus's harm, the clock started ticking.

Feeling privileged with the luxury of space and accompanied by my second mother, Juanita, I thought of so many people alone in a tiny apartment. So I took to Instagram, looking to inspire and came out inspired.

Inviting people for a casual chat first, it was only about fashion, then I understood I needed more diverse stories, besides fashion was always in the mix. Then came stories from people from the arts, music, gastronomy, photography, nutrition, models, makeup gurus, stylists, and cancer survivors like myself. We even made a challenge of writing a letter to an older adult who taught us a lesson. Rejoiced with five "Teen" Tik-tokers who not only made you laugh, proving that to be funny needs intelligence, openly bragging about studying, earned scholarships, and being conscious of being good role models to their base, Centennials, now.

On achieving 100 lives in the midst of finding incredible stories that have nurtured my creative process in ways I could not expect. Reaching out and reconnecting with people I had not heard in ages and even making new friends in the process.

I have taken so many years to come to terms and write about my Challenge, and now I am facing a new one, only this one is shared.

Again, contributing what I know has kept me sane, even in the most troubling days. I now have evidence that we all need inspiration to booster our creative spirit, and there is no creative process when we look in the mirror and look lousy.

These "live streams" have helped me dress every day in a different crazy comfy outfit. Certain to this day, I have not worn the same dress for sure on the first sixty lives. Realizing I have enough clothes to play around with for quite some time. And pondering on the question, what do I need? Which is only health and love?

Life may seem to be on hold, but this has been my most creative time since the main focus is Me.

I know that even when alone, on taking care of myself, how I look, and how my space feels is enough to make me happy. We will open our minds to new ideas that we will share with others to create a better world for the ones waiting to hug us tight.

All through the protection period, I have woken splashed water on my face, been grateful for the new day, and still have never stopped putting some lip gloss on.

Rosina Ramón

Printed in the United States
by Baker & Taylor Publisher Services